Kingdom

The Fortress Book 3

T. A. Styles

TRANSCENDANCE PRESS

Contents

Prologue

THIS PLACE HAS SO much room! It's bigger than Magic Kingdom.

It's our fortress, indeed.

Is that what we'll call it? Not a kingdom?

A kingdom sounds a lot bigger than what we have here. What we have here is just a small part of a kingdom. Maybe from here we can build a kingdom. There's an expression I remember from all the reading I used to do: "Prepare your heart as a fortress, for there is no other."

What does that mean?

It means your heart should be stronger than any house. So, this house can sure enough be our fortress, but there is also a fortress inside of us. And from there, a kingdom can rise.

One

Alyssa and Uncle Mike started their journey down from Saratoga roughly six weeks after Alyssa's mother died.

Her mother had told her to pray every night and do everything her uncle told her. Alyssa held her mother's hand until the end, and then she went with her uncle to his house and waited to see if either of them were going to get sick.

"Do you think if we were going to get it, we would have by now?" she asked.

Uncle Mike put a log on the fire he had going in his fireplace and the embers scattered.

"I'm guessing we would have," he said. "That's why we're leaving tomorrow."

He had grown more serious since the disease killed everyone. He was always funny and cracking jokes, an easygoing type of guy who was comfortable to be around. And even though he was still the one person she wanted to wake up with each day, he had changed. There was an urgency in his voice and to everything he did.

"Where are we going?" Alyssa asked.

"South," he said. "Down toward Albany."

"Why?" she asked.

"I heard some things from someone who came up from that way and I want to check it out."

"Who?" Alyssa asked. "We haven't seen anyone in days."

"*You* haven't seen anyone in days," he said. Alyssa stared at him with a *don't-treat-me-like-a-kid* look because it wasn't like him to do so. He must have felt her gaze on his back.

"Sorry," he said. "When I was out the other day getting supplies, I ran into an old buddy of mine who had just come back from Troy. You remember Cypress, don't you? Just something he said made me curious, so I wanted to check it out, but I can tell you more on the road."

"It's a long walk," she said as she pulled a blanket over her. It was spring, but there was a chill in the air. Plus, there was something about being in front of a fire that made her want to be covered.

Alyssa and her mother and father would always spend Halloween at Uncle Mike's. He lived in a development where there were lots of houses, so they would go trick or treating, then come back to Uncle Mike's for a fire and pizza; memories of which were all she had now.

"That it is," he said. "I got my map handy, and our path outlined. We'll take Route 9 down instead of following the highway so we can stick close to houses and stores for supplies while keeping out of the open."

Alyssa smiled. "The scenic route."

Uncle Mike smiled too. Like her, he knew how much Alyssa's mother, *his* sister, loved the scenic route. He would sometimes vacation with them, and even though driving the highway to Maine was an hour quicker, she would always insist on taking the winding mountain roads through Vermont.

"We can probably take a car," she said.

Uncle Mike remembered seeing survivors still driving around while they could, but it wasn't his preference.

"I don't know if it's a good idea," he said. "It'll attract too much attention, and I don't want to get into a situation where some hoodlum is trying to run us off the road."

"What if they get us anyway?" Alyssa asked.

He placed his large hands on her shoulders. "I'll kill anyone who tries to hurt you."

That was Uncle Mike. Fierce. Protective. He had had no kids of his own, but now he did. It was hard for Alyssa to tell how he felt about that.

"We'll walk, and it'll be fine," he said. "We won't box ourselves in and it'll be easy to elude anyone who we might run into that doesn't have the best intentions."

The pair set off the next day, each with a backpack of supplies. They traveled cautiously while taking in the reality of the new world around them. It looked much the same as the old one, only hollow, quiet, and still. Stores, offices, restaurants, and schools stood vacant. They saw streets without purpose, and telephone and power lines that no longer flowed with power.

The soundlessness of the world was surreal. It wasn't like normal quiet as some define the stillness of night. It was a sick absence of sound where one could only question whether it was truly the world or if they had all gone deaf.

They saw the men on horseback within the first three miles of their journey. There were five of them, though Alyssa counted six horses. They were stopped at a gas station eating sandwiches.

Alyssa and Uncle Mike held up across the street next to a house and watched. Uncle Mike pulled out a pair of binoculars and peered through them. There were no women in their company, and they all looked to be between the ages of twenty and forty.

"What are we going to do?" Alyssa asked.

"No sense trying to trust they're friendly," Uncle Mike said. "We have to keep to ourselves for now."

"I guess they didn't want to travel by car either," she said.

There was no shortage of horses in Saratoga with the nearby racetrack being such a lively tourist attraction before the virus.

"They might have the right idea," Uncle Mike said. "I'm not fond of riding horses, personally, but it's going to be the wave of the future once this gas goes bad. You can't really pump it no more anyway, and trying to find keys to any of these cars that are sitting around would be a task in and of itself."

"Well, then find us some," Alyssa said.

"Hey!" one of the horsemen called while the two were conversing.

"Shit," Uncle Mike said, quickly ducking down and pulling Alyssa with him.

"It's kind of late now," she said. "Did that call sound friendly?"

"We're not waiting to find out," Uncle Mike said.

The two ran alongside the house as the horsemen saddled up and gave pursuit.

Alyssa and Mike jumped the backyard fence, and it led into another yard. They heard one of the men calling as they closed in on them.

"Get back here!" he said.

Mike and Alyssa continued to hop fences in zigzag fashion to throw them off. They ducked into one of the homes through a Bilco basement door that was open in one of the yards. Alyssa proceeded down the concrete steps as Mike closed the metal doors over their heads and readied his weapon in case they were discovered.

They waited while listening to muted voices and the faint trotting of horses on concrete.

"We'll wait here for a while," Mike whispered. "They won't spend much time searching. We're like a needle in a haystack."

"Maybe they didn't want to hurt us," Alyssa said.

"We can't take that chance," Mike said.

"Then maybe we shouldn't have let them see us," she said.

"Alright, now," he said. "Little Ms. Attitude. This is the first time we've ventured out so far from home, so there's going to be a bit of a learning curve. Maybe they heard us chatting. With practically no sounds in the world now to drown out normal conversation, I guess even a whisper can catch someone's ear. Something to keep in mind."

"How long are we going to stay here?" she asked, looking around at the dingy, dark basement.

"Let's give it an hour and we'll pop out and see," he said.

"How will we know when an hour is up since we haven't got a clock?" she asked.

Mike rolled up his flannel shirt sleeve to reveal a watch wrapped around his thick right wrist. "Still keeping time pretty good."

"Does it tell the date?" she asked.

"It's June first," he said after pressing the button to light the watch face.

Alyssa nodded. "Mom got sick on April sixteenth. The TV was still working, and I remember her coughing for the first time while I was watching the news and hearing about how the first symptom was a deep, hoarse cough. I turned around and she was looking at the TV, then back at me. She gave me a reassuring smile, but she knew. She knew *I* knew."

Mike put his arm around her and pulled her close. "Those were tough weeks."

"Why do you think we lived when most everyone else died?" she asked.

"I don't know," he said. "Lucky. Unlucky. They never did have a chance to study this because it swept through the world so quickly. The dinosaurs went out with a bang and people with a cough—'Getgone.'"

"Even dinosaurs lived years after that asteroid hit," she reminded. "At least they had more time."

"Yeah," Mike said. "Some of them. I try to forget that the ones that died right away were probably the lucky ones."

An hour later, after hearing nothing and no one again, he opened the basement doors and the two climbed out and continued with their journey. They walked several miles, making frequent stops in various stores and homes, looking for supplies and weapons. They only had so much room in their packs, so they prioritized. With each visit, it was clear which places had been visited previously and which ones hadn't.

Many of the stores had been looted during the brief period before the virus ravaged the larger population. Little good the looting did for anyone. Alyssa and Uncle Mike discovered many of the homes had not been touched. Most had rotted or rotting corpses in them, a sight which Alyssa had to brace herself for each time they entered a home.

Mike found several weapons along the way. He disregarded rifles and shotguns for the pistols. Silver and black, small and large. He tried to stuff each one into his bag, not wanting to leave any behind.

They continued down Route 9 at a good clip, and in the late afternoon as the sun was dipping in the sky, they had to take cover in a car, one of many sitting on a Mercedes lot, to avoid the horsemen again.

Alyssa gave Mike a look as they hunkered down below the dash.

"You don't want us boxed in, huh?" she commented.

"Well, hell," Mike said. "They would have seen us if we ran for the building."

The men came to a stop on the road in front of the car lot. Alyssa and Mike scooched up in their seats just high enough to catch a glimpse of a couple of them over the dashboard. They were sitting atop their horses looking every which way. One of them was smoking a cigarette, which he flicked from his fingers.

"What the hell do they want?" Alyssa asked. "They're on horses. If they're going our way, they should already be to Albany by now."

"I don't think they're going our way by coincidence," Mike said.

"Then where *are* they going?" Alyssa said.

"They're tracking us," Mike said, "for whatever reason."

Alyssa pursed her lips. "We got the guns we found. We don't need to be afraid."

"The last thing I want is to get involved in a shoot-out," Mike said. "If we have to, we will, but until that time comes, we're just going to avoid these yahoos."

The two stayed in the Mercedes until dark. They both napped so they would have enough energy to make more progress on the road at night. As soon as the pink and orange hues in the sky gave way to blackness, they forfeited the sanctuary of the car and continued their journey down Route 9, staying clear of the roadway.

They were headed to an unknown destination following not the north star but an old paper map marked with a black streak of ink that went from Saratoga to Troy.

Mike hadn't told Alyssa anything about the place they were going. He claimed he didn't know much about the place himself, but was told it was a sanctuary for children, as well as some sort of survival camp.

Survival camp? For children? What about you? I'm not leaving you.

I could always stay nearby, Alyssa, if this place was in your best interest. It would be sort of like sending you off to boarding school.

Boarding school? What's in my best interest is to stay with you. Besides, what would you do without me?

This isn't about me. He had made this statement, but deep down he wasn't so sure if it was true.

The real truth was, he didn't know if his motives were selfish or selfless, but it likely didn't matter until he found out if this place was real or merely a fantasy created in his mind from loose pieces of information.

Kids in training to survive the apocalypse at a fortified orphanage.

Could it be?

They continued their journey south, but the horseman caught up with them again in Malta. Mike pulled Alyssa aside into some bushes next to a residence.

"Shit," Uncle Mike exclaimed. "Here we go again. There's only one way we can get these bastards off our tail."

"By using your guns and killing these assholes?" Alyssa asked.

"It's too risky," Mike said. "Clearly they have guns, and if we get in a fire fight, we may not make it."

"Well, then what?" Alyssa asked.

"It's time," Mike said.

Uncle Mike handed her the map, which highlighted the route from Saratoga to the green bridge in Troy. "Take this map and follow it to the intersection just over the bridge." He followed the line on the map with his finger to the bridge. "I'm told good people will find you there."

"People?" Alyssa asked confused.

"I told you it's a refuge for children. A school. An orphanage."

"I know what you told me," she said, growing frantic. "I'm supposed to find this place on my own...without you?"

"You have to!" he said. "It is the only way."

"Are you crazy?" she said. "They know there are two of us. They'll keep looking for me. And what about you?"

"Don't worry about me," he said. "I'll lead them in the opposite direction then circle back and find you. You keep south, stay low, and follow the map."

"No, wait," she pleaded.

He clutched her head between his large, warm hands and kissed her on the forehead. "I love you."

Before Alyssa could say another word, Uncle Mike bolted from the bushes and ran. The men on horseback spotted him and gave pursuit.

Alyssa cried as she watched her uncle run off, after which she ran south in a hurry, following the map he had handed her.

Orphanage?

Training camp?

What the hell?

Mike ran off feeling a sense of guilt and shame. He caught the attention of the men on horseback, and they followed him in the opposite direction. As they caught up with him about a half mile north of where he left Alyssa, he ducked behind a former roller-skating arena.

The horsemen followed him there and the party came to a stop.

"Did Hawk stay on her tail?" Mike asked as the group formed a semi-circle around him.

"Just like you told us," a man by the name of Cypress said. "Are you sure this is what you want to do, Mike?"

Cypress was the only surviving member of Mike's lumberjack crew, and he was so nicknamed in honor of his trade.

"I intend to stick to her like glue," Mike said. "If this place is real, it'll be better for her."

"Better for her, or *you*?" Cypress asked.

Mike would only accept a line of questioning of this nature from Cypress, with whom he went back fifteen years. The other four, including Hawk, Eddie, Fisher, and Zippo were only random others they had connected with after the fall.

Mike remembered the conversation he had had with Cypress before devising his plan for Alyssa.

Hey, I just got back from Troy checking on my brother, Cypress had said. *No surprise he's dead, but while I was there, I heard about this place that is a sanctuary for kids. Like an orphanage. Thinking about Alyssa and all. From what I hear, it's fortified, and there's some guy there training these kids with survival skills.*

Who told you that? Mike remembered asking.

I crossed a couple of them when they were on a supply run down in that area, Cypress told him. *Oldest couldn't have been more than fifteen and the youngest was probably ten, but they weren't fucking around. They nearly killed me. They said if I found any kids, they would take them in because they had a few more beds in their place to fill. They told me to bring them across the green bridge going into Troy and wait at the intersection and they would see me.*

Interesting.

"I'm surprised she didn't recognize me," Cypress said.

Mike tapped the binoculars that were hanging around his neck. "I kept her eyes off you. She hadn't seen you in a while anyway. She wanted to kill y'all though. Good thing I had the guns, or she probably would have done it herself without permission."

"She's a little warrior, that one," Cypress added. "You left her without a gun?"

"As long as we stay close," Mike said, "she shouldn't need one. Or maybe she'll find one on her own in short order."

"Why didn't you just get her down there, Mike?" Fisher said. "You could have left after you made sure she made it safely."

"Trust me," Mike said. "It was the only way. She would never have left my side. After we follow her to that doorstep and make sure everything is safe, we'll take up nearby."

Mike approached his horse and put one foot up on the stirrup in preparation to mount. "I hate riding horseback," he mumbled.

"Yeah, yeah," Cypress said. "You're the only one I know who gets cramps on a horse."

Mike glowered at Cypress over the top of the horse, a slight smile etched across his face. He took horseback lessons when he was a kid, and not only was the instructor less than kid-friendly, she made him and Alyssa's mother ride even when his side cramped up from bouncing up and down for a half hour straight.

It surely had been a mistake telling the boys that story.

Mike mounted his horse and the group of five proceeded stealthily south to reunite with Hawk and follow Alyssa down to Troy.

They caught up with him less than an hour later, according to Mike's watch, which was still working soundly. He had pulled off alongside a drive-through coffee shop.

"How I wish this place were still in business," Hawk said.

"Relax, sunshine," Mike said. "We'll make you some coffee when we stop for the night. Where is she?"

"In that store across the way," Hawk said. "She's doing a good job with the cloak and dagger act. You want to know the first thing she did, no less than ten minutes after she gave up running?"

"She found a gun?" Mike said.

"Damn," Hawk said. "You spoiled my surprise."

"I've been telling you she's no fool," Mike said. "We better just make sure she doesn't spot us, because she'll shoot at us."

"Well, truth be told," Hawk said. "She's good at keeping a low profile, but she doesn't seem to be looking over her shoulder all that much—a skill she'll have to acquire in time, we should hope."

"For now, she has us to do that for her," Cypress said.

"She's a good girl," Mike said. "I won't let nothing happen to her."

"You just better hope she don't run into any baddies when she goes into these stores," Fisher added.

With that in mind, Uncle Mike sighed with relief when Alyssa came out of the store, a pack on her back stuffed with items. She maneuvered around some cars, crossed a street at the crosswalk, and then ducked behind another building.

That'a girl.

He watched her longingly and wondered if his sister would approve of what he had done. He did love her so.

"Cute," Fisher said. "She's using the crosswalk and looking both ways and everything."

"No need to check for cars anymore," said the quieter one of the group, Zippo.

Zippo was self-named after the shiny metal lighter he always kept in his hand. It had run out of lighter fluid long before, but he constantly flipped the top up and down, which drove the others bonkers, yet they knew it helped settle his anxiety, so they dealt with it.

Given Hawk was the best tracker, they kept him about a mile ahead of the rest of them, figuring one rider would attract less attention than the six of them together. He would track and they would catch up. Track. Catch up. Track. Catch up.

For eight days, the gang rode as Alyssa made her way on foot down from Malta to Ballston Spa, Clifton Park, Latham, and then finally Troy. She veered off on the highway just after Latham. Hawk worried about remaining concealed on the highway, so they proceeded with extra caution.

Alyssa didn't stick to the center highway. She used the trees that paralleled the interstate to make her way to the bridge. Hawk did the same and was able to stay tucked away enough so that she didn't see him.

When Alyssa arrived at the green bridge, she crossed. Hawk hitched his horse to a guardrail close to the bridge and scurried across, keeping low. The intersection Mike had mentioned was just over the bridge, but he noticed Alyssa wasn't waiting there as directed. Instead, she made her way up a steep hill that was at a sharp right at the intersection. She entered a home on the hill, which is where she remained.

The others, following Hawk's cues, hitched their horses and caught up with him over the bridge. He had pulled off the road into a ditch near the intersection.

"Where is she?" Mike asked.

"She ducked into that house," Hawk said, pointing across the street.

"This is it," Cypress said. "This is the place those kids told me about. The bridge...the intersection. It's just like they said. Their place is here somewhere."

"Unless them kids were just fucking with you," Mike said.

Cypress ignored his comments.

"Fisher," Mike said. "Can you take Eddie and Zippo back to the horses and wait for us? I don't want our rides to go missing."

"This fool don't have to take me," Eddie said. "I can walk myself."

"Are you sure you don't want to hold my hand?" Fisher mocked.

"I would, but God knows what it's probably touched," Eddie said.

"Want to smell?" Fisher said, sticking his hand in Eddie's face.

Eddie swatted it away.

"Alright, come on," Mike said. "Get back to them horses and stay put."

The three split, while Hawk, Cypress, and Mike continued to keep their eyes on the house. They continued to follow her for a few more days as she explored locally for food and other items, always returning to the same house, until she emerged one day in pursuit of an older man who had come down the hill from some other place.

"What the hell is she doing now?" Mike said.

"Maybe that's the guy the kids were talking about?" Cypress said. "Alyssa's smart enough not to just wait around and be caught...she's been doing recon this whole time."

"Impressive," Hawk said. "My daughter...God rest her soul, same age, but she would have crumbled in this world. Sometimes I think what happened was for the better."

Cypress issued no response. Mike knew he had a young son and daughter who both died from the virus. Mike had met them many times. Cypress never talked about them after they died but carried a picture of them in his breast pocket. Mike often caught him looking at the photo, in tears, before putting it away.

"Can you go back to the others, Cypress, and just let them know that Hawk and I are going to follow them? We'll catch up with you soon."

"Will do," Cypress said. "Make sure you don't spoil eight days of work."

Hawk and Mike followed Alyssa, who was tailing the mystery man. The pursuit lasted all day, until Mike finally witnessed this mysterious man emerge from a residence holding a young boy's hand and a large bag of unknown things. He grew hopeful but was also a bit leery.

Hawk put a hand on his shoulder. "Hard to tell what's what."

The two followed the man, boy, and Alyssa back to the intersection, where the man proceeded up the hill. The front doors of this three-story brick home opened from inside as he arrived, and the pair walked through them. As the house swallowed them up and the double doors closed behind them, Alyssa continued to watch covertly from a hidden location across the street.

"It's real," Mike said.

The brick home was halfway up the hill. It loomed tall between a large grassy piece of land to its left, and a sloped wooded area to its right. It cast all the other homes on the street in shadow.

As he stared, enraptured by the sight of what once was only a rumor and now a full reality, he heard Alyssa's shouts.

He watched as the man with the boy returned to the door. He couldn't hear the exchange he had with Alyssa, but within minutes Alyssa was walking up the steps to this place, and behind her the door closed.

She had made it. She was safe.

Mike cried that day. And in the days after, he and his group settled in Pinewood. He checked on Alyssa regularly. Sometimes there was nothing to see, and sometimes he caught glimpses of her. He dared not get too close, but he could see in those moments from different vantage points, that she seemed healthy, safe, and happy.

As happy as anyone could be in these days.

For the time being, he hoped it was enough.

Two

When Sky came to, while lying on the foyer floor, Misty and Wyatt helped her up while the others came running, weapons drawn. Mike unmounted his horse and started up the steps to the fortress.

"Hold on there a second, mister," Wyatt said raising his pistol.

Mike held up his hands, but as Sky recovered her senses, she pushed down Wyatt's arm. But she did not run into her uncle's arms like she had so many times envisioned would happen if she were ever to see him alive again. Truth is, she never thought she would. After all these years, how could he still be alive?

Is this why she had thought about him so often? Did some part of her know deep down that what happened on the road was not the last of his story?

She protested his arrival. "It can't be."

"It's me, sweetheart," Uncle Mike said, his teeth still pearly. He didn't look a shade different from what she remembered, except for his hair graying.

"It doesn't make sense," she said.

Uncle Mike walked the rest of the way to the top of the stairs and opened his arms to offer a hug. When he saw she was not pulling away, he embraced her carefully, though she did not return his gesture. Instead, she stood there in shock.

He pulled away from her, and she stared at him as if he were a ghost returned from the dead. Perhaps Vash had accidentally conjured him instead of Zagan.

"You knew where I was going," she said. "Where have you been?"

"I understand you're confused, Alyssa," Mike said. "And I'm not saying you're going to be pleased with all the details of my story, but it was finally time for the past to catch up with us."

"Who's Alyssa?" Teddy asked, scratching his head.

"*She* is," Misty said pointing at Sky.

"That's Sky," Teddy said.

"I don't know exactly what's going on here, so someone might have to catch me up," Wyatt said.

"Do I blast the cowboys?" King crackled in on his walkie from the rooftop. "I got clean shots."

"No, King," Misty said. "We're not shooting the cowboys. Anyway, just because they're on horses doesn't make them cowboys."

"Yeah," Baby said. "They don't even have hats."

"Sky?" Mike said. "Interesting."

"You know what's more interesting?" Sky said. "*You* showing up here on my doorstep four years after you sprinted out of my life to save me from those men who were chasing us. I thought you were dead."

Sky began to cry, and Mike bowed his head in shame. "I can explain it all, Sky; maybe not to your satisfaction, but I can explain it all. Can I come in?"

Wyatt exchanged glances with Misty and Baby.

"Sky," Wyatt began. "You remember what happened with Ms. Betty. This man may be your uncle, but we don't know him from Adam, and maybe you don't either."

Mike frowned.

"How about a walk?" Uncle Mike said.

"If you're going on a walk, I'm going with you," Misty said. "And the cowboys stay here."

"I thought you said they weren't cowboys?" Teddy said.

Wyatt sized up the other four horsemen. They were a bit grungy, but didn't appear threatening, but neither did Vash when he first came knocking.

"You carrying any weapons?" Wyatt asked Mike.

"My rifle is holstered on the nag," Mike pointed.

One of the other men was holding the reins on Mike's horse.

"Fine, then," Sky said.

She led Mike down the steps, and the two made their way up the street in the direction of the heights as Misty followed behind several paces, her gun at the ready. It was a quiet walk, at first, as Sky was still trying to process that her uncle was there.

"I don't even know where to begin with the questions I have," Sky said. "I'm so happy you're alive, and I don't think my mind has caught up with this reality, but over the years I thought of so many horrible things about what happened to you, and not knowing has been driving me crazy. You gave me that map and left, so I always felt if you were alive you would have to have been trapped or imprisoned. But in the end, I just thought it was unlikely and that those horsemen just caught up with you and killed you."

"I'm sorry," Mike said. "I was scared as hell, Alyssa. That I couldn't protect you, and then God forbid if something happened to you, I would have had to carry the guilt of that. And so when I heard about this place, I thought it might be the best solution for you in these times. And my God, look at you now."

Sky stopped to face him. "So, what are you saying, Uncle Mike?" she asked.

He swallowed hard and his face went flushed. "Those men back there...those are the men that chased us out of Saratoga. But the thing is...I knew them all along. I enlisted them to help with my plans to get you to this place the way we did, because I knew if it was real, you would never have left me. We followed you the entire way after we separated and watched to make sure you got in. Then we went and settled in the Pinewood area. I watched you from afar, and I made sure they were taking care of you, and—"

"You mean to tell me you made me think for four years that you had been tortured and killed so I could escape, and you planned the entire thing just because you were afraid?"

"Alyssa, I—"

"*I* was afraid!" Sky yelled. "I've been afraid for four years! For you, for me...for everyone! And if you were so keen on watching me from afar, maybe you would have known this place was attacked twice. I nearly was killed, and I lost people I loved as much as you, Mom, and Dad while you were living out your glory years with a bunch of grubby horse wranglers up in Pinewood, wherever the hell that is."

"It's where I lived," Misty offered somberly.

"Alyssa," Mike pleaded. "It wasn't all that glorious."

"My name is Sky, not Alyssa!" she said. "Alyssa died four years ago, thanks to you, and this conversation is over. You can take these men back to Pinewood, because I don't know you anymore."

Sky turned away with tears in her eyes. Misty stood by Mike, and the two watched as Sky walked down the hill, up the stairs, and into the fortress.

"All she talked about was you over these years," Misty said. "It was kind of a shitty thing you did."

"I know," Mike said. "But at least she knows. I couldn't live with it any longer. Now, in time, she can do what's best for her with the information." Mike turned to Misty. "You lived up in Pinewood?"

"I sure did," Misty said. "It's where Sim found me. That's the man that took us all in and trained us. Sky loved him. We all did. He died fighting for us while you were in hiding."

"I'm sorry to hear that," Mike said. "I truly am."

"Where are you living up in Pinewood?" Misty asked. "In case we need to find you."

"A nice farmhouse with lots of land around it and a big silo draped with an American flag, which has seen better days," Mike replied.

"The old Livingston place," Misty said. "Quarter mile from my old home. They were a good family."

"That's the place," Mike said. "Their mailbox is still there with their name across it."

"I remember it," Misty said. "I'll talk to her. But not for you, for her." She turned to Mike. "She is the closest thing I've ever had to a sister."

"Understood," Mike said.

Misty led Mike back down the hill, and he and his men galloped off and away. Sky watched her Uncle Mike leave from the second-floor window and collapsed on the floor, a flood of emotion washing through her.

When she composed herself enough, she picked up her journal, which she had continued to write in as she had vowed after burying Sim's in the ground next to his gravesite.

Dear Diary,

All of these years. The longing. And Uncle Mike came back. It's hard to believe, but he came back. He left me on purpose. I would never have dreamed that he would do such a thing. I have learned family is everything, no matter if we have to face death to protect one another, and I'm only a teenager. He is a middle-aged man and never figured that out. He never had a child of his own. Or a wife. And he wasn't close to his mother or father. He did love my mother. His sister. Maybe he was just so used to being about himself, that he

*never realized what family really meant or was. The things we don't know
about the people we love most.*

*I'm angry. I'm sad. I'm awestruck. I'm full of emotions I cannot fully
describe. I don't know what to do. Life presents us with these dilemmas, and
we have to decide what is best. Sim, do you have the answers for me? What
would you do? You sought forgiveness from Amanda and Sarah. You bought
this house to make it right. To show your effort. And they forgave you. You
sought forgiveness from the world when you killed them both, and the world
forgave you by bringing us all together.*

*Sim...I miss you. I wish you were here. You have blessed my life in so many
ways, and to think this all came about because you forgave yourself. I realize,
forgiveness...it is the only way, no matter how difficult it may be. Maybe that
is why King went to talk to Zagan. Maybe King wanted to forgive him so he
could feel whole.*

My Uncle Mike. He is here. Oh, my God, he is here.

Misty tapped on Sky's door just after she put her journal aside. Sky slid
to the edge of the bed.

"All this time...I wish he *had* been tortured and held captive from you,"
Misty said. "It's too bad how it all turned out."

"You can stop, Misty," Sky said. "I have a right to be mad."

"Yes, you do," she said. "But he's still your uncle and you still love him.
I could see it in your eyes. You can't fool me, only yourself."

"Of course I still love him!" Sky said. "But I can be mad. What he did
was wrong. It was selfish. Sim taught us the opposite of selfishness, so I'm
not going to make it easy for him. I'm almost an adult now. I'm not a kid. I
see things for the way they are. Maybe he wasn't the man I thought he was,
even when I was a child in a normal world."

"You aren't a kid anymore," Misty said. "Maybe none of us are, but
that just means you learned that adults aren't perfect. They are flawed.

You would have learned that either way. But let's consider the future. The kingdom, not the fortress."

"The kingdom," Sky scoffed. "I have enough on my mind trying to keep the fortress together."

"It doesn't matter," Misty said. "It was Sim's vision to see a fortress become a kingdom. That's what was revealed in his journals about who we were and what we could become. Your Uncle Mike could be part of that. These people that brought Yamil and Miracle home safely could be another part. A spark becomes a flame, becomes a fire."

Sky shook her head. "Just give me time. That's all I need, Misty. Time."

"There's plenty of that," Misty said.

Sky brushed herself off and made her rounds. Miracle, Yamil, Leo, and Baby were continuing their work on the wall. They first used the brick that King and Teddy had discovered across the street, and since Vash's death two months earlier, they had made some missions to scour for more. They had made decent progress, and they were all hopeful that by winter, the wall would be fully completed.

King had taken up roof duty since Skinny Jim was killed, but he didn't like it one bit. They had interviewed several people that were recommended from the heights and settled on a thirty-year-old named Holly that seemed to fit the bill. She had been a welder in the previous world and was as tough as nails. She didn't mind being on her own, and she was more than willing to commit to a twelve-hour roof assignment.

You don't have no chair up there? Just get me a chair so I can sit down once in a while. And bring me some food. Food and a chair. That's not much to ask for, is it? If you can do that, I'll make sure nobody gets a hundred miles within the place without me knowing it.

They were still looking for one more person to share the other half of the shift. They had never officially had two roof men but felt it would be a good idea moving forward. They were homing in on another guy named Rodger. He was older and quiet and didn't seem to mind the terms.

I prefer nights. I'm a night owl. Mornings, I suck. Afternoons I can handle.

The committee wasn't sold on the idea of having more adults in the house. They feared it could alter the vibe of the younger people in charge of carrying out Sim's vision.

Sleep on it, and we'll decide at the next committee meeting.

Sky walked out to the back where the crew was hard at work. Leo was the first to complain.

"Oh, there you are," Leo said. "These little ones are annoying. They keep putting the bricks in the wrong place and all crooked and I have to keep fixing it."

As Sky looked, Miracle was placing a brick on top of the wet concrete while leaving a gap.

"Well," Sky said. "It was you who wanted them to start getting more involved with all the duties around the house. They are younger and have to learn. You can teach them."

Sky watched Yamil and Miracle at work and smiled at their careless attention to the details. They were still little, but the only thing she could think about was how they had escaped their captor after they had been kidnapped during the last threat. They had been underestimated by everyone, including her. And they showed everyone.

The day Yamil and Miracle returned home from their great escape, Sky let them sleep. She did not ask them any questions and though some of the younger ones did, she cautioned them not to badger. She insisted they needed food, rest, and a chance to recover.

The boys slept through the day and night, and in the morning time, after breakfast, they were invited into the living room with the others to tell their tales as a days-gone-by story. Normally, these stories would be hinted about on the wall, but this was a story that Sky did not want to wait for. She assumed none of them did.

The boys sat on the couch side by side, as all the others gathered around, wide-eyed.

They all waited for the boys to say something, but they only sat on the couch holding hands.

"What?" Yamil finally said.

"Tell us everything that happened," Sky said. "If you can. I mean, you don't have to, but it would be nice. But I do want to tell you boys...we did come looking for you. Me, Baby, and Charlie came to find you where you were. You were gone. I don't want you to ever think we didn't come looking for you." Sky knelt, teary eyed, before them. "I would have searched forever to find you. Like the book I read you."

Sky had read them a book about a mother bird who was asked by her baby bird what she would do if they ever got lost.

I would fly the lengths of the sky until blue faded to black and black returned to blue. I wouldn't stop flying until the day I found you.

"It's okay," Yamil said. "We left the house because Ms. Betty said Sim was waiting for us, and that someone would bring us to him, so we went out."

Sky fumed.

"He took us and tied us up and brought us in a wagon to a bad place. It was cold and ugly. But I remembered a lot of things Sim taught us, so I got out of the ropes, and me and Miracle went out a window and into the woods. It was cold, but we found a house and made rice and started the grill and got our clothes warm."

"It was fun," Miracle added. "We found Gigi and she licked our face and we felt like we were home."

"But then we were at a store looking for stuff and this girl showed up," Yamil said.

"I liked Harlow," Miracle said. "She was nice and held my hand when Yamil went running."

"I saw the store," Yamil said. "That JZ was from. I saw her picture on the mirror. It was sad."

"We got McDonald's!" Miracle said. "The chicken nuggets."

"We didn't get McDonald's," Yamil chided. "We only *saw* the McDonald's. There were no chicken nuggets."

Miracle slapped Yamil. "I remember them."

"We didn't get them," Yamil said. "But Harlow brought us to the bridge and then went into the ground."

"Ground?" Sky said.

"She lifted the thing and then went down the ladder," Yamil said. "Then she went into it. She said she would see us again soon."

"A storm drain," King said, when Sky looked for clarification.

"We'll check it out," Sky said.

"But then we got home!" Yamil said. "We got away from the bad guy and saw a lot of things. It was fun."

"Yeah," Sky said. "I can imagine. I think we are all very proud of you for getting away and finding your way back to us."

They pieced together more and more information over the course of the following days, but in the end, nothing really mattered except that they had gotten home. The most intriguing part of the story was about Harlow and her friends who supposedly lived in the storm drain tunnels beneath the city. They couldn't let that go, but none of them wanted to explore the underground system. They felt it could be too dangerous.

Sky and Misty, typically on the same page, differed in their opinions on the matter, with Sky wanting to play it safe and Misty looking to take risks.

If they have been down there all this time without bothering us, then let's just leave it be. This Harlow said she would be back, so if she does return, we'll explore it more then. In the meantime, just keep an extra eye on the storm drains.

Aren't we trying to reach more people? Remember, the Kingdom Initiative?

The Kingdom Initiative was implemented at the second council meeting after the fall of Vash and his men. It was established that the fortress, along with the heights, were not going to be enough to build an allied network strong enough to dissuade dissidents, thugs, gangs, and marauders from constantly threatening the territory. They all decided that the Kingdom Initiative would involve a sweep at a prescribed radius for other communities that they could network with to establish a regional presence.

I'm sure, in time, we will meet. She told the boys she would be back. We cannot send a group of our people into those tunnels. Whoever's been down there for four years knows that underground network much better than we do. And if they are foes, we don't stand a chance.

In the end, the committee,which now included more representation from the heights via Malayah and Frankie, resolved the disagreement and voted to avoid the tunnels and wait and see if the gophers returned.

Ironic given how things turned out, Sky thought.

Three

KING PRETENDED NOT TO know where he lived before the fall. He remembered, but he didn't want to—just like he wanted to go back to see if his mother had survived, but he was afraid. He was angry. He thought about it more often as the others decreed their interest in returning to their former homes. The idea was as fervent as the virus itself.

Going home.

Teddy had talked about it for a long time, wondering if going through that door might stop his nightmares. Then, Misty started talking about it after Sky's uncle visited. Now, King, though he had resisted the thought of returning to his roots, started wondering if he should.

It was four years since they left. Not only left their homes, King thought, but their old lives. And even though they had found love, shelter, and meaning in a new and unfamiliar world, there had to be a piece of them that never escaped those years before.

What piece of him did he leave behind from those days?

It was all too obvious. He left his mother. He never dreamed the last conversation with her would be a fight. She often told him never to leave the house angry, but that's exactly what he did. She wasn't that bad, only weak. He wasn't a man back then, or he would have saved her from the same life he was trying to save himself from. He would have stuck by her unconditionally. That's what family did, he had come to learn, but too late to save the relationship with his mother.

He not only ran away from his problems in the old world, but twice in the new world. But Sim wouldn't let him go that easy, like his mother had.

The first time was not too long after Sim found him. Sim was short with him about falling asleep on watch, and King rebelled and left. Sim tracked him down in the city center and brought him back. On the second occasion, when he met Zagan and fled to the heights, Sim sent a search party out for him. In hindsight, he could admit his instincts were childish and selfish, then *and* now. Who does such things, he often wondered? Him. A boy who would be named King, ironically. A king of mice, not men.

Being on the roof with nothing more to occupy his mind than his own thoughts didn't help. He couldn't wait for the others to take over the roof assignment so he could get off the shift.

Holly and Rodger. He wondered how that would work when they verified a communication with one another. "Roger that." It might confuse Rodger. They would have to change it. Yes, many, mostly random, things occupied his mind while he was alone.

The morning was in stark contrast to the previous night, which had been cloudy and starless. The sun was bright and the air still. The overnight showers left puddles across the flat rubber roof platforms.

Leo came up at one point with his Rubik's Cube, and King was excited for the company. At breakfast, Leo promised he would, but King didn't think Sky would allow him to escape for a leisurely trip to the roof when so much work needed to be done. They reminisced as King scouted with the scope.

"What happens when we have to replace the roof on this place?" Leo asked. "Sim said the roof was only ten years old, so it should last a while. But eventually...yeah, someone will need to do it."

"You know Jack and his buddies are 'jacks of all trades,'" King laughed at his pun. "Just look how fast they patched things up after you had the skirmish downstairs. Anyway, isn't that what the Kingdom Initiative is? To find new places and people so we can start doubling and tripling our resources and collective brain power?"

"Well," Leo said. "It's quite the initiative. We don't even know if there are other communities out there near enough to join us."

"We know Sky's sketchy uncle is out there with his horse riders...and what about that tale Yamil and Miracle told us about the girl popping out of the storm drain?"

"Do you think they fantasized that?" Leo asked. "As a way to cope on the road?"

King laughed, "Listen to you. You'll sure make a good therapist one day."

"I feel like I've been a therapist at this place since I got here," Leo said.

Leo twisted and turned his cube.

"Hey, Leo," King said. "Do you ever think about going home? Just to see it again?"

Leo put his toy down and leaned back, placing his hands on the roof and gazing into the sky, eyes closed. He absorbed the warmth of the sun on his face. "Sky asked me that not too long ago. I don't know. I guess, maybe, but I don't feel like Teddy. I think he really does need to go home. Me...probably not. My mother...she was thinking that we should all die together. She actually...tried to smother me with a pillow just before she died. I get afraid thinking about that being my last memory of her. She was always so...amazing. I tried to save us at one point by building a Lego rocket ship that would take us to space. I thought it was really going to work."

"Little kids," King said. "They sure are a different sort. But I'm sorry your mother did that to you. She must have been afraid. But you shouldn't remember your home that way."

"Maybe not," Leo said. "But my home is here. That's what I know now. Why complicate things by trying to cling to some past? It doesn't exist anymore unless you let it."

"You don't think the others are right in wanting to go back?" King asked, more thinking of himself, realizing he might be taking advice from someone several years younger.

"I don't think it's necessary, unless it'll help them move forward," Leo said. "Some part of them is trapped. Me...I don't feel trapped."

King understood. He might be trapped like the others by a past that would not let go. A past that kept him from enjoying the moment-to-moment reality.

As King peered through his scope toward the front of the fortress and down toward the intersection, he became less interested in discussing Zen and more interested in something he was seeing.

"What in the world?" King mumbled.

Leo, basking in the sun, turned to him. "What?"

"I don't know, but something strange is going on," King offered.

Leo stood and stepped closer to the edge of the roof in the direction that King's gun was aimed. "You see something?"

"I don't know," he said. "Wait. There it is again."

"What?" Leo asked. "I don't see anything."

"It's definitely something," he said. "It might finally be that person Yamil and Miracle talked about all this time. Do you see that storm drain cover on the street near the intersection?"

"Yeah, barely," Leo said. "What about it?"

"It's moving," King said. "I think it might be a gopher...this Harlow girl."

Leo squinted through the sun, using his hand as a visor. Sure enough, though, he saw the cover pop up from the ground. The cover remained suspended in air, likely by a pair of hands, for a few seconds before it came to rest again.

"Should you take a shot?" Leo asked. "When it's up?"

"I don't know," King said. "I'd have to be really good to get a shot through that sliver of space, and we don't know exactly what we would be shooting at. I don't want to kill someone who helped Miracle and Yamil get home."

What would Sim do?

Leo didn't think Sim would shoot at a target that was unidentified. The thought of someone being in the ground was concerning, even though Yamil and Miracle had warned them about this.

"Maybe we should go down?" Leo said.

"Let's radio," King said.

He picked up his walkie and pressed the side button. "Yo, King here. We got possible spies at the intersection in the storm drain...maybe Yamil and Miracle's person."

Seconds later: "You can see them?"

"The storm drain is popping up," King said. "There is definitely someone with eyes on us. I can send Leo down and have he and Wyatt investigate."

Leo looked at King in surprise and slapped him on the arm. "Why me? I don't want to be killed by some underground mongrel."

"It's your turn to vet," King reminded.

"Ugh," Leo said. "You *would* pull that."

"Send him downstairs," Sky said. "He can have a look with Wyatt and Baby."

King lowered his walkie. "You're up, kid."

"No thanks to you," Leo said. "Remember this moment when I'm killed by some underground mutants."

"Mutants?" King said. "You must have watched too many Saturday night movies on the Horror Fest channel back in the day."

"I'm a reader," Leo said. "I hardly remember television."

It was an interesting reminder of all the things that had changed that they had once taken for granted.

When Leo got downstairs, Baby and Wyatt were ready to go.

"You say you finally saw something in those drains?" Wyatt asked.

"That's what King said," Leo said. "Maybe they've always been watching us. We were just never watching back until Yamil said something."

"I want to go!" Yamil chimed in. "I want to see Harlow."

Sky looked at him warily. "I don't know."

"It might be a good idea," Wyatt said. "She knows him, after all. She might just be looking for him and Miracle."

"Well, she shouldn't be," Sky remarked. "He has a home. If she's looking for him, then she's looking for all of us."

"Copy that," Wyatt said. "You ready, Yamil?"

"Let's go!" he yelled.

"What about Miracle?" Baby said. "Where is he, anyway? These two are never apart."

"He's helping with the wall," Sky said. "He thinks he's the project foreman now. Let's just let him keep doing what he's doing. These two are finally diverging a bit. We don't want to spoil it."

Wyatt, Baby, Leo, and Yamil left the fortress, guns loaded and headed down to the intersection. King kept a close eye on them as they proceeded. They moved in cluster formation, as they typically did when they knew there was a potential threat. North, south, east, and west.

They approached the storm drain safely and peered down through the holes in the iron cover. They didn't see anything at first, but after a minute or so they did see movement beneath the grill cover.

"Hey!" Leo cried. "Who are you?"

Wyatt had his rifle pointed down as he prepared for the encounter. "Should we go down?"

Leo, pistol in hand, debated. "I don't know. We don't really know what's down there, and they aren't any sort of threat unless they come up, so what's the point?"

"Same ol' story," Baby said, reiterating the mindset of the committee.

"No!" Yamil protested. "It could be Harlow."

As they peered down into the storm drain, someone made another pass.

"Hello!" Leo cried. "Who are you?"

"Parker," a ghostly voice spoke faintly from the abyss.

Wyatt gave Leo a passing glance and both kept their guns aimed. The voice was that of a child.

"We saw you from up the hill," Leo said. "Show yourself."

"We see you all the time," Parker said.

"We?" Leo asked.

"Us moles," Parker said. "We don't mean no harm."

"If that's the case then you can reveal yourself," Leo said.

"Or you could come down here," Parker whispered.

"How 'bout I drop a grenade down there if you want to continue to debate," Leo said.

Yamil kneeled and peered through the holes. "No. Where's Harlow?"

"You know Harlow?" the voice said.

"Yes," Yamil said. "Where is she?"

Parker answered the question with one of his own. "How do I know you won't kill me if I come up there?"

"I'll tell you what," Leo said. "If you come to the ladder and let me get a look at you first, I'll come down."

"What are you talking 'bout?" Wyatt asked. "You aren't going into that hole."

"Just wait," Leo said.

Leo tucked his gun into the waistband of his jeans and got to his knees. He put his fingers through the drain cover and pulled upward, but he wasn't strong enough. "A *kid* pushed this up all by himself? No way."

That should have been the first red flag, but he ignored it.

Wyatt put down his rifle with a sigh and helped from the other side of the cover, and the two of them were able to slide it off. Wyatt bounced back to his feet and aimed the rifle into the hole. Leo remained on his knees, peering into the hole alongside Yamil.

"Well, let's go," Leo said.

"I don't like this," Baby muttered, still pointing her gun.

Thirty seconds later, a child of about ten appeared at the bottom of the hole staring up at Leo with large brown eyes. He had a head of curly hair, and his face was streaked with dirt. He was wearing gloves with the fingers cut off, a pair of jeans, and a long-sleeve shirt that was either black or stained black with dirt. Leo couldn't tell.

"There you are," Leo smiled.

The boy smiled back, a thin grin that revealed no front teeth. He had his hands on his hips.

"What are you doing down there?" Leo asked.

"I thought you said you would come down if you saw me," Parker reminded.

"Oh, yeah," Leo said. "Right."

"I don't know if that's a good idea, Leo," Wyatt said. "We don't know what's down in that tunnel other than that dirty kid."

"It's only me," Parker said. "The others aren't here. I know Harlow, though. How do you know her?"

"She walked us home," Yamil said. He turned to Leo. "I want to go down and see her."

"You *live* down there?" Leo asked, ignoring Yamil's pleas.

The boy didn't answer, only glanced at Leo expectantly.

"Oh, right," Leo said as he thrust his body into the hole and onto the ladder.

He climbed down to the bottom of the hole, which reminded him of climbing in and out of the fortress tunnel, and as he placed both feet onto the ground, he drew his pistol. "Okay now, back up and let me look around."

There was not much to look at but the grayness of the tunnel illuminated by random rays of sunlight traveling through the hole in the street. The tunnel proceeded in linear fashion to the east and west. The tunnel height was taller than the one they dug at the fortress, which made it comfortable for standing.

"Wow," Leo said arching his head in a circle. "Why didn't Sim ever think to explore down here?"

"I want to come," Yamil said from above. He started moving onto the ladder, but Wyatt stopped him.

"Come back up," Baby said. "I can't see anything."

Parker shone a flashlight into Leo's eyes and Leo shielded his eyes instinctively.

"Stop that," Leo said.

He heard Parker laugh followed by a series of fast footsteps, which led to him being knocked over the head with something hard. Leo blacked out, but remained lucid enough to hear the sounds of his friends calling him, cries that quickly grew fainter as he was carried off over someone's shoulder down the tunnel.

Up top, Wyatt and Baby screamed Leo's name repeatedly but got no response.

"Dammit, I knew it," Wyatt said. "Why the hell did I let him go down there?"

"Where's Harlow?" Yamil asked.

"Enough with Harlow!" Baby yelled. "They just took Leo."

"Shit," Wyatt said. He looked back to the fortress and down the hole. "We have to go down."

Just then their walkies buzzed. "What's going on down there?" King asked.

"Leo went down that damn hole and someone snatched him up," Wyatt admitted. "We're going down. We'll send Yamil back up."

"No," Yamil protested. "I'm going down."

Yamil jumped on the ladder and headed down.

"Damn," Wyatt said. He pressed the walkie button. "We're all going in. We have to find out what's going on."

"Going in?" King said. "Wait."

"What's happening?" Sky chimed in. "Don't you dare go into that hole. I'm coming down."

Wyatt ignored Sky while he, Baby, and Yamil proceeded down the hole in the ground to find out where Leo had gone.

Sky and Misty raced down to the storm drain, but they were too late. The cover was still dislodged, but everyone was gone.

"What the hell were they thinking?" Misty asked.

"Here we go again," Sky said. "Can there ever be a moment's peace?"

"We just have to trust them," Misty said. "We knew this day might come with these people in the underground. We were warned. At least we know they helped Yamil and Miracle. They can't be that bad."

"The just kidnapped Leo!" Sky yelled.

"The others will find him," Misty said. "There's nothing we can do."

She and Misty left the cover open and returned to the fortress, their only hope being that everyone that went down would eventually emerge.

Four

THE HEIGHTS HAD MOVED on from Tony's attempted coup. Charlie appointed Malayah and Frankie to the head of the defense taskforce, mostly because what transpired with Tony solidified his trust in them as the ones he wanted behind the guns.

He held a gathering where he thanked the community for their support and celebrated Mrs. Chandler's actions in stirring the community to action in order to thwart Tony's takeover. She promised to always have her eyes out and vowed that nobody was ever going to disregard the people of the heights when making decisions about leadership.

The next committee meeting was at the fortress in a couple of days, and while he was preparing his thoughts, Malayah came crackling over the radio.

"Charlie," she said. "You read?"

"I'm here," he said, putting down his pen.

"We have a visitor here on the west side," Malayah said. "He says he knows you and wants to meet."

"He *knows* me?" Charlie said, puzzled. "Who is it?"

There was a pause. "Says his name is Kane, from the old days."

Kane? Could it be? *Insane Kane.* The drug dealer from the south end of the city? Charlie knew him, but they weren't close friends. *He* survived? Of all the people to survive this mess of a new world...Zagan, Vash, Insane

Kane...if he didn't meet another hoodlum again in his life it would be too soon.

What did he want? Was this going to be another enemy to contend with right as they were pushing the Kingdom Initiative? Kane surely wasn't coming to discuss how to make the world a more peaceful place. The man had served prison time. Back in the day, he ran a large crew, and they supplied drugs not only to their city's residents, but he also had major drug connections in New York City at the time.

Fuck. Kane. Insane Kane.

"Charlie?" Malayah said.

If he were smart, he would tell Malayah to put a bullet in him right there and then and be done with it. A proper vetting. But if he killed Kane, that could only stir up a larger nest of bees, as Charlie was quite certain Kane wouldn't be operating solo. It was more prudent to see what he wanted first.

"I remember him," Charlie acknowledged. "Bring him down."

As he waited, he took out the bottle of Jack Daniels and put it on the coffee table. He poured himself a shot and threw it back. Then he threw back another one. He tied back his hair and cracked his ringed fingers to settle his nerves. Then came the knock.

Three. Two. One. He would have to change that code after Kane left.

He opened the door for Malayah, and standing in her shadow was a man he had not seen in years. He was heavier than Charlie remembered, and the tattoos on his thick neck were faded, but his hardened face was clean shaven and looked the same. Dark eyes. Thick lips. Black hair cut close to his large head, and a scar that ran from his right eye vertically down the side of his face, courtesy of a knife fight he had gotten into when he was a teenager.

He stepped past Malayah when he saw Charlie and raised an arm. "Charlie boy!"

Charlie grabbed Kane's hand mid-air, and Kane pulled him in for a chest hug. While he was gazing over Kane's shoulder, he gave Malayah a wide-eyed look, that tipped her off that she should stay close. She nodded.

"While I'm here, Charlie," Malayah said, "I need to visit the pharmacy."

Of course. The pharmacy was Charlie's pantry closet, so Malayah walked in and proceeded to the kitchen.

"The pharmacy?" Kane said. "Man, you are running a racket here, Charlie. I knew you would be. That's why when I heard that Charlie from the heights was still in business, I just had to come see it for myself. They said you was growing weed, too, in this motherfucka."

"Oh, come on Kane," Charlie said. "You know I was small time shit back then. Where have you been all this damn time?"

"I fled to Brooklyn when all the mayhem broke out," Kane said. "Brooklyn is whack, though. Tore the fuck up. Bodies everywhere. People didn't even have the goddamn sense to die at home. Got me a following though, which paved my way back to the Troilet."

The city of Troy had been referred to by many bougie people back in the day as such.

"Then, as soon as I got back, I got the best idea ever."

Charlie pointed a thick finger at the table.

"Why don't you sit down, Kane," Charlie said. "I pulled out the whiskey."

"Now you're talking, Charlie," Kane said.

The two sat down and Charlie poured them each a drink. He started to feel warm inside, and it helped relax his nerves. He wondered what Malayah was thinking in the kitchen. Charlie could hear her shuffling through the cabinet, though he knew it was just for show. Then he questioned why he had to pretend.

Because you don't want to do anything just yet to undermine mutual trust with this guy.

Kane tossed back a drink and licked his lips. "Ah, it never gets old." He breathed in a deep breath of air. "Thank God for the shelf life of whiskey and all the other fine beverages in this world. It's all that's left."

"I'll say," Charlie said.

"So, Charlie, baby," Kane said. "I brought many people back here and we carved a stronghold out of that Green Island in the Hudson. You know where they had all those pretentious apartments back in the day? We blew the fuck out of the two bridges on both sides. Youknow where I'm talking about?"

"We heard the explosions," Charlie said. "We never did take time to explore. That was a couple of months ago. So, that was *you*?"

"Right on," he said. "Only way to go back and forth is by boat unless you want to swim it. The isolation is perfect. Nobody can get in or out without us knowing. Like motherfucking Rikers or Alcatraz."

"You always had a knack for figuring it out," Charlie said, adding an uncomfortable laugh.

Malayah popped out of the kitchen and sat down on a chair in the living room, making herself at home. She laid her assault rifle across her lap. Kane eyed her suspiciously.

"You got the ladies running the show around here, huh?" Kane said sipping more whiskey. "Our ladies are a bit more...trained in the arts of domesticity."

"Malayah is head of defense," Charlie said. "As long as they can kick ass and take names, we don't care if they're male or female, and Malayah kicks ass."

"Oh shit," Kane said. "That's what's up. She looks like a warrior top to bottom. Fine specimen."

"You mess with this fine specimen," Malayah said in monotone, "and I'll stick this gun right up your ass and empty the clip."

Kane looked at her with reddened eyes. Then he burst out laughing. Charlie followed suit and the two were laughing hysterically while Malayah shook her head.

"She has some big balls, Charlie boy. I like her," Kane said, turning to Malayah. "Maybe you come visit me out on the island soon. We'll have some fun."

"As tempting as that sounds, my girl, Frankie, may have a problem with that," Malayah said.

"Oh, fuck," Kane said raising his glass. "Playing for the other team. Damn shame. Damn shame."

Charlie cleared his throat. "So, what brings you out my way, Kane? It's been a long time, and things aren't what they used to be. That old life...seems irrelevant now."

Kane smiled. His teeth were yellow. "This from the man growing weed, warehousing pharmaceuticals, and laying claim to the territory along with some other community...the fortress, is it? I hear they got mad guns and other fun toys."

Charlie's stomach sank. Same old Kane.

"Kane," Charlie said. "Malayah started the farming of marijuana for trade and for medical use. Our committee has since squashed the trade idea and we only retain a small field so we can use it for medical purposes. The pharmaceuticals are for our people. For sickness or surgery. What do you care about drugs now, anyway? There's no money in it."

Kane leaned forward in his chair, his eyes swelled. "Charlie, even our own government back in the day knew well enough how to control people. That's what this is about. Not drugs. Subtle oppression." Kane leaned back. "The people think you're doing them favors, but in reality, you got them by the balls." Kane raised a hand and it squeezed it into a fist.

"It's control you want, then?" Charlie said.

"Oh, Charlie," Kane said. "People want to be controlled. Why do you think your people came here to the heights? Why they came to me in Brooklyn. Community...that's just what people make when they want protection. I don't want protection, personally; I want to offer it. For allegiance."

Insane Kane.

"We're trying to develop a regional network here," Charlie said. "To rebuild. Not on the foundation of fear and oppression, but cooperation and workmanship. We call it the Kingdom Initiative."

Kane leaned down and put his glass on the table. He smiled with downcast eyes. "That's exactly what I'm talking about, Charlie. This whole area...a kingdom." Kane threw out his arms to his right and left. "And you and I...the kings."

"We're building a democracy," Charlie said.

Kane burst out laughing. He threw himself back on the couch. "A kingdom without a king? What kind of initiative is that? It's either a democracy or a kingdom. Right? Unless I missed something in the seven years of schooling I had."

"The kingdom...it's more of a metaphor," Charlie said with ill confidence.

"A metaphor?" Kane said. "Wow, Charlie, you gone soft on me, boy. You must have read some good books over the last few years."

"You never knew me back then, Kane," Charlie said. "You only thought you did."

"Maybe not, Charlie," Kane said. "But I think it is only fair to advise you, that I *am* looking to build a kingdom—a real kingdom...and there are only so many people left. It would be too bad if we were in a tug-o-war over the same survivors."

"It'll be just like the old days, Kane," Charlie said. "The people that want what you're selling will come to you, and the people who want what we're selling will come to us. We can all work together, respectful of one another's turf."

"Turf," Kane said. "Now there's a term from back in the day. Even still, we have turf to stick to, in a day and age when you can have any turf you want without limits. I have much to consider with my people, but keep in mind, with the limited amount of local resources, we may end up having to discuss how to equitably share weapons, medicine, and other things. It's only democratic, right, Charlie?"

"Exactly my point, Kane," Charlie said. "We have a committee you can join, and we can discuss your needs. That's how it works."

"A democracy," Kane mumbled to himself.

"It was good seeing you, Kane," Charlie smiled. "I'm sure you can find your way out."

Kane stood and stretched. "It was indeed eye-opening catching up. Come by the island sometime. We have a bunch of small boats housed under the Green Island bridge...or what's left of the bridge. I'll show you around and we'll have a good time and discuss this...*democracy* some more."

"Maybe I'll do that," Charlie said.

"Ask for Jesse at the river's edge," Kane said.

Charlie nodded.

Malayah rose to escort him out, but Charlie grabbed her arm.

Kane turned around as he reached the door. "Thanks for the whiskey."

"It wouldn't be a party without Mr. Daniels," Charlie laughed.

Kane laughed and then Charlie closed the door behind him.

"What in the hell is that all about?" Malayah asked.

Charlie ignored her and grabbed his walkie from the table. "Frankie, you copy?"

"What is it, Charlie?" Frankie said. "Where's my girl? Last I saw her she was leading some overstuffed *puta* into your apartment."

"Good!" Charlie said. "You saw him. He can't..."

Charlie paused and lowered the walkie.

He can't leave here. Consider him vetted and shoot to kill.

Then what? Have his men from the island show up for a war? Maybe Kane *would* consider democracy. Maybe he *could* be an ally. As badly as he wanted to issue the order, he couldn't.

"Walk him to the edge of the property with caution," Charlie said.

"If that's what you want, Charlie," Frankie said.

"I'll go out and make sure he leaves and that nobody else is with him," Malayah said. "I don't trust that fool for half a second."

Charlie agreed. As he returned to write up notes for the next meeting, he scribbled "Insane Kane" at the top of the ledger.

Five

LEO CAME TO AS he was being carted through the drainage shaft on top of someone's shoulder. As his limp body bounced up and down, his head, the back of which throbbed, was nearly hitting the top of the concrete shaft. He explored his head with one free hand and felt an egg-shaped lump. Though his glasses remained on his face during the attack, he could not see anything as the underground passage was dark, except for when they passed by the occasional outlet to the streets above. He heard the scurrying of feet as he was being whisked further and further away.

When he came to his full senses, he started to scream.

"Let me go!" he yelled.

His abductor had firm hold of both his legs so he couldn't kick, but he pounded away at the man's back with his closed fists. The man grunted but continued further down the shaft. He heard Parker's distinctive giggle ahead of them.

"Parker!" Leo yelled. "Tell him to put me down and stop this nonsense now."

Another giggle.

As they continued forward, the sides of the shaft started to reveal themselves, courtesy of the natural light that was seemingly ahead of them. With each passing second, it got brighter until finally they were out of the shaft and on the shores of the Hudson River. The tall man that was carrying Leo put him down on the ground just outside the exit to the shaft. Parker was there as well.

Leo picked himself up quickly and shimmied away from the pair until his backside hit a tree. Parker was giggling, and the other man, double Parker's size, was a muscle-clad behemoth that was probably no more than twenty years old.

Parker pulled Leo's gun from his pocket but kept it pointing to the ground.

"Hey," Leo said. "That's mine."

"Nothing belongs to anyone anymore," Parker laughed. "But you'll get it back when I know it's safe."

"You're talking to me about being safe, when you and your hulk friend just knocked me over the head and abducted me?"

"His name is Messiah, and he doesn't talk much," Parker said. Then he placed his hand to the side of his mouth to use it as a shield while he whispered away from Messiah, "I think he's autistic, you know. He's very awkward, and believe it or not, even though I knew he was there, I had no idea he was going to clock you on the noggin with his flashlight. He usually doesn't do anything I don't tell him to do, but he might have been scared this time."

Leo looked the giant black boy up and down. "Why did you hit me?"

"I thought I was supposed to," he shrugged. "I was confused."

"I only asked you to hit the last guy because he scared me," Parker said to him. "He probably would have hurt us, but that doesn't mean you have to hit everyone, Messiah."

"Okay," Messiah said.

"What is your name?" Parker asked, turning his focus on Leo.

"Leo," he answered.

"That's funny," Parker laughed.

"No more funny than the name 'Parker,'" Leo snapped, rubbing the back of his head. He turned around and saw the river a few feet off, the same part of the river he could see from the fortress if he looked out any east-facing window. "So, what is your story, anyway? You're about my age. You could have lived with me all this time, had Sim found you back then. He looked everywhere for children. Had he only looked in the sewer—"

"Excuse me," Parker said. "But I don't live in any sewer. Don't you know the difference between a storm drain and a sewer? I thought kids with glasses were supposed to be dorks and know everything."

"Well don't you know the difference between a dork with glasses and a regular person who isn't a dork but wears glasses?"

"Clearly not," Parker said. "What is that place you live at?"

"It's called the fortress," Leo stated proudly. "I've lived there since the fall and have great friends there."

"They all looked weird," Parker said. "Who was that old greasy fart with you?"

Leo thought of Wyatt. "You sure have a knack for making fun of people," Leo snapped. "While you stand there covered with grime and don't even have any front teeth, which would be fine if you were a six-year-old."

Parker's face reddened. "Another mole knocked them out. It hurt a lot, but thankfully Messiah got him good." Parker perked up again as he threw an air punch. "He punched him so hard in the head that the guy flew about ten feet and then he started having those convulsions. Then he just...died."

"I'm sorry about your teeth," Leo said. "But you shouldn't make fun of people. It's not nice."

Parker shrugged.

"Anyway, I think I know another mole," Leo said. "Someone who helped my friends get home when they were lost. You said you know Harlow?"

"Yes, I know Harlow!" Parker exclaimed. "We're like besties."

"So, she's your family?" Leo asked.

"I don't know if you would call it a family, but there is her and about fifteen or twenty others that me and Messiah hang out with. Most of them are legit. Sometimes we stay under, and other times we come up, but it's the coolest place to play hide and seek, and you can get anywhere in the city without having to be in the open. It's really awesome, but I never had any other kids to play with. It'll be fun to have a friend. Do you want me to show you around down here?"

"Show me around?" Leo said. "I need my gun so I can get back and tell the others what happened. I got friends. A life. I can't be playing around in the sewers."

"They aren't sewers, I said!" Parker yelled.

Messiah put a large hand on Parker's shoulder as the boy sulked.

"Here's your stupid gun back," Parker said, thrusting his arm forward.

Leo took the gun but felt ashamed.

"Look," Leo said. "I'll let you show me around for a while, but only after I go back and tell my friends that I'm okay."

Parker smiled. "Maybe one day me and Messiah can meet *your* friends."

Just then they heard voices coming out of the tunnel. It was the voices of the others screaming his name.

"Looks like you won't have to wait too long," Leo said. "You can't mess with us. My friends don't play."

As he said this, Wyatt, Baby, and Yamil appeared from out of the mouth of the tunnel. Messiah pushed Parker behind him, and Leo raised his hands.

"Wait!" Leo yelled. "Put your guns down. They aren't hurting anyone."

"Well, what in tarnation are they doing stealing you away like that?" Wyatt asked, eyeing Messiah up and down.

"I think the big guy thought we were a threat," Leo said. "This is Parker and Messiah. They know Harlow."

"You know Harlow?" Yamil asked. "I want to see her."

"She's around," Parker said.

"Let's go!" Yamil cried.

"Yamil," Baby said. "We're not just running around some sewer tunnel looking for a girl you haven't seen in two months."

Parker tossed up his arms. "How many times do I have to tell you...it's not a sewer!"

"Sure smells like one," Wyatt said.

"We're going back," Baby said. "Radio the others and tell them we found Leo."

Wyatt jumped on his radio. "You all hear us up there?"

"There you are," Sky said. "Where's Leo? Why did you all jump into the sewer? You had us frightened to death."

"Look, Sky," Wyatt said. "The people we're with...they kind of get offended when you call it a sewer down here. It's actually—"

"Who the hell cares, Wyatt?" Sky said. "Is everybody okay?"

"We're all fine," Wyatt said. "The Harlow mystery is partially solved, though. These guys down here know her."

"Where even are you?" she asked. "Isn't it dark down there?"

"We actually came out of the drain at the riverbed," Wyatt said. "We'll be back up in a few."

"Make it quicker than a few," King said. "We got more company. Coming over the bridge. Five people. Armed."

Everyone looked at each other, then Wyatt turned to Parker. "Get us back there quick."

Parker and Messiah led the way back into the tunnel, with the others following behind, Leo first in line. Leo was thankful to have his gun back but was kicking himself for entering the storm drain without a flashlight. Wyatt had a flashlight and was shining it over everyone's heads from the back. Parker had a light in the front, but Leo was stuck behind Messiah, which was like walking behind a moving wall, so it was hard to see anything.

"Can I get in front of you, big guy?" Leo asked.

"Sure," Messiah answered as he stepped aside.

As it were, Messiah had to walk hunched over, as he was taller than the height of the tunnel.

"Just as long as you don't go knocking me in the head again," Leo said.

"I won't do that," Messiah said.

It was a much better view being behind Parker and his ray of light. With each ladder they passed, Leo wondered which storm drain it connected to. The walls on either side of them were graffitied in various places, and Leo wondered if it had all been done after the fall or if people used the tunnels to squat even in old times.

"Wait till I show you the network," Parker said. "The tunnels connect everywhere. It's not so convenient when it rains, but if it is dry up there it's good down here. Unless you like to surf."

"How do you know which hole leads where?" Leo asked.

"When you're down here long enough, you just get to know. We marked a lot of them with spray paint though. The outlet you came down has a missing step on the ladder. You see."

Parker pointed his flashlight at the ladder they had arrived at, pointing out the missing step. "We'll mark this as the fortress outlet," Parker said.

"That makes sense," Leo said, grabbing a ladder wrung in preparation for his ascent.

"Hurry, Leo," Baby cried from the back. "It's hot down here and I can't see."

"I'm going," Leo said.

One at a time, they climbed out of the storm drain. Leo, Parker, Messiah, Baby, Yamil, and finally Wyatt. As they got out, they saw the people King was referring to on the walkie. The group hadn't noticed them come out of the drain. Wyatt got back on his radio.

"We're at the intersection," he said. "What's the word on these people?"

"Proceed with caution," Sky said. "Undetermined."

Baby, Wyatt, Leo, and Yamil came up the hill. Wyatt, Baby, and Leo had guns drawn while Yamil hung back with Parker and Messiah, who proceeded cautiously behind the lead three.

As they got closer to the crew in the front of the fortress, the visitors noticed them, but none raised their weapons. Either it was because they realized Wyatt and his group had gotten the drop on them, or they wanted to assert passivity.

"Leo and Baby, run up the hill behind them and stay to their right," King said. "Wyatt, you stay put."

They did as they were told, and before long the fortress had them surrounded.

"Well," an auburn-haired woman with rosy cheeks said. "Impressive. A child army with precision movement."

"What was it you wanted, again?" Sky said.

"I can imagine visitors concern you," the woman said. "We come on a diplomatic mission to network with other communities who are like-minded in the way of progress."

She turned to Wyatt and the others on her right and left. "My name is Ember. To my right is Avi, a child not too much older than many of you. A lovely man in our community, named Pierre Dumas, discovered him a few years ago. He tried so hard to save orphans, but Avi was the only one he could come up with. Maybe it was because somebody else had already found them all."

"His name was Sim," Sky said. "Where exactly are you from?"

Sky thought of the Kingdom Initiative and how much easier it would be if other communities fell into their laps instead of having to search for them. Right before her sat the seeds of two potential groups in the two boys that had emerged from the storm drain, and this woman, Ember, who stood before them.

"We are from a community about ten miles southwest of here," Ember said. "It's a former environmental center. We call it the preserve. Not only have I and others maintained the land throughout, but we developed it with the help of engineers, scientists, builders, and architects. I think you would all be impressed."

"We got good things happening here, too," Sky was quick to mention. "Vegetable gardens, fruit bearing trees, and many other things."

"We've heard," Ember said. "In fact, we've heard from someone you know."

"Who?" Sky said.

"Your uncle," Ember said. "Michael and his men have been friends of our community for a couple of months now. It's no coincidence he came here the other day. We all feel like you, that the time is right to see our individualist communities evolve into a sizeable district. We even have a name for this new district...*Pangea*!"

"Pangea?" Misty said, raising an eyebrow.

"Yes," Ember said. "You see, before there were seven separate continents on earth, they were all merged into a single land mass that scientists called Pangea. That's what we liken our vision to."

"Clever," Misty said.

Sky seethed inside, thinking of her uncle networking for months with this woman while he knowingly let her, and the fortress, sit in isolation and under threat with no offer of support or help.

"If you think bringing my uncle's name into it is going to make us kneel and kiss your feet, you've come here with the wrong strategy," Sky said.

Ember shook her head. "I don't want anyone kneeling at our feet. And we aren't here to force you to do anything. We're offering a proposal for partnership."

Misty whispered into Sky's ear as she stood at her side atop the steps. "Don't let your feelings about your uncle get in the way right now. This is what we have been talking about. The kingdom. Sim's vision."

"We have another community," Sky said. "The heights, not two miles from here. They are allied with us and would be interested in what you are proposing."

"Wonderful," Ember smiled.

"I don't know enough about my uncle of late to know where he fits into all of this, but we've recently found another community it would seem...underground, who might also be interested in organizing. It's still too early to tell."

Sky looked beyond Wyatt at Parker and Messiah who were standing with Yamil.

"It's all coming together," Ember said. "There are so many of us out here no longer just fighting for survival. We have all managed to get over that hump, so now it's time to grow. To come together as one. Imagine if we bring a regional policing presence to the area, a government, a school, and start rebuilding infrastructure. We can do this. Together."

"And what did you expect to accomplish in coming here?" Sky asked.

"I want to invite a few of you back to the preserve to see our progress," Ember said. "We can leave a couple of our people to see the wonderful initiatives at the fort—"

"No," Misty interrupted. "Nobody is staying here. Not yet. We have a committee that votes on everything."

Ember nodded. "Interesting. The roots of government. Right here. Maybe a couple of your people can follow us back and see for yourselves. We can develop a trust and from there..."

"The only way our people go back is weaponized," Sky said. "We don't turn our weapons in at any gate, and if anything happens to our people, we will find you, and we will kill you."

Just then, Sky caught Avi smiling at her.

"What's so funny, boy?" Sky said, trying to forget he was probably two years her senior.

"I like you," Avi said.

"No flattery in the world is going to take away from our protocol," Sky said. "Using Mike as a reference hasn't instilled anymore trust in you than if you were unknown to him."

That was a lie, of course, as she knew her uncle would never put her in harm's way.

Just then, Gigi poked her head out the door.

"She's not barking," Misty said. "That's a good sign."

Gigi went down the stairs and Avi reached down and petted her on the head.

"We understand your reticence," Ember said clasping her delicate hands together. "So, who are the lucky liaisons with whom we get to travel with, back to the preserve?"

"We can't decide that now," Sky said. "Not until after our committee meeting. It's not scheduled until tomorrow morning, though. We can take you quickly through the fortress as long as you are willing to leave your guns with us and are subject to a pat down. Then, maybe our friend, Wyatt, can take you to the heights so you can meet Charlie. You can all travel back down together tomorrow, and after our meeting we will have more resolved."

"Sounds fair enough," Ember said. "And we are humbled."

As Baby, Leo, and Wyatt closed the distance and disarmed the members of the preserve, Yamil turned to Parker and Messiah. "Go get Harlow and bring her back."

"We don't even know where she is right now," Parker said.

"Go find her," Yamil said.

"Okay, okay," Parker said. "Who made you boss of the world, anyway?"

"I want to see her," Yamil said. "She brought us home."

"We'll come back when we find her," Parker said. "Tell that Leo kid we'll see him later."

Parker and Messiah climbed back into the storm drain, and Messiah pulled the iron grate back over their heads. Everyone else was too busy with their guests to notice them depart. King shouted at Yamil from the rooftop.

"Where are they going, Yamil?" King yelled. His voice echoed through the street, and everyone turned their gazes downhill.

"He's going to find Harlow!" Yamil yelled back. "They will come back later."

King put his hand to his ear and shrugged. Yamil completed his distance up the hill as the preserve members entered the fortress. Miracle weaved around them as the others, Ember in particular, stood in awe of him.

"Look how little," Ember said, trying to pat his head as he dashed by to get to Miracle. "My people would be enthralled by him and the other little one. Kids this age...they just don't exist."

"Trust me," Teddy said. "*Here*, they do."

"And what's your name?" Ember asked.

"Teddy," he said, redirecting to Leo. "That's no fair. You guys found new friends to play with in the sewer."

"It's not a sewer," Leo said. "They'll be back."

"Where's Harlow?" Miracle asked Yamil.

"Parker is going to get her," he said.

"Was he that big giant guy?" Teddy asked.

"No, that was Messiah," Leo said. "Guys, we got work to do. We can't stand around here asking questions all day. We have company. This is embarrassing."

Sky took them on a tour of the fortress. She did not bring them to the basement to highlight the arsenal storage or the tunnel exit.

"For security reasons, we can't bring you to the basement, but we do maintain indoor gardens down there and grow lots of shade-tolerant vegetables and herbs. We funnel some light from the subfloor windows, and it's quite successful. Perhaps one day we can show you. But not today."

Though the fortress was only a microcosm of larger-scale possibilities, the preserve members were highly impressed and loved interacting with the orphans. They held good conversation as they visited the well, the outhouse, the fruit trees, and outside gardens, and all were regaled with the stories of how the fortress was founded, of Sim and the others who had died, and their struggles against Zagan and his cult, led by Vash. They regarded the wholesomeness of the small community in awe, observing with much interest the handprint mural, the fortress pledge, and the days-gone-by wall filled with hashmarks.

Ember not only observed her surroundings but soaked in the details, as if visiting another planet. It was surreal to see how others had survived since the fall, and she became hopeful that their visit would pave the way to their unification.

Six

PARKER AND MESSIAH WEAVED through the underground labyrinth of tunnels. They sloshed around in pooled water as they made their way with a flashlight in random directions hoping to bump into Harlow.

That's how it went in the tunnels. Parker stuck with Messiah to ensure protection, but he knew most everyone else who he ran into down there. On occasion, they did come across a stranger, but if he or she posed any threat, he had Messiah deal with them. It was rare, though. Most people in the tunnels were trying to escape the dangers of the world above.

Nobody in the network bothered with Messiah because he was mentally limited. Even Parker didn't know how the boy survived before the two hooked up. Instinct only, perhaps, or because he was so big and muscly that people didn't mess with him. Parker ran into him on the street one day, and after he got a sense for him, he invited him into the drains. He would admit it was for selfish reasons, but he had grown close to Messiah over the years. Now, their relationship was much more than that.

They came across a man who was sitting with a bottle of wine under a gateway. Parker stopped.

"Bobby," he said. "Have you seen Harlow wandering around?"

"I saw her at the Fourth Street gate about an hour ago. She was blabbing to Marianne. You know how they like to chat."

"Fourth Street, then," Parker said. "Come on, big guy."

Parker led them another quarter mile or so until they hit the Fourth Street gate. He let Messiah up first to lift up the cover.

"Is it clear?" Parker asked.

"Yeah," Messiah said. "It's quiet."

"We'll go up for a bit," Parker said. "Maybe find something to eat. I've got to take a piss too and it's hotter than the sun down here."

Harlow spent more time above than down below. She loved using the tunnels to travel and she did find recessed areas in the tunnel system in which to light fires and sleep, but she spent the larger part of her day up top. If Bobby had seen her at the Fourth Street drain, it was more than likely she was wandering above ground in that area.

The pair came up in the middle of downtown and drifted in and out of some stores. They called out with a signature noise which was well known among the moles. *Coo. Coo. Coo.*

They got no response.

"I'll bet she's at the library," Parker said. "Let's go, big guy."

"Okay," Messiah said.

They made their way around the courthouse to the others side. Down the road a bit was the city library. Harlow spent a lot of time there. The pair stepped into the foyer of the historic building. *Coo coo coo.*

Seconds later, a return call came. *Coo coo coo.* Parker ran up the spirally granite staircase, and in the center of the second floor Harlow was sitting in a cushioned chair, book in hand.

"There you are," Parker said. "I knew you would be here."

"Hello, my fellow underground urchins," Harlow said.

"How are you doing, Harlow?" Messiah asked.

"Just dandy," Harlow said, slapping her book shut. "Enjoying a peaceful afternoon in the fresh air. Honestly, I don't see how you spend so much time down there in these hot months."

Parker fanned himself. "It's not much better up here. We need to take a river plunge."

"Maybe later," she said. "How did you know I was here?"

"Bobby told us that he saw you with Marianne near the Fourth Street gate," Parker said. "We looked around, but then I figured you would be in here reading another book."

"You should try it sometime," she said.

"I can't read," Parker said.

"I'll teach you," Harlow said. "They have a kid section, you know."

"School's out for the summer," Parker laughed. "Maybe in the fall. You can get me new clothes, a backpack, and a lunch bag, and it will be just like old times."

"I'll even put you on the school bus," Harlow said.

"Yeah, cool," Parker said. "Me and Messiah slept on a bus one night. It was a city bus, though."

She looked to Messiah. "And how is everything with my favorite warrior of the underground?"

Messiah smiled wide as he shuffled on his feet. "Good."

"As always, a man of few words," she said.

"We met some friends of yours today," Parker said. "They wanted me to come get you."

She cocked her head. "Friends?"

"Yes, Leo...and there was a few others," Parker said. "I totally forget the name of the one kid who bullied us to come find you. He was little, though. Tan, dark hair. Scrawny."

"Yamil!" Harlow said.

"That's it," Parker pointed.

"I don't know anyone named Leo," she said, appearing starry-eyed. "Oh, wow, I had forgotten all about them. I would remember them sometimes, but then forget. And it went on and on like that. Right now, I remember."

Parker slapped Messiah gently on the arm and spoke out of the side of his mouth. "And this is the smart one."

"Intelligence and memory are two different things," Harlow said. "Oh, but I remember the boys. We had a nice walk back. It was quite an adventure, and I did promise to come back and see them. I just got so busy."

Parker looked around. "Busy? That's what you're going with? Maybe for their sake, you can tell them you got lost or were abducted and only just managed to escape."

"I'll tell them...I wanted to let them get settled before I came back. After all, getting lost was quite traumatic for them. They had me in some nail and hair salon, and Yamil was picking up hair from the floor and smelling it."

"I knew he was weird," Parker said.

"What about Miracle?" Harlow's eyes beamed.

"I don't know any Miracle," Parker said. "I met Yamil, Leo, some girl with blonde, curly hair, and some crusty white man with wrinkles on his face. But there were others at the house. I just left before I could meet the rest of them."

Harlow jumped up from her chair. As it skidded backward on the marble floor, the scraping sound echoed throughout the hollows of the library.

"Well let's get back there!" she cried. "Maybe we can take the street? I'm not in the mood to be in the dark humid tunnels right now."

"Whatever you want, but don't expect me to wait around if we run into trouble," Parker said. "First sign of marauders and I'm diving."

Harlow raised her arm and put a hand on Messiah's shoulder. "No worries, you coward. My warrior will save me."

Messiah grinned and the three left the library and headed down Fourth Street toward the fortress.

Back at the fortress, they were wrapping things up with Ember and her crew. Wyatt led the group out the door and returned their weapons, which they had earlier stored in Ms. Betty's shopping cart and left under Baby's guard.

Sky gave them plenty of bottled water, as they were running low, and then sent them on their way.

"I'm looking forward to seeing you again," Avi said to Sky as he last exited the fortress.

Sky retained her poker face, remembering how Kellogg always tried to flatter, but he was only a little boy with a crush. With Avi, it seemed like the fascination was different.

"Keep your pants on," Sky said with a half-smile.

"I'm sorry," Avi said. "I didn't mean to—"

"You'll be back tomorrow," Sky said.

"Sky's got a boyfriend, Sky's got a boyfriend," Teddy said as he giggled with Yamil and Miracle.

She snapped her head back and they went running. She yelled after them. "Get back to building that wall!"

"Sorry," Avi said.

"Boys will be boys," Sky said.

Avi joined the group and watched as the six of them made their way up the hill and out of sight.

Baby climbed the steps. "Interesting group. The boy was cute. Avi? I wonder if that's his real name."

"Likely not," Sky said. "Anyway, who has time to notice boys?"

Sky turned away briskly, and Baby smiled. *I saw the way you looked at him. You can't fool me.*

A few hours later, as most of the fortress orphans labored over building the wall, King alerted them of more visitors.

"We got more people coming up from Fourth Street," King said. "It's just those sewer people, though. If we're going to start seeing visitors like this all the time, maybe the roof job will hold my attention after all."

"They aren't sewer people, King," Leo reminded. "Storm drain."

"Whatever," King said. "Anyway, there are three of them. Two males, including the Hercules-looking guy, and one female. Maybe some pocket weapons, but nothing visible."

"Misty and I will handle this," Sky said. "But send Yamil and Miracle up to the front of the house, so they can confirm if this is the girl who walked them home from Valley Hall. They'll probably want to see her anyway."

Sky, Misty, Yamil, Miracle, and Gigi met the trio as they came up the hill. Yamil and Miracle wanted to run to Harlow, but Sky stopped them.

"Wait until she gets closer," Sky warned.

When the three arrived at the doorstep, Harlow smiled at the boys. "So, we meet again."

Sky nodded to the boys, and they ran down the steps with Gigi and hugged Harlow.

"She was abducted," Parker said. "That's why it took her so long to come back to see you."

"Uh huh," Messiah laughed.

"I was not, you goofball," Harlow said. "I wanted them to get settled before I bothered them."

"We can't thank you enough for helping them get back," Sky said. "If something were to have happened to them...let's just say it would have been a deep struggle."

"They would have found their way back, regardless," Harlow said. "Persistent little buggers, and in my opinion, born for the road."

"They surprised us all," Sky said. "But the road is no place for anyone right now. By the time they are older, we should hope."

"It's been good to me," Harlow said. "But I have friends that watch out for me. It's a unique community underneath, but I'm sure they would all love to see a day when being on top makes sense. Though I do spend a lot of time wandering above ground. One day it could catch up with me."

"She likes the library," Parker said.

Sky's eyes lit up. "We've visited the library on occasion, but most of the books in our own library were scoured from homes and stores. We try to avoid the city center."

"The city is quiet most times, and usually you can hear trouble coming. But nobody thinks to look for you underground, so it's easy to get away quick when you have to."

"We should go on another adventure!" Yamil said.

"Yeah," Miracle parroted. "Another adventure."

"I just said that, you goofball," Yamil said.

Parker put his hand on his head. "And I thought *one* was annoying. Now there are two."

Harlow gazed downward, ignoring Parker's comment. "Maybe through the tunnels."

"I was down there," Yamil said, plugging his nose. "It was smelly, dark, and hot."

Parker shrugged. "I guess you just get used to it."

"We'd invite you in," Misty said. "But we're cautious about visitors. Even in this case."

"You let those other people in," Parker pointed out.

"That was different," Sky said. "They knew a family member of mine, but we were still a little hesitant and only gave them a peek."

"I'll take a peek," Parker said.

Misty stepped aside. "Take a peek."

Parker arched his neck. "Ohhh, a staircase," he said.

Misty moved to block the entrance again.

"Anyway," Harlow said. "I guess we'll get going. I just wanted to see these guys again. I was in the middle of a vampire romance novel and I'm dying to find out what happens next."

"No," Yamil said. "Come in."

"How many of you are there?" Sky asked. "And is anyone in charge?"

"No more than twenty of us roam the tunnels," Harlow said. "We know all of them. But nobody is really in charge. We're not organized like that, but we help each other out."

"We have a special call," Parker said, making a funnel with his hand and placing it over his mouth. "*Coo. Coo. Coo.*"

Yamil and Miracle laughed.

"It's a bird," Miracle said.

"Perhaps we can meet more of your friends?" Sky suggested. "We're trying to organize the region so we can make the streets safe again and start rebuilding at a larger scale. The people who were here earlier were from another community. We would like to ask your group to take part in our initiative that we're calling the kingdom. The other group has another weird name for it, but it's all the same idea."

"Hmph," Harlow said. "I can mention it to people, but what do we have to do?"

"Right now, we're just trying to get in touch with other communities and start discussions. The more people we have involved, the better our chances of success."

"And by the way," Misty said. "If any of your people want to get out of the underground, we have another community not too far from here called 'the heights' with plenty of room. Any of you are welcome there. The leader of the community is a good man and old friend of ours."

Harlow considered this idea. She couldn't envision being part of an actual community. Though more dangerous, she had always enjoyed the freedom of travel, the thrill of escape, and the challenge of survival outside an established order.

"It's a lot to think about," Harlow said. "But I will start talking to some people."

"Our committee convenes tomorrow, and members of two other communities will be here," Sky said. "You're welcome to come and see what, if anything, is determined about our next moves related to this. We typically meet a couple hours after sunrise."

"Yay!" Yamil said.

"Well, me and the big guy have nothing pressing to do," Parker said. "I mean, there are your basic chores, like graffiti art at the 110th street gate, and ironing my clothes. I also have a new pair of gloves I need to cut off the fingers on. We planned to visit the Presbyterian church on Broadway and break out all their windows, do some shopping, take a swim..."

"Will you shut up?" Harlow scolded.

"Wow, you have a good life," Yamil said.

"Really good," Miracle said.

"Boys," Sky said. "Time to say goodbye."

"I'll get this urchin out of your hair for now, but we'll be back tomorrow," Harlow said.

She hugged the boys while Parker and Messiah offered them a high-five. The boys were enthralled with how big Messiah's hands were. After the farewell gestures were concluded, the boys headed inside while Misty and Sky remained, sending them off with a wave.

"She's kind of cute," King said through the walkie as they strolled away. "Scrappy, maybe, but cute."

"Can we keep our conversations on the walkie to business, and not personal fantasy?" Sky said.

"Copy that," King said.

"The hormones are starting to fly around here lately," Wyatt said through his radio.

For the rest of the day, no more visitors showed. King was bored, but hopeful that the next day's committee meeting would solidify two new rooftop guards so that he could get back to being mobile.

Seven

THE NEXT DAY WAS sunny and humid. They kept the windows to the fortress open for the breeze, and they had several battery-operated fans around the house, but they added only mild relief. It was typically sticky and hot. Wyatt, Charlie, Malayah, and Frankie arrived with Ember, Avi, and their crew in the early morning. Harlow, Parker, and Messiah had not come back, and Sky wondered if they even would.

Ember and her crew waited out front taking in the rising sun while the seven members of the committee convened at the dining room table.

"We might have to start holding over any tie-breaking votes on committee issues so either Frankie or I can stay at the heights on these days," Malayah started. "I don't fully trust Dylan's competency holding down the security force while we're away. Merrick and Watson are great, but Dylan is responsible for the entire east side, and he's a nitwit."

"We could consider it," Charlie said. "But I don't think you give Dylan enough credit. He's a bit awkward, but I think he's responsible. Plus, Mrs. Chandler is stepping up a lot."

"Yeah," Frankie acknowledged. "I think that whole thing that went down with Tony and how she handled it went to her head. She's a regular mother hen now."

"It's called empowerment," Charlie said. "It's great to see people stepping up."

"I'm just worried with that guy, Kane, who showed up the other day," Malayah said. "We can't let down our guard with that guy lurking around."

"Kane?" Sky said.

"It's on the agenda," Charlie said.

"Why don't we start with that, then," Sky said. "A new threat?"

"Let's hope not," Charlie said. "But it is possible. He and his people are the ones that blew up the bridges a couple of months ago going on and off of that small island outside of Troy."

"Mystery solved," King said. "What's his deal? Is it just someone else who's head I need to put a bullet in?"

"Why do you get to have all the fun?" Frankie asked.

"I knew him back in the day," Charlie said, ignoring the banter. "Drug dealer. Lots of connections. Murderer. Prison time. The usual."

"And now we're lucky enough to have him here," Sky said. "Just as we're finding new people and communities to spearhead our Kingdom Initiative."

"By the way, Ember and her group seem lovely," Charlie remarked. "Perfect timing, too."

"They seem to be," Sky said. "What did this Kane want?"

"Oh, nothing more than what *we* want, except to rule the land personally and through oppression. Democracy isn't much in his way of thinking. He sees a landscape to conquer and subdue. He spent the last few years in Brooklyn, and I can only imagine the people he gathered down there are nothing less than your typical street soldiers from back in the day."

"We don't know much about that," Sky said.

"Speak for yourself, babydoll," Frankie said. "They're pretty much like the *putas* out there today, only back then they had to hide from law enforcement to avoid jail. Now, who are they hiding from?"

"Well, us, if we can organize and start policing this entire region again," Sky said.

"That's not going to happen overnight, Sky," Charlie advised. "In the meantime, we may have to fight fire with fire until this initiative gains momentum. They used to call this man 'Insane Kane.' His visit to the heights was nothing more than a courtesy announcement that he's back. It won't be long before he starts doing what he came here to do."

"Just what we need," Sky sighed. "Then, what do we do?"

"I will take him up on his invitation to visit the island," Charlie said. "It'll stall him, so we can have a chance to strategize. Maybe I'll feign interest in partnership. I can take Malayah with me. It'll give us a chance to probe their setup and formulate a plan to nip this in the bud. He did us a favor by showing us half of his hand. Now, we just need to see the other half."

"Won't that be a bit dangerous, Charlie?" Wyatt said.

"It's more dangerous waiting for him to act," Charlie said. "We can't just sit around hoping he goes away. Because I know this man, and he's not going away."

"You want to take my girl into the lion's den, Charlie?" Frankie said.

"Don't worry, babe," Malayah said. "I see beneath his layer of filth. We're smarter than he is on any given day."

"She'll be fine," Charlie said. "He won't try anything in this context. He's got no motive to want to hurt us at this point. He's just out for control."

"He'll certainly kill anyone who opposes that control," Sky said. "I think you're right. Let's get a look at his operations inside and strategize to either capture or kill this man. We're on the edge of a new frontier. We can't let anyone get in the way of what we need to do to get to where we need to be in forming a regional presence."

"All in favor, then, of Malayah and Charlie's mission to the island?" Misty said.

Everyone raised their hands, and the meeting moved on.

"The preserve," Sky said. "They seem nice, and my uncle has a relationship with them."

"We didn't verify that," Misty said.

"Uncle?" Charlie said.

"Yes, Charlie," Misty said. "In the last couple of days, we've been approached by Sky's uncle and a group he rode in with on horses, this other group that helped Yamil and Miracle get home from Valley Hall that live in the sewers—"

"Storm drains," King corrected.

"And then this group from the preserve," Misty continued.

"Uncle?" Charlie repeated.

"Yes," Sky said. "My uncle. He stranded me in Malta under the guise that we were being attacked by a group of men on horses. I thought he was dead, but much to the contrary, he and these horsemen were friends and devised this whole plan to abandon me at the fortress, so he didn't have to take care of me. In the meantime, he started his own new life in the Pinewood area while we were being attacked and killed over the years, and just now decided to come out of hiding and share the whole story with me...while smiling with his big white teeth."

"It sounds like it didn't affect you too much," Charlie said.

"That *puta*," Frankie said.

"Is everyone a *puta* in your eyes?" Sky asked.

"Not everyone," Frankie said. "Just *putas*."

"What the hell is a *puta* anyway?" Misty asked.

"Maybe we should just get back on track," Wyatt suggested.

"And if Yamil starts using that word, I'll know where he got it from," Sky said.

"Oh," Frankie cooed. "Yamil. I've been working with that little dolly on his Spanish. It's a little rough around the edges."

"You should talk," Sky said. "Anyway, I've been thinking about my uncle's visit, and although I could use more time to digest his return, I think it's best if we go to Pinewood and let him know we met with Ember. He's already familiar with the preserve, apparently, and even though I disagree with what he did, he will make a strong alley."

"I'll go with you!" Misty said. "I've been wanting to visit home. I can kill two birds with one stone, and I know right where he is."

"So, you tell this guy off only a day ago, and now we're chasing after him the next day?" King said.

"It's only a few miles from here," Sky said. "Barely a day trip."

"I would advise no more than that," Charlie said. "We have to make sure defenses are tight with Kane settled and prowling about now, and Malayah and I will be gone as well."

"It's a good point, Charlie, but we can't just keep letting these crazy people dictate everything," Sky said. "If we constantly play defense instead of offense, we might as well just be dead, because no progress will be made being trapped in place all the time. There is always going to be some whacko out there waiting to oppose us."

"You said it," Frankie said.

Everyone raised their hands to Sky and Misty's mission to Pinewood.

"In the meantime," Sky said. "We have this group, the preserve, as well, inviting a couple of us back with them to see what they're doing. I thought...if Harlow and some of her people were inclined, we could arm them and send them along with Leo."

"Who will that leave us with after tomorrow while everyone is off and about?" King asked. He held up his hand to count on his fingers. "Me, Wyatt, Baby, Teddy, Yamil, and Miracle..."

"King, we have two hundred fifty people at the heights," Malayah said. "Good people. That celebration here, when Vash was killed, was the first time most of them even saw the fortress, and we're talking about becoming

Pangea? Some of your orphans never even saw the heights more than once. You have to start looking at the resolve of this place outside of Wyatt and a handful of...well-equipped children. We got your back!"

"Well said, Malayah," said Charlie. "To me, as I always said, this place, on the edge of the city, is like a lighthouse. Lighthouses were home to the keepers and sometimes their families, and that's it. You orphans are the keepers of the light, but this is only an outpost where the keepers live. A community in its own right, but lighthouses are isolated on islands. Safe from intrusion. It's not the same here. With only keepers in place, you will always be vulnerable, even when the wall is done. We should stack this place with guards when some of the keepers are away, and I argue even when the keepers are here, though it has never been our regular practice. It's on our agenda to vote on Holly and Rodger coming down and taking up residence to provide support on the roof. That's a start. Let's be smart, because as the years turn, you children are the first and last generation of kids who knew Sim, and eventually you'll all either leave here, or stay here as adults. This orphanage...will no longer serve that purpose."

"We're not afraid of adults being on the premises, and neither was Sim," Sky reminded. "He was only afraid...worried about corruption. Whoever comes through these doors must respect and appreciate our history, culture, and the orphans' authority over this domain, regardless of any age differences."

"Understandable," Charlie said. "So, shall Holly and Rodger make their journey here tomorrow, then?"

No one opposed, though King, Misty, and Sky all knew it would be monumental to have three adults living along with the orphans at the fortress. But they also felt confident that they could hold their own as authority figures in their home. It was a notion that Wyatt fully respected, and was why he had been a perfect fit for them in the previous year. The orphans would not be keen on keeping anyone at the fortress who didn't fit that mold.

"With that settled, we'll need to rearrange the rooms," Sky said.

"What about this trek to the preserve?" King reminded. "Leo? Alone? With the sewer...*storm drain* people?"

"Leo can hold his own, and we can send Gigi along," Sky assured. "But let's bring it to a quick vote."

"Are we really going to vote on volunteering Leo for this ten-mile trip to some unknown place?" Misty said.

Sky smiled. "I already talked to him last night about my proposal, and he was thrilled."

"All in favor?"

Five of seven votes. Misty and King *weren't* thrilled with the idea.

"Back to bedrooms," Sky said. "Just a few little tweaks. Misty...Baby will be your new roommate. Her room will go to Rodger and Wyatt. Sim's old room is big enough so that Holly can shack up with me, and King, you'll have your own space, for the time being."

"Hot damn!" King yelled.

"I guess it's only fair since I've had my own room for almost a year now," Sky said.

"I want a turn," Misty whined.

"I don't see that happening any time soon, unless King wants to move in with Teddy and Leo."

"Oh, no," King said. "That's no way for a King to live."

"You've been with Wyatt, so you should be able to handle anything," Misty said, tossing a smile at Wyatt.

"Hey, watch it," Wyatt said.

"I don't know how y'all do it," Frankie said. "All cooped up in this place with each other. Y'all can have your little lighthouse. But me...I'm going back to building five, apartment six, and stretching out!"

"Now let me present from my agenda," Charlie said, as he reached beside him on the floor and took up a box of walkies. "My contribution to the kingdom. Long-range radios!"

"What's the so-called range?" King asked. "Because we tried about a dozen long-range sets over the past year and none of them work beyond a mile. The ones that take standard batteries just aren't sophisticated enough."

"The package says thirty-eight miles!" Charlie stated proudly.

"Bullshit," Frankie said. She covered her mouth. "Excuse my French."

"Did you test them?" Misty asked.

"Charlie hasn't been thirty-eight *feet* from the heights over the last week, let alone thirty-eight miles," Frankie said.

"I will ignore that rude comment," Charlie said. "At the moment, we would all be happy if they worked simply from here to the heights. So, let's check it out." He pulled one from the box and looked at it like it was a long-awaited birthday present. "These ones take lithium polymer batteries, so it may be the difference. Mrs. Chandler has one of these babies on her right now just waiting for the maiden communication."

"Well, turn it on," Misty said.

Charlie turned the knob on and twisted the volume all the way up. "Drum roll, please."

Everyone banged on the table drum roll style and then froze. "Mrs. Chandler...this is Charlie at the fortress. Do you copy?"

Seconds seemed like minutes before Mrs. Chandler came through loud and clear. "I hear you, Charlie. Dylan is driving me crazy up here. He needs a babysitter. You almost done?"

Everyone cheered. Progress.

"We'll be up soon," Charlie said. "Let Merrick or Watson handle it."

"I told you about Dylan," Malayah said. "But now you'll listen because old and wise Mrs. Chandler has spoken."

"How many of these puppies you have?" King asked.

"They came with seven in a box, and thankfully my runners had the foresight to take every box the electronics store had...eight."

"Whoa," Wyatt said. "A total of forty-two."

"Um," Sky said. "You better see me for math lessons after the meeting, Wyatt. The total is fifty-six. And it will be amazing being able to finally reach each other from a distance. Maybe Ember was right...maybe things are coming together."

The kingdom.

Pangea.

The beginning of a beginning.

The meeting ended and everyone went outside to convene with Ember. Harlow, Parker, and Messiah had also shown up during the proceedings, and it was quite the street gathering.

Harlow approached Sky. "I'm here."

"I'm glad," Sky said. "Did you have a chance to talk to anyone?"

"Some people," Harlow said. "But most are afraid, or just have grown too comfortable with their existing arrangements."

"I was wondering if you might do us a large favor," Sky said.

"Spit it out," Harlow said.

"My friend, Leo, here, is joining another group back in their community. It's located at a preserve. It's about a ten-mile walk, but we're trying to build something here. It's important we see for ourselves what they have going on. I was wondering if you could join him on the journey."

Sky grabbed Leo by the arm and pulled him forward. He had a backpack on him and was ready to go.

"I know Leo," Parker attested. "He's cool. And funny. You should go, Harlow."

"Ten miles?" she said. "I do like a good adventure, but that sure is a long way."

"Not as far as it seems," Leo said. "We'll cover ground at two miles per hour or even better. That's eight to ten hours round trip."

"And you say you aren't a dork," Parker said shaking his head.

"We can also provide you with some weapons," Sky said. "I'd feel more comfortable knowing that Leo was going with someone we can trust."

"Can I come too?" Parker asked.

"I thought you had church windows to break?" Harlow said.

"It can wait," Parker said.

"I guess we don't have anything better to do," Harlow said. "Are the little ones coming as well?"

"They're sitting this one out," Sky said. "They'd be complaining after the first mile."

"Trust me, I know," Harlow said.

Sky handed Leo one of Charlie's new walkies. "Make sure you have it with you at all times."

"Yeah, yeah," Leo said.

"I want one!" Parker said.

"Not today, young man," Sky said.

She gave a walkie to Ember as well, who clipped it to her waistband. King came out with some extra guns for Harlow and handed Parker a pistol.

"Wow," he said.

"Haven't you ever handled a gun?" King asked. "In all these years?"

"Well, I stole the one from Leo, but no, I never had a gun of my own."

"You still don't," King said. "That's property of the fortress, and we'll be expecting it back when you return."

"Calm down, fella," Parker said. "You're so serious."

King eyed Messiah up and down. "Hey," he said.

"How you doing?" Messiah said.

"Just fine," King said.

Sky next approached Charlie. "Good luck on the island."

"It'll be fine," Charlie said. "Try not to worry too much about Kane. Just get up to Pinewood, make amends with your uncle, and let's keep tightening the screws." Charlie took a step back and took in a breath. "Look at all these people. Kane will be running back to Brooklyn by the end of summer, if not sooner. This is not the place for him to be right now."

"Or ever," Sky said.

"For sure," Charlie said. "We're just going to walk Frankie back and then we'll head out. We will make sure Rodger, Holly, and a few others from the heights are here first thing in the morning to keep the fortress in good hands while everyone is off and away."

"Misty and I will leave when things break up," Sky said.

"Stay in touch," Charlie said. "Now that you can. And don't forget to bring one of these new walkies to your uncle."

"I will," Sky said.

Sky, along with all the orphans, met on the street to bid farewell to Charlie and his group, Leo, Gigi, the moles, and the preserve group as they all left in opposite directions for their various destinations.

Before setting off on their own journey to Mike, and while Misty prepared her travel bag, Sky took a minute to update her journal.

Hello Journal,

It's been a crazy few days. When Miracle and Yamil returned, I thought things would be, even without JZ, somewhat back to normal. Then, all of a sudden, the Kingdom Initiative got a full greenlight from the committee, Uncle Mike shows up on my doorstep with a tale that was hard for me to accept, Harlow and her friends spring from the depths of the underground, the preserve members arrive, and now we have possibly a new local threat in a man from Charlie's past named Kane. At least it's not someone from Sim's past this time.

These could be great times, or they could be terrible times. Or both. It depends on so many things. We've been forced to throw caution to the wind in order to embrace new people in our lives and trust that they have our best interests at heart. If we are going to grow and become stronger, we must put a layer of trust in the unknown and embrace some risk. The reward in doing so could be more freedom and hope. I wonder what Sim would think about all of this? Did he ever dream we would get this far? Sitting on the edge of a new frontier where we might one day be able to walk out our door and not have to worry?

I'm heading off to see Uncle Mike again. Perhaps I shouldn't have let him go. Perhaps I should have embraced him more. He is my blood after all. He would never have purposely done anything that put me at risk. I hate to say, I may be chasing him down more for myself than the kingdom. I need to know more to make his motives make sense to me. I yearned for so long to know what happened, and after all these years I can learn the answers.

I suppose I can't argue what fate dished out to me. I'm one of the leaders of an important community. I met a great man who taught me many things Uncle Mike might not have been able to. I've loved. I've lost. I've lived in this world where so many have died. There's no reason to be anything but grateful. Should I die today, it would have all been worth it.

Misty and Sky were joined at the doors by King, Wyatt, Baby, Teddy, Miracle, and Yamil. King handed Sky an extra walkie talkie to give to her uncle.

"Good luck," King said. "And don't be too hard on him. These years have challenged us all with the choices we've had to make. The sacrifices. I'm sure he loves you and always has, like my own mother, but not everyone is cut out for guardianship. Maybe the worst disappointment is learning that he wasn't like Sim in that way, when you always had it in your head that he was."

"Thanks, King," Sky said. "No one is perfect. Not Sim. Not you. Not me. But I'm not a little girl anymore, and so now that guardianship is no longer needed. We're over that hump, and there are other matters at hand that must trump my personal drama. Still, it will be nice getting to know him again."

"No fair," Teddy said. "I want to go see where *I* lived when Sim found me."

Sky cocked her head compassionately. "Your old home is going nowhere, Teddy. When the time is right, you'll see it again, if that's what you want."

"Bring us back some horses of our own," Baby said.

"I'll second that," King said.

"See you soon, my little ones," Sky said to Yamil and Miracle. "You've been a great help lately. You're growing up on me."

Yamil and Miracle ran and hugged her, and then Misty and Sky set off. Before they reached the intersection, the walkie buzzed.

"When are you coming back?" Yamil asked.

Misty and Sky smiled at each other.

"We just left, silly," Sky said. "Maybe before you go to bed, if we're lucky. Or maybe in the morning. But guess what."

"What?" Yamil answered.

"We have the new walkie talkies now, and you guys can talk to me whenever you want, and no matter how far we go from home."

"Yay!" Yamil said. "I'll talk later. In a half hour."

"Okay, then," Sky said.

The streets were quiet and the air still as they walked their way into the future.

Eight

CHARLIE, MALAYAH, AND FRANKIE returned to the heights, leaving Frankie to deal with security while they prepared for their journey to the island. Not many in the community were aware of this mission, nor of Kane's visit or the significance of it. Mrs. Chandler was, however, and wasn't shy about voicing her opinion.

"I wish I was a member of that committee, because I would have firmly voted against it, Charlie. This man you have described sounds sneaky and vile."

"I didn't mean to panic you, Jenny," Charlie said, putting a gentle hand on her arm. "I only needed you to understand so you could be mindful of this situation while I'm away. But I think you're in good hands with Frankie and the security team until I get back."

"We'll conduct a community muster drill while you're away," Frankie said.

The muster drills were something Malayah and Frankie came up with when they took over security detail. They conducted the drills with a bullhorn siren on a random schedule, so the community never took for granted that the siren was a drill. They wanted to keep the community on their toes, in case there was ever a real call to action.

"Perfect," Charlie said. "We should hope to be back by evening, if not sooner. And with our new communications system, we can stay in touch quite easily."

"We never discussed protocol should we fall out of communication with each other on these new devices," Malayah said.

"We haven't tested them more than two miles," Charlie said. "God knows if they even work in a wider radius. But should they not work, or we should go silent, don't send backup. It's pointless. Your first priority is always community protection. We all know anything can happen on the road, so no sense turning an unknown situation on the road into a community event. Plus, it's unlikely we'll bring these devices onto the island and risk Kane getting hold of them, should something happen to us."

Frankie and Malayah hugged. "You be safe, girl, because I'm making dinner tonight."

Charlie and Malayah headed off into the unknown to see Insane Kane. This time on *his* territory.

They arrived at their destination a couple of hours later and turned off their long-range walkies before stashing them in a street-side trash can. They made their way carefully down an embankment under the blown-out Green Island bridge, where several small boats bobbed on the water at the shoreline. There was a lone boatman pissing when they arrived. He didn't notice them, so the two waited alongside the row of small vessels for him to finish.

"If this is reflective of the quality of his help," Malayah whispered, "then we shouldn't have to worry about much."

The Green Island bridge was a drawbridge that spanned the distance from Troy to the island of Green Island. The island part of Green Island was a parcel of land surrounded by the Hudson River on all sides. The suspension bridge on the west side led from the island over to the village of Green Island and the highway.

They had all heard the explosions two months earlier, and the orphans saw the smoke plumes from the fortress, but they never investigated it. In hindsight, Charlie thought maybe that could have been a mistake. They had given Kane time to get settled and find his groove, and his appearance suggested that he had enough in place that he was comfortable to start making moves—the first one being his visit to the heights. He likewise knew of the fortress, which was telling about what he had been up to.

Charlie cleared his throat to get the man's attention.

The boatman whirled around and zipped up his pants as he stumbled forward. Malayah scowled. He was dressed in scurvy clothing and had a head that was as thin as a pencil with large ears that resembled a couple of cauliflower stalks. His teeth were crowded and crooked in his mouth, and he had blackheads dotting the coarse skin of his face.

"Who are you?" he said in a panic. He fumbled for his side arm, which was holstered. "What do you want?"

"Please, Jesse, my name is Charlie," he said. "And this is one my people, Malayah. Kane and I go way back. He invited me here. That's how I know your name."

On his unholstered hip was a walkie talkie. He grabbed for it. "Yeah, Kane, it's me. We have a couple people over here on the Troy side. They look nice. Charlie and Mayla. They say they know you."

"Send them over, Jesse," Kane said.

"It's *Malayah*," Malayah corrected.

"Oh, yeah, right, sorry," Jesse said as he leaned down and held one of the boats still. "Jump right in, guys. I'll get you to him quick. They gave me this job because I'm a fast rower. My arms are nothing but muscle. Since I got this job, my biceps are popping."

After they stepped into the boat, Jesse flexed for them. His arms were as thin as rubber bands, and his flexed biceps resembled two small potatoes. Nonetheless, Charlie nodded while Malayah tried not to laugh.

"I'm glad you're able to keep busy, Jesse," Charlie said.

"I love the water. I'm a swimmer, too," Jesse said as he pushed the boat from the shore and hopped in. "Hey, tell Kane I was nice to you, and don't tell him I was taking a piss while you snuck up on me. He wouldn't be happy. I don't want any trouble with the big man."

"We will tell him nothing," Charlie said.

As he rowed, Jesse grinned ear to ear. "Nice, thank you. I just like to help people."

"And you are in charge of monitoring the entire eastern bank?" Charlie asked.

"Yes, well, usually there are three of us, but two of the guys are out on a mission," Jesse said. "One day, Kane will let me go on a mission. Just waiting for the call."

The row across took ten minutes. They hit the ground on the island with a thud. Jesse hopped out and pulled the boat onto land and Charlie and Malayah stepped out. They glanced up the embankment to the complex that stood before them. Before the fall, the small island portion of Green Island was home to a double set of posh apartment complexes. One development was on the south side of the island and bridge, only recently completed and populated before the fall, and the other was an older complex on the west side of the bridge and island.

"I'm going back across," Jesse said. "Just go up the embankment. There's a security booth near the plaza, and those guys will show you to Kane. And remember to tell him I did good."

Charlie and Malayah ignored Jesse as they climbed up the embankment, which was composed of large stones that rolled down the hill into the water with each step they took. They arrived in the former parking lot of a strip mall plaza that in the past offered a restaurant, convenience store, and wine and liquor store for the residents. They ventured across the lot and turned into the complex parking lot, the entryway of which was secured with a tollbooth as Jesse had indicated. Armed guards were at the ready as they approached. One was a young man whose expression indicated boredom, and the other a middle-aged man who appeared inconvenienced as he blew a big bubble with his gum. It popped with a loud snap as the two came to a stop.

"Hands up, please," the man said. "We need to take your weapons while you're here. You'll get them back when you leave."

The younger guard patted Charlie down and took his side bag, which contained a couple of small firearms. He had another tucked in the backside waistband of his pants. The man took it and put it into his bag. The older guard did the same for Malayah and took away her Remington 750 rifle. She had a knife buried in a sheath on her lower leg as well that the man confiscated.

The older man raised his walkie. His younger counterpart returned to the booth and sat down.

"Yeah, Kane," he said, chewing loudly through the device. "They're clean."

The radio crackled. "Okay, bring them to me, please. I'm at my apartment."

He snapped another bubble. "On the way."

"Many thanks," Charlie nodded.

They entered the compound and proceeded to Building C. The normal door, which was always locked electronically in regular times, had been replaced with an all-access door. They took the stairs up to the second floor, and their guide knocked on the door to apartment eleven. Along the way, they only spied one other person walking the perimeter.

Security looked lax, Charlie noted.

Kane answered the door to them and smiled ear to ear, a gesture that Charlie could easily see through, in being aware of the man's former and present nature. Yet, Charlie was inclined to indulge the man's fake enthusiasm. The escort left them, and the two entered his apartment as he stepped aside.

The complex was nothing like the heights. In regular times, the heights was housing-authority apartments, which were low income with less square footage and none of the perks. Kane's apartment was more fitted for a king. With views of the Hudson River from the balcony, a breakfast bar with a granite top, two sizeable rooms, and a fireplace, it was a convenient setup.

"Charlie boy," Kane said. "I never dreamed you would actually come, let alone with such quick turnaround. That tells me you are either eager to re-evaluate my offer, or you are sizing up your competition." Kane laughed. "Which is it, Charlie?"

"Perhaps a mix of both, Kane," Charlie said. "I showed you mine, so it is only fair that you show me yours."

Kane laughed and turned his stare on Malayah. "Oh, and you brought along the sassy warrior."

"I hate to tell you, but I didn't come in answer to your marriage proposal," Malayah said as she scanned the room.

"That's too bad," Kane said. "Because every king needs a queen."

"What about the escort?" Malayah said with a sarcastic tone. "She seems lovely, and she likes...gum."

"I've already had her," Kane said. "She's not queen material."

"So," Charlie said. "This is quite a nice place you have for yourself. It was a good move taking out the bridges for added security. Too bad we didn't think of it three years ago. But then again, I've always loved the heights."

"And so did we, back in the day," Kane said. "We sold a lot of product to the residents."

Charlie knew all too well. But back then, Kane's goal was to make money; now, his goal seemed only about controlling the local population through dictatorship, which was a scarier proposition.

Charlie wandered freely around the apartment and stood before the sliding glass doors. He pulled them open and took in a breath. He saw Jesse had made it back across and was under the bridge.

"Spectacular, isn't it?" Kane said, sidling up to him. "To be out here enjoying such views and knowing that you are untouchable by the rest of the rogue world."

How untouchable would a sniper find you to be?

Charlie kept that thought to himself as he gathered intel.

"Interesting you should mention this being a rogue world," Charlie said. "You've only been back a couple of months, Kane. This area is developing in a more sophisticated way. As I told you, our goal is to bring rogue communities and people together and rebuild. I'm still not quite clear what you want, though. It seems like you have everything you could need right here."

"That's a small-minded thought, Charlie," Kane said. "You yourself have a vision far greater than the heights, yet you want my vision to stop at the island?"

Charlie turned to Kane, deciding it was time to offer perspective. "We've been here for the past four years spearheading our initiatives in this territory. You've been here only a matter of weeks. Let's just say my plan to develop this area is years ahead of your plan, and we…we were here first."

"Oh," Kane said feigning disappointment. "So, what you are really saying, is that I'm infringing upon your…turf?"

"I don't look at us as rival gangs, Kane," Charlie said. "But there is an entire fallen world out there, where you could go to bring your particular brand of…*leadership.* Here, we just want to fulfill our goals, without opposing forces getting in the way."

"But I like the island, Charlie," Kane said. "I like Troy. I like this entire area. It was always my turf back in the day, and just because I went away doesn't make it any less mine than yours."

Charlie studied the man's hardened face, marred by the long scar. It was clear he was not going to listen to reason. It made him think of the time he was being bullied in the seventh grade. Mr. Ford, Sim, gave him advice about how to handle it back then.

Here's what you do, Charlie. You find out where he lives. You go to his house, and you confront him there. Show him yourself outside of school. Make a connection. Make him see you as a person. He'll never expect it. I guarantee he'll remember it, and it will make a difference.

Do you know for sure it will work? What if he kicks the shit out of me right there?

He won't. He'll be in shock.

Can this really work?

Who knows, but it's worth a try.

Oddly enough, King had done the same thing when he confronted Zagan at the prison, and it seemed to work there. In the situation with Clyde Borrows in the seventh grade, it did work. Charlie went to his house, surprised him at his door, and asked him to please leave him alone. He learned that Clyde's house was a rat hole, that his mother was paralyzed and wheelchair-bound, and his father long since gone. Clyde was as helpless as Charlie, exerting control the only place he could. It made sense.

He was trying the same tactic with Kane, but felt it was not a strategy that was going to work. "Let me ask you something," Charlie said. "Why did you leave Brooklyn after nearly four years? Wouldn't it have been easier on the feet just to push into Manhattan and inhabit Ellis Island? Call it a day."

Kane burst out into laughter. "You kill me, Charlie boy. Ellis Island. Or even Liberty Island!" He continued to laugh.

"Or Staten Island," Charlie laughed.

"Coney Island, too," Malayah chimed in from behind.

"Wow," Kane said. "Had I only known about all those islands, maybe you're right. Maybe I would have just stayed."

"It's not too late," Charlie added with a laugh.

Kane shook his head. "Oh, boy, Charlie...you always had a sense of humor. I wish I had more time to show you around, but once you've seen one apartment, you've seen them all. I think it's safe to say, you showed me yours, and now you've seen mine. But daylight is wasting. I will see you out and consider your points."

Charlie and Malayah left out the door ahead of Kane and all three exited the building. As they passed the intake station, Charlie stopped.

"What about our weapons?" Charlie asked.

"They were given to Jesse before he went back across, and you will get them on the other side," Kane said.

They walked past the plaza, and as they approached the rocky hill that led to the shoreline, Charlie and Malayah paused.

"Well, it was good seeing you again, Kane," Charlie said. "I hope we can keep talking and find common ground. The city is big enough for all of us."

"I'm more than sure we'll figure this out," Kane said. "But there is one last thing I wanted to ask you before you left."

"What would that be?" Charlie said, growing impatient, and feeling vulnerable without a weapon.

"How did you find security to be on the island?" Kane asked, his nostrils flared, and a wide grin etched across his large face.

"It seemed fine," Charlie humored. "I particularly like the ferryman, Jesse. He's...well prepared."

"Eh, he can be a burden," Kane said. "Normally we have three—"

"Yes, he told us," Charlie said. "Three men, but two are out and about."

"He even told you that?" Kane said. "Did he tell you where they were?"

"No," Charlie said. "He didn't mention that, but I'm sure it's nothing that concerns us, so, we should really get going."

"Are you sure?" Kane asked.

"Sure *what*?" Charlie said.

"That it doesn't concern you?" Kane said.

There was an awkward silence.

Kane drew a revolver from his pocket and shot Malayah in the stomach.

Charlie's eyes widened and he screamed. "Malayah!"

Two soldiers came rushing to Kane's side.

Charlie knelt and pressed on Malayah's wound, but he knew it was not a wound she could recover from. She was already coughing out blood. "Malayah," he mumbled.

Charlie looked up at Kane. He was seething, but powerless. He had no weapon, and he couldn't even run because he wasn't going to leave Malayah.

"What did you do, Kane?" Charlie. "Why?"

Kane's demeanor changed. All pleasantness, fake or otherwise, dissipated as he held Charlie at gunpoint. "You didn't think you would come to my island as a guest, to deliver a message that I wasn't welcome in my own city, and get away it, did you? Truth is, you could have come or not, and it didn't make a difference. While you spent the last two months with your head up your ass, my soldiers have been doing local reconnaissance, and finding out everything we need to know about this area. Currently, they are out formally introducing themselves to all our wonderful new neighbors and enforcing our first governing protocol for this territory. That being, that all firearms not belonging to my soldiers and outside of this island, will be considered contraband. We will disarm and confiscate, with force, anyone opposing that first and most important rule. But the good news is, you will all have the protection of my soldiers, so you won't need them! It may not be the exact model of democracy you and your fellow communities were looking for, but you guys had four years to make something work, and what do we see when we arrive here? Just a scared, disorganized people. No, no. Not in my city. My city will be one of glory, and the hallmark city of our growing empire."

Kane's eyes glazed over as he stared into the sky. Charlie could see the man fantasizing about his new world while Charlie thought of his own people at the heights, the fortress, and those on the road. The idea of a unified territory full of peace suddenly disappeared in his mind, like a candle flickering out in the wind. A scary new thought about a land governed by tyranny and oppression and ruled by Kane replaced his visions of grandeur.

Was Kane right? *Did* they blow it? *Did* they wait too long? *Did* they not take the bull by the horns when they had a chance? Had they tried, they could have secured Troy and been ready for Kane. But they weren't. They let this happen, and now the Zagan and Vash battles would pale in comparison.

"As for Brooklyn," Kane laughed. "Who said we ever left? I'm just branching out, Charlie. Brooklyn is ours. Just like every other territory north and south of here and along the Hudson will be, before long. The land, the river, the ports...Your dream...was only that. A child's dream. My dream is the dream of a king. An emperor, even. The bad news is, I just don't think there is room enough for all of us in my plan."

Kane stood and kicked Charlie in the face. He fell on to his back and the other two soldiers stomped him as Kane picked up a heavy boulder from the ground. It was the size of a large pumpkin. Charlie curled into a fetal position and covered his head as the men rained down their feet upon his body. He felt every blow, but the pain was nothing like seeing Kane lift the boulder over his head.

"No!" Charlie yelled.

"I'm just trying to end her suffering, old buddy," Kane said.

Malayah turned her head and Charlie locked eyes with her. "Tell Frankie—"

Kane threw down the boulder before she could finish her sentence. Charlie closed his eyes as the boulder landed on Malayah's head. Kane then shot her two more times. His soldiers then picked Charlie up by each arm and held his bloody body before Kane.

"This won't go the way you think," Charlie coughed.

"It's amazing that you believe that, Charlie boy," Kane said. "But I'm very good at bringing despair to the hopeful. You'll see."

Kane punched Charlie in the face. His body collapsed onto the stony slope and rolled down the embankment, landing at the edge of the water. The soldiers carried Malayah's body down behind him, preparing to toss her into the river. Charlie was only halfway conscious but knew he had only one chance to escape while they were distracted, so he pulled himself into the river and dove under water. The current took him away swiftly, and as he struggled to conceal himself beneath the surface, he heard gunshots being fired from the shore. The bullets cut through the water on either side of his flailing body. Thankfully, he was not hit, and when he came to the surface, he was relieved to be a safe distance from the island, such that he was no longer a target. He saw the three men standing on the rocks watching as he floated from their reach.

As much pain as he was in, he couldn't help thinking about Malayah and how hard her death was going to hit Frankie. He thought of the rest of his people, too, and the likely confrontation they were all about to endure while he lay maimed at the side of the river.

How foolish he was in underestimating Kane. He was so organized back in the day. Why would he have thought it would have been any different this time around? They were careless not to investigate the bridge explosions when they occurred. They let it go.

His thought, even as he floated on his back and kicked his feet, was how they had to get ahead of it, but it seemed as if they were already grossly behind.

Then he thought of the fortress and the heights. They were no fools either. If Kane thought his soldiers were going to stroll into either one of their communities and make them passively submit, he would be the one in for the rude awakening.

The one positive of everything that had transpired, was that Kane was no longer a question mark. His intentions were now out in the open, and there would be no more surprises. At least not for them.

Charlie made it to the Troy side of the river and dragged himself onto the shore about a quarter mile north of the Green Island bridge where he had gotten the ride from Jesse. His body hurt all over, and it felt like they might have cracked one or more of his ribs. He either had to travel back up-river to get his walkie talkie, or get to the fortress, though in his condition, it would be a feat no matter what he decided to do.

Regardless, bloodied and bruised, he had to do something.

Shortly before Charlie and Malayah arrived at the island, one of Kane's lieutenants sought him out in his apartment.

"Wasp!" Kane cried. "Are you excited about the upcoming proceedings? By now, this should be second nature."

"We've done enough reconnaissance to know what we're up against in the initial phase, but information is still coming in," he said. "The landscape is expanding rapidly with some new groups suddenly appearing. We aren't fully aware of all the dynamics yet, but our scouts are keeping lookout. Should we postpone our first engagements, perhaps another week until we can fully identify all the threats in this area?"

"We have to act now, Wasp," Kane said. "The cat is out of the bag with my visit to the heights. We don't want to give them any time to plan. Just tell me how many groups are required and where they need to be so we can make sure we're covering all our bases."

"Our intel tells us that we have four distinct groups to follow up on," Wasp said. "I am leading my men to the brick house...that fortress on the hill. We have the unit going to the heights, and we'll need two additional units, as they have a couple of groups going mobile...who will lead us to other potentially equipped communities. It looks like they are trying to organize..."

Kane waved his hand. "Yeah, yeah. Democracy. I heard all about it."

"Maybe we should plan to set off with more firepower," Wasp suggested. "At least at my location, I don't think we'll be too convincing at trying to get them to open their doors and let us in to confiscate weapons. They'll have no reason to do that unless we can show that we're a real threat to their home."

"We need to call up more munitions from the lower settlements," Kane said. "We're running low. We have some strong firepower we can engage, but let's announce ourselves first, explain our goals and resolve, and where we don't get the cooperation we need, we can always return with more persuasive tactics. This protocol has been effective in seventy-five percent of the territorial attacks we have lodged to date, don't forget, and with the other twenty-five percent, all it took was...more convincing."

"So, we should or shouldn't lodge an aggressive attack in this first round of introductions? I just want to be clear."

Kane put a hand around Wasp's shoulder. "I'm not going to delve into specifics with the men. As always, the goal is to acquire what these settlements have amassed. We want to disarm them. We want them to have nowhere to turn to...but us, for protection. The means to that end, we will leave to the discretion of each lieutenant in charge, and it will be based on many factors that will present themselves in the moment." Kane smiled. "Have fun, and get it done."

Wasp nodded and left.

Not long after, fifty of Kane's soldiers gathered in the former parking lot of their freshly inhabited island apartment complex. He used a second-floor balcony as his pulpit from which to address his people, who were assembled in a mass drove.

Kane was excited with the calm of the summer day. The blue skies. The gently flowing Hudson River beyond the eager crowd. He placed both hands on the railing before him, sucked in a large breath and quietly prayed.

Thank you for delivering me back home. Fate has been kind. Let us renew the world.

"Good morning, my esteemed military," Kane said. "We have been here in Troy for two months. We fortified ourselves. We watched. We learned. And, like we did in Brooklyn, Yonkers, Poughkeepsie, Kingston, and Hudson, so too must we act now on our ongoing trek north to secure the mighty river's territories so we can fulfill our vision of a revitalized, New York State. New York...It's always been known as the Empire State. And so it shall be with the death of the world, as it was before."

The soldiers stood unflinching as Kane spoke.

"This island is our military base of operations," Kane said. "Fit only for soldiers, their wives, and children, and the territorial arsenal. The goal is always the same for the others in organized pockets off-base: to understand that a new territorial government is in place that will secure the entire area. To keep it safe. To keep it from being overrun by any other ambitious parties. But in order to do so, we must have rules. And we must have consequences for breaking rules. Today, in fulfillment of protocol one, all community pockets must be disarmed so they are not a threat to government. Your team leaders have been briefed on the identified locations where there are likely weapon caches. Our goal is, as always, not simple, but clear.

To engage. To disarm. To seize. And let them know that documentation on future protocol will be hand-delivered by military liaisons forthcoming. They must know that we do not want their homes. We just want their allegiance to our protocol. Do what you must to help them understand the new order. As I earlier told one of our esteemed lieutenants: Have fun, and get it done. Eventually, they will come to accept the security wrought by larger scale organized territorial policing and control. Perhaps not at first, but in time." His eyes drifted off for a few seconds of silence. "We will see you back here later for festivities."

The crowd dispersed, and Kane watched them from his perch cross the river in their collection of boats. He relished what he knew would be their initial success at enforcing operational protocol number one, and he looked forward to finally bringing the city to its knees.

Nine

MISTY AND SKY PROCEEDED to Pinewood at a speed walk with the soft wind at their faces. As they made it to a country road a mile outside of the city, they continued until the buildings got smaller behind them and their surroundings gave way to pastures, barns, and rolling hills. Misty felt a surge of excitement to be going home. She always loved her country house in the middle of nowhere but around the corner from everything.

We live in the only spot where you can have cows and a Walmart five miles away.

Misty's parents didn't even own cows, and neither were farmers. Her father was a state worker and her mother a nurse. Neither wished to live in what they called a "cookie-cutter neighborhood." They wanted land, privacy, peace, and quiet. Yet, they didn't want to be far from everything. Misty always loved her house even though there weren't a lot of neighbors. She had friends over all the time, and she got to have chickens and ride horses. When Ace and Sim came for her, she left in haste, and was more than curious to see what had become of her house in the past several years.

She guessed nothing at all had happened to it, as houses often stood the test of time. Not like people. Or animals. They died and disappeared.

It's not too much farther now.

Sky might be wondering, as she didn't know where Misty was taking her. Three miles was not far, but the geography changed substantially in the short distance. As Misty got closer to her house, she picked up her step, and she was going faster every minute. Sky shouted for her to slow down, but Misty had tunnel vision as she departed from one country road and took them up another.

They continued walking until they approached a home that stood in isolation behind two trees that looked like they were keeping guard over the property. It was about a hundred yards away, and behind it was the sun, casting it in golden light, almost like the manger at the time of Jesus's birth, aglow under the light of the north star.

"That's my house," Misty said, standing in awe as if she was witnessing an unprecedented event. "I'm home."

They crossed a field overgrown with dry yellow grass and made it to the front steps.

She climbed the stairs to her wraparound porch and paused at the screen door before entering. It all looked the same, only much more weathered.

"You might want to get your gun ready in case someone's in there," Sky said, her mind flashing back to her experiences at Valley Hall.

"There's nothing but ghosts in here, Sky," Misty said.

"Don't be so sure,'" Sky said.

Misty scanned the porch and saw the rocking chair she remembered quite fondly from her youth. She unslung her rifle and laid it down beside the chair. She sat down and rocked with her eyes closed as Sky quietly climbed the stairs, which she noticed sloped to the right and had partially rotted away.

"I hate to interrupt your trip down memory lane, Misty, but we promised the others we would get back as early as possible."

Misty continued to rock, her head back, eyes closed. "Do you know my mother used to hold me in her lap in this chair?"

A summer breeze whistled as rusted wind chimes clanged together.

"It's good you have those memories," Sky said. "Memories are all we got most days."

"She would read my favorite stories here, and when it got dark, we would look at the stars. Out here, the stars are everywhere."

Sky smiled. She shouldn't be surprised by the moment. She knew Misty was planning to revisit her home. It was something Teddy wanted to do as well, and she suspected King did too, even though he feigned disinterest. Maybe one day she would as well, though the trip back to Saratoga would be much more than a three-mile walk. She remembered how grueling the journey was on the original trek with her uncle Mike.

Misty closed her eyes and rocked in silence for another minute before jumping up. "I'm just going to take a quick peek at my house," Misty said, opening the screen door. "You want to come?"

Sky turned back to her. "No, thanks. You enjoy. I'm going to sit here for a moment. I'll touch base with the others and see if these long-range walkies actually work out here."

"It's basically the same distance as the heights," Misty said. "So, they should."

"It's farther," Sky said. "By about a mile."

Misty shrugged and entered the house. She stood in the foyer and looked around. The air was cold and damp, and it was hard to see. She retrieved her flashlight and lit up the area. She smiled at the pictures on the wall. She had nearly forgotten what her mother and father looked like. Seeing them in the photos flooded her mind with old memories. She stepped forward and shined the light into the living room. All the furniture she remembered was still there, coated with inches of dust. There was a television mounted on the wall that still loomed large in the small room. Her mother had been mad when her father came home with the seventy-inch monster. It took up much of the wall.

That's just ridiculous that you need a television that big. The sound will probably shatter the windows.

She smiled and turned back around toward the entryway staircase and made her way up each wooden step. They creaked and moaned with old age but held firm. Her room was the first one on the left, the biggest room in the house.

For the princess.

She pushed open her door and flashed her light in. Everything was as she remembered it in her mind. Her canopy bed, vanity, pearly white dresser and mirror, television stand and TV with a shattered screen. She recalled the day she threw the remote at it in a state of despair, about six months after her parents died. There were the soft white lights strung up fancifully around her room. They used to twinkle at night and make her feel warm and cozy, until the electricity went out.

Everything seemed so much smaller though, but she knew it was because she had grown. Yet, her bedroom still called to her in much the same way it did in the old days. She sprawled out on the mattress, and it was cold and hard on her back, but it was still a comfort as she gazed upward and danced the flashlight around the translucent canopy above her. She had spent so much time alone in the house, and for the life of her she couldn't imagine how she had survived so long on her own before Sim came—especially after her chickens died and the food ran out in the cupboards. She was only nine years old and having to figure out all on her own how to live day-to-day. She visited nearby houses to steal food, and even cooked eggs her chickens laid. Her parents had stocked up on kerosene and propane and taught her how to use it to light fires, and how to be careful when doing so. They tried to teach her everything they could, even in their last days, to ensure she could have a chance.

Will I die?

I don't know, her mother had said while caressing her cheek.

I'm scared.

I'm not. Because I know you have the tools, and you didn't get sick, and that's a blessing. Keep your gun close, your heart open, but don't trust anyone until you know for sure they won't hurt you. And don't be afraid to pull that trigger when you must.

She took in a deep breath and imagined her white lights illuminated, and it made her smile. When she came back down the stairs, she removed the picture of her mother and father, holding her three-year-old self, from the wall and stuffed into her satchel, and when she let the screen door close behind her, she lingered.

Sky was still waiting for her on the porch steps, and she must have sensed Misty's melancholy.

"How are you feeling?" Sky asked.

"Like...rain," Misty admitted.

"That's when you find rainbows," Sky reminded as she went in and hugged Misty.

"I just want to see one more thing," Misty said. "Then, I promise we can go see your uncle. He's not far from here."

Misty led Sky around back, and behind her garage there was an elm tree, under which were the graves of her parents. She stood over them. Sky stood beside her and took her hand.

"Hello, Mom and Dad," Misty said, wiping a tear from her eye. "It's strange being back here. I see you everywhere, but that makes sense because you're still here. I sure do miss you both. I don't dwell on it, though. We can't. As much as it sucks, we have to let go, so we can be free. I don't know if I'll ever be back, but I remember the good times. It's part of who I am. Well then, goodbye."

Sky hugged Misty again, and the two set off for the old Livingston's place that Uncle Mike had made a home over the years.

"Enough of my drama," Misty said, wiping the remaining tears from her eyes with the short sleeve of her shirt. "Did you reach the others?"

"Crystal clear," Sky said. "These new devices are a Godsend. How we didn't discover them until now is beyond me, but I'm glad we have them."

"Follow me," Misty said.

The two made it the short distance to the former Livingston residence, presumably the place where Mike had established himself. It was a single-story ranch house with a long dirt pathway leading to the front door. On either side of the path, there were lawns of yellow grass. Back in the day, when the lawns were properly watered, those stretches of grass would be bright green and well-manicured. Behind the house was a classic red barn and silo, as well as a two acres of fenced-in land. Misty remembered visiting the Livingstons and riding their horse, who she named Chocolate.

As they stood at the foot of the path leading to the ranch house, the front door swung open and Uncle Mike stood at the entrance, hands on his hips. The girls, seeing him, advanced. When they arrived in front of him, he smiled.

"Glad you decided to come," Uncle Mike said. "I wondered if you would. Let's go on in and get something to eat. We have a lot to catch up on. My friends will be coming along too. You can meet them. They're good people."

"I saw Cypress already," Sky said. "I remember him. He was one of those men supposedly chasing us down from Saratoga."

Mike's face became awash in shame. He hung his head. "Yeah."

There were a million things Sky could have said with that confirmation, but she held her tongue, for she knew if she said anything, it could doom their mission. Instead, she allowed her uncle to lead them into the ranch house. He brought them to the living room where they all took seats, the girls on a couch and Mike in a lounger.

The house was just as Misty had remembered it, and it was almost as surreal sitting in the Livingston's living room as it was going through her own house.

There was awkward silence. She looked around the living room.

"So, this is what you've been up to this whole time," Sky said. "Only a few miles away from me."

"That's about it," Mike said. "Just...surviving."

"We could have done that together," she suggested.

"Sky," Mike said. "I see you've become a strong young lady. But back then, you were just a kid. Kids think their parents and the adults in their lives are perfect. It isn't until they get older that they start to see their flaws."

"But you dumped me before I could see yours," Sky said. "Kids learn to accept those flaws, the same as parents accept their children's flaws. It's called unconditional love."

Misty stood. "I'm going to step out front and give you guys some time." Misty left Sky and Mike in silence.

"Look, Sky," Mike said. "I thought about the perfect excuse that I would give when I saw you again about why I made the choices I did back then. There was only one that was perfect enough that I thought you would accept, and it's the God's honest truth."

Sky waited for him as he gripped the sides of his chair tightly. "I was terrified. That's the perfect excuse I came up with."

Sky didn't think that was much of an excuse at all.

"I was scared too," Sky said. "Probably more than you. Everyone was scared. If that's the best you—"

"No, wait," Mike said. "There's more. But I have to take it back a ways. Your mother and father never told you this, Sky, but...when you were no more than two, I was babysitting you at my place and I dozed off on the couch. You managed to open the front door, and when I woke up...you were gone. I was frantic. Your mother came, and I called the police. Thank

God a good Samaritan found you walking around the neighborhood and brought you back safe, but...I could never really shake the feeling I had when I thought about what could have happened to you that day. Your mother...well she never completely trusted me to be alone with you again after that, and who could blame her? I didn't even trust myself."

Sky paused to think about her history with her uncle. As much time as she had spent with him over the years, she had never gone anywhere alone with him. Not to a movie, out to eat, or to his house for a sleepover. She never thought anything of it at the time.

"I was only little," Sky asked. "You just weren't used to having a baby around the house. It could have happened to anyone."

"But it happened to me," Uncle Mike said. "Look, Sky, we had a lot of fun times, but I couldn't take care of shit. Not a cat. Not a dog. Not a plant. Most certainly not a child. For me, being a caretaker or guardian was like someone just waking up one day and putting on surgical gloves and going in to operate on someone. Had you stayed with me after the fall, you'd probably be dead by now. Plus..."

Sky waited for him to complete his thought. His eyes wandered. "I wasn't even sure if your mother would have wanted me taking care of you. She never really did forget what happened that day, and though I was always thankful she didn't let it get between you and me, I knew she would never trust me to care for you again."

"If that's the case, then it was ridiculous of her," Sky asserted.

"No, no, Sky," Uncle Mike shook his head. "She and I...as opposite as could be. She was the churchgoer and the apple of our parents' eyes. She did everything the way people are supposed to. College. Job. Husband. Family. Children. Church. *I* was the rebel. A bachelor. Trade school. Just...living the life. I don't know, Sky. Maybe chalking it up to psychological wounds isn't enough, but I had terrible anxiety about what to do when I inherited you. I love you dearly, but I would wake up every night after your parents died and think I might die too. That's how scared I was. I tried not to let it show, but it was eating me alive inside."

"And now?" Sky asked.

Mike half smiled. "Now...you've become what someone else made you. But I look at you and see you're not that child that needs me to protect you anymore."

"So, it's the perfect time to come out of hiding," Sky said. "Now that I don't need your protection."

"I didn't mean it like that," Mike said.

"For your information," Sky said. "I could have died just as easily under Sim's care. I almost did. That I made it this far is as much due to the care and training I received as luck. Your regret should not be leaving me alone to wander the streets when I was two. It should be that you'll always wonder how great you could have been for me had you fought your demons and kept me by your side."

"There's only the one path, Sky," Mike said. "Good or bad, it led us here. So, what is the point of entertaining the notion of some other path that wasn't taken? The big question is, where does the path we're on lead us tomorrow?"

Sky wiped a tear away as she saw her Uncle Mike, in many ways, for the first time. "We'll know tomorrow night."

Uncle Mike laughed. "That we will."

"How about we just keep it simple, and let's just live until we die," Sky said. "Together, this time."

"I'd love that, Sky," Mike said. "I'm so happy you're here."

The two swapped smiles as Misty came back through the front door. "It looks like your friends are here."

Mike moved to the kitchen where he had scrambled eggs and instant coffee already made. Misty and Sky stumbled into the kitchen and sat at the table.

"The boys come over every afternoon at this time," Mike said. "They live in other homes on this stretch. We have a unique compound. They're spoiled."

"I'm surprised none of them occupied my old place down the road," Misty said.

"Your house, Misty?" Mike said. "That the one with the country porch and the two trees out front?"

"That's the one," Misty said.

"It's our munitions depot," Mike said. "It's kind of central to the other homes we occupy, but we thought it would be best to house our larger arsenal separate."

"I just went through the house," Misty said. "I didn't see anything."

"Exactly," Mike said. "We emptied out your oil drum and turned it into a makeshift storage locker. Did the same thing at each of our homes, but we keep the larger stash at your place. We collected quite a bit over the years."

"Hmph," Misty said. "Us, too. I think I'll have some of that instant coffee now. I've gotten used to it over the years."

"The simple pleasures," Mike said.

Just as he said this, the door opened and a bunch of men filed in. Five, in total. Some of them looked weary and others bright-eyed. Mike responded as if he didn't even notice the intrusion.

"What's up, boss?" Cypress said. Then he noticed the girls sitting there. "Oh, my God, Alyssa."

"Hello, Cypress," Sky said.

"I never thought you would come here," Cypress said. "Let alone the next day after we showed up on your doorstep."

"It was too tempting to avoid," Sky said. "But don't think I'll ever forget what you did. I want to shoot you!"

"That's on me," Mike said.

"You're all adults here," Sky said. "Everyone needs to be accountable for his own choices. But let's not go on about it."

"I can agree to that," Cypress said.

"I can't believe you're that little girl," Hawk said. "Not so little anymore."

"She could kick *your* ass," Zippo said while flicking his lighter lid up and down.

Click, click, click.

"You're the one that got beat down by that other little girl on the road," Fisher laughed. "This little thing, probably no more than twelve, kicked him in the balls and smacked in the face. It was the funniest thing I ever saw."

"He approached her like he was trying to feed a stray cat," Cypress laughed. "And then he was surprised when she beat the shit out of him."

Click, click, click.

"Here kitty, kitty," Fisher mocked.

"Well, I wasn't going to hit no little girl," Zippo said. "Even if I wanted to, she jumped into that storm drain before I could even bat an eyelash. Crazy little thing. Good for her."

Misty thought of Harlow. *Could it be?*

"You meant well, Zippo," Mike said.

"So," Hawk said. "To what do we owe the pleasure of this visit, ladies?"

"Aside from seeing my uncle again, we're in the middle of tying together some local communities for peace and posterity," Sky said. "We call it our Kingdom Initiative. Of course, you already know Ember and her community at the preserve, but there are some others we know who live in the storm drains. We want to secure a zone, not just a single house or apartment complex, so we can rebuild and get back to some level of normalcy for the sake of future generations."

"Admirable," Fisher said. "Kudos. All Mike here has wanted to do was sit on his ass and make eggs all these years."

"Screw you," Mike said. "What have you done? These girls were led by a man who out of the gate was trying to save the world, and Alyssa is taking over where he left off."

"I remember that guy," Cypress said. "Whatever happened to him?"

"He died with some of our brothers and sisters trying to protect us," Sky said.

The group fell silent, some with a spoonful of eggs at their mouths.

"I'm sorry to hear that, Alyssa," Cypress said. "I guess all of us here have been a bit selfish. Out in the middle of nowhere, accomplishing nothing but to keep ourselves content, while little kids are fighting for a new world."

"And that's another thing," Sky said. "As I told my uncle yesterday, my name is no longer Alyssa. Not anymore. I'm Sky, and I don't wish to be referred to by any other name."

"So, gentlemen," Mike said, "she is Sky. And though we have dropped the ball all these years in thinking our fates were out of our control, it's more than clear that we can make a difference outside of the small bubble we've been living in."

Eddie put down his plate. "With all due respect...what if we're happy with the way things are? This...bubble. This is your niece. None of us sitting here has any family to fight for. It's different, Mike."

Click. Click. Click.

"It's true," Mike said. "My niece is a motivating factor, but aren't we *all* family? There isn't anything I wouldn't do for Sky that I wouldn't do for you, Eddie. And I mean that. If you don't feel the same way, I understand. Truly, I do. But I love all of you in this room, regardless. They call that unconditional love."

Mike looked to Sky, who smiled.

"What do you need from us, Sky?" Cypress asked.

"Yeah," Fisher added, rubbing his hands together. Fisher was a younger guy with wild eyes. "I love a good mission."

He reminded Misty of a grownup Teddy.

"I know you do," Mike said. "Let's finish eating, and then we'll talk shop."

There were six places around the kitchen table. The others dug in while leaning against counter tops or pulling around chairs from the dining room table. It was quiet for a few minutes as everyone shoveled eggs into their mouths and drank from the well of instant coffee, but when Mike rubbed his hands together and discarded his plate, the others knew he was ready to move on.

"Gentlemen, and Fisher," Mike laughed. The others joined in the taunt with short laughs. "I'm ever so grateful that my niece, Sky, has returned to me. She is a better young woman than I'll ever be—"

"You're still a fine lady," Cypress said. All the guys laughed, as did Sky and Misty.

"What I meant is, she is a better *person* than I'll ever be," Mike said. "Whatever she needs, I'm in for. We are at a crossroads here, and I know which way I'm going. But my path...doesn't have to be yours. I want you to know that you are free to enjoy the survival you have had over these years without regret. I appreciate all you have done for me. Truly."

"Well," Eddie said. "Honestly, if we were to go separate ways from here, I don't know that I'd ever be able to make eggs as well as this. So, I have to stick with you, buddy."

"You know which way I'm going," Cypress said.

"A man ain't nothing without a purpose," Fisher said. "I look at these young ladies and feel like, if I walked out these doors, I would be nothing more than a coward. I'm in."

Click, click, click. "I'm in," Zippo said. "And for what it's worth, Sky, I'm sorry we scared you back then."

"I forgive you," Sky said. "Or maybe there's nothing to be forgiven. If even one little thing had been different from my past, I might not be sitting here now, the person I am. I don't have any regrets."

As they all sat around the kitchen table, Sky's long-range walkie crackled.

"I think we're gonna need help." It was King's voice. "This is messed up. There are just the six of us. Heights? You hear me?"

"King?" Frankie crackled. "We're under attack over here. Our men are mustering. I don't know what I can do."

"Shit!" King tried. "Try to get some of them out and down here. We got a slew of armed men approaching."

"I'll do what I can," Frankie yelled. "Two miles on foot...It's a lot of ground to cover. Thirty minutes?"

"It could be too late," King yelled.

"Charlie?" Frankie called. "You hear me, Charlie? Malayah?"

"Leo, you out there?" King said. "Leo?"

Sky and Misty jumped from their chairs.

"Oh my God," Sky yelled. "Kane?"

"Who's Kane?" Mike asked.

"We have to get there," Sky cried. "Fast."

"Saddle up!" Mike yelled.

Everyone threw their plates down and headed for the front of the house. As Cypress opened the door, he saw a group of a dozen men with readied guns had created a semi-circle around the ranch house. He had only a second to react before the men opened fire.

"Everyone down!" he yelled as he slammed the door shut.

Everyone dove to the floor as a hail of gunfire erupted and lit up the ranch house in a furious blaze of bullet spray. Smoke, as well as debris from furniture, glass windows, and woodwork, filled the house.

"What the fuck?" Zippo shouted.

"We have to get out back to the stable," Mike cried.

"What's going on?" Eddie yelled.

"To the back. To the back!" Cypress yelled.

The gunfire continued as they all tried to move to the rear of the house toward the exit. Sky and Misty kept their heads covered as bullets whizzed over their bodies. Old memories from Zagan's attack stirred in their minds as the thunder of bullets roared.

Ten

KING WATCHED MISTY AND Sky disappear around the corner and radioed down to the others.

"So, I guess it's just the few of us," King said.

"Guess so," Wyatt replied. "How much brick is left back there? We could continue the wall."

"Not much," King said. "We have to go out and get more. I swear that thing will never be done."

"Just think how long it took to build the Great Wall of China," Baby chimed in.

"Where are you, Baby?" King asked.

"In the dining room straightening up," she said.

"And Teddy?"

"He's bossing around the little ones," Baby said.

"I'm sure," King said.

Teddy was with the boys in the living room showing them how to flip back his eyelids.

"I wanted to go," Yamil whined. "We never get to do nothing."

"It's ten miles!" Teddy said. "That's a long way. Your legs would be hurting bad."

"My legs are strong," Miracle said. "My legs wouldn't hurt."

"We walked far before," Yamil said.

"You'll go next time, so quit your whining," Teddy said. "Did you guys make your beds this morning?"

"You're not the boss," Yamil said.

"I'm just asking," Teddy said.

"I made mine," Miracle said.

"What are you all fussing about?" Baby said, rounding the corner.

"Nobody's fussing," Teddy said.

"How about you guys get the empty jugs from the basement and go to the well and fill them," Baby suggested. "We only have about two more full jugs left, last I looked."

"Chores, chores," Teddy said. "Why can't we ever just have any fun?"

The three boys paraded down to the basement and obtained several empty jugs and brought them back up. Wyatt was in the kitchen gnawing on an apple.

"Need a hand there, boys?" he asked.

"You can fill mine up?" Teddy said, handing over his empty jugs.

"That's not exactly what I meant," Wyatt said. "Since you have your hands full, I'll get the key and unlock the well cover for you."

"You get the easy job," Teddy said.

"My arms are going to be tired," Yamil said.

"Mine, too," Miracle copied. "Water is heavy."

"And these guys wanted to walk ten miles," Teddy sighed.

Wyatt led the way, and Teddy, Yamil, and Miracle followed behind him toting their jugs out the kitchen door, down the patio steps, and into the yard. King viewed them from the roof.

And to think I didn't like being up here.

"Fill them jugs, boys!" King yelled from the roof.

For the moment, everything was calm.

—◦◦✦◦◦—

Ember, Avi, and their extra three led Leo, Gigi, Harlow, Parker, and Messiah along the road toward their destination: the preserve.

Parker studied his firearm, a small .38 caliber revolver. Leo saw him flippantly managing it and chided him.

"Parker," he said. "Be careful with that. King didn't show you how to use this?"

"I just have to point it and shoot," Parker said. "Right?"

"For the most part," Leo said. "As long as the safety is off, and it shouldn't be, at the moment. And you never point this at anyone you don't intend to shoot."

Leo took the gun from him, showed him the safety feature and how to use it. "Did he give you any extra bullets for this?"

"All he gave me was the gun," Parker said. "Can I have it back?"

"Oh, brother," Leo said. "It only has three bullets in it, and I didn't bring any extra."

"Don't worry," Ember said from her lead position. "We have more ammunition we can give him once we arrive."

"Do you have a lot of guns and stuff?" Leo asked.

"We are comfortable with our supply," Ember said. "The preserve doesn't attract too much attention from outsiders, so we've been able to retain for many years what we recovered in the beginning. Just making sure our weapons are taken care of and maintain their functionality is the biggest effort."

"We haven't used our weapons a lot either," Leo said. "We had a big fight last year, and another fight a couple of months ago, and we used a lot. But we still have a lot."

"What happened in these...*fights*?" Ember asked, slowing her pace so that she was walking alongside Leo.

"In the last one, the two little guys got kidnapped, and I had to bring them back home," Harlow stated proudly.

"Oh," Ember said.

"Last year, this crazy guy got over a hundred people to attack the fortress," Leo said. "It was a huge fight, and some of us died. But we defended ourselves and won. Our leader died, though. His name was Sim."

"Sorry to hear that," Ember said.

"Then, two months ago, friends of the crazy guy who attacked us showed up and tried bringing him back to life at the fortress."

"They tried bringing him back to life?" Ember said.

"It was some cult," Leo said. "They were following the devil, but their ritual didn't work, and we just killed them too and burned them in the same pit as the crazy guy."

Ember looked at Leo cross-eyed and then turned to Harlow. "Where are *you* from?"

"Me, Parker, and Messiah live in the underground storm drains," Harlow said. "It's dark, but we haven't run into any devil worshippers down there."

"If you want a tour, I can bring you down," Parker said. "There's a gate near here. We can play hide and seek."

"As lovely as that sounds," Ember said, "we better stick to the road, because it's quite the long journey. We should keep a steady pace."

"Is your big friend a mute?" Avi asked, having taken the lead from Ember.

"What's that mean?" Parker said.

"He talks," Harlow said. "Just not often. If you have a question for him, you can ask *him*, as he is no less here than the rest of us."

"Avi," Ember said. "Let's remember to be tactful."

"I'm sorry," Avi said. "I didn't want to put him on the spot."

"Anyway, these other three you brought along don't say much," Harlow said.

"We're trained to keep quiet and observe," one of the three men said. "That's our role."

"Timothy and the other two are former military," Ember said. "They've been invaluable members of the preserve, especially when it came time to amass weapons. We haven't had one fatality since our inception, which was sixty days after the fall."

"Easy to say if you've never been attacked," Leo said.

"Fair enough," Ember said. "But sometimes your best offense is a strong defense."

"Sim was military too," Leo said. "Did you know him?"

"Sim?" Timothy said.

"Gabriel Simpson Ford," Leo said.

Timothy shook his head. "Didn't know him."

"I guess that makes sense," Leo said. "You're half his age. Anyway, he knew a lot of military tactics as well, and taught us kids a lot."

"He sounds like an honorable man," Timothy said.

"He was," Leo said. "And we will never forget him."

"Where did he find you?" Ember asked.

Leo didn't like thinking about those days.

"In my house. I was playing with Legos," Leo recalled. "Trying to build a spaceship so we could fly away to another planet and be safe. He wanted me to come with him, and I did."

"You weren't scared?" Ember asked.

"Back then I just...was," Leo said. "I don't remember feeling anything after my parents and dog died. But when Sim came, and I went to the fortress, I started to feel something again."

"That's wonderful," Ember said. "Look at you now."

Leo smiled. *Yes, look at me now, Sim.*

—◦❖◦—

Charlie found solid earth on which to plant his hands, and he pulled himself from the Hudson River. He laid on his back and found himself staring at trees and gasping for air. He had to take a minute, even though he was astutely aware that every second counted. He wasn't even sure if he could move. His body was numb all over and he was soaked to the bone.

He had to keep moving, no matter what. He had to warn the others of impending danger. Kane wasn't a distant threat, but an imminent one. His soldiers could be attacking the fortress or the heights as he lay there.

It will be an hour-long walk back to the fortress. It could be too late. What would he do, anyway, injured and without a weapon?

He rolled himself onto all fours, wincing through the pain. He crawled a few feet and collapsed.

Get up, Charlie. Get up!

He couldn't. He wanted to, even if it was only to get to the fortress to die, but he simply couldn't move. As he lay there disgusted with himself while thinking about Malayah and how he had unwittingly walked them both into a trap, he wanted to scream. How could he have been so naïve? Frankie was going to be devastated.

"You need help?" a voice called from the shore.

Startled, Charlie, still lying on the ground, positioned himself on one arm to see who was there. It was Jesse, the ferryman. His eyes were wide, and he was sitting in his boat, which he had brought close to land.

"Jesse," Charlie said. "What are you doing here?"

"I saw what they done and how you got away," he said. "I thought maybe you could use a hand."

"Why?" Charlie said.

"I like to help people," Jesse said. "You guys were nice. That lady you was with...I feel sorry for her."

"So do I," Charlie said. "Can you bring me down river? Just a mile or so."

"I can do that," Jesse said. "I can't go back, though."

"That's fine, Jesse," Charlie said. "We have a place for you."

Jesse backpedaled the boat, then brought it straight into shore. A new sense of energy overcame Charlie as he realized that by boat, he could get to the fortress much quicker and without expending any energy.

Charlie clutched his battered ribcage as he stumbled over the aft side of the boat. Jesse held it steady with both hands as it rocked on the water.

"What weapons do you have?" Charlie asked, trying to pull himself up onto a seat.

"Just a pistol," he said. "That's all they give me."

Jesse pushed off with an oar and reversed from land. With a couple of quick motions, he had the rowboat zipping with the current down the Hudson. Charlie felt some relief, though he shuddered to think about what he might encounter when he got back to the fortress.

"Kane said he had a lot of the soldiers out on missions," Charlie said. "He made it sound like they were attacking places."

"They don't tell me much, but those boats brought a lot of people from the island to the mainland not too long before you got there," Jesse said. "I figured they was up to no good. They're just doing what they do every time we land at a new place. Kane wants to take over the whole state."

"Have you ever been to the island?" Charlie asked.

"Sure have," Jesse said. "Kane throws wild parties all the time. I even get to go."

"Good," Charlie said. "We can use you later. You made a good choice, Jesse."

"I just like to help people," he reiterated.

Charlie hadn't met too many of Kane's associates, but he couldn't quite understand where Jesse fell in the mix. He didn't seem to be the type that would be accepted by an ambitious gang of thugs.

"Where are you going with that man, Jesse?" a voice cried from up-river.

Charlie turned quickly and noticed another rowboat bearing down on them. There looked to be three men in it. "Oh, shit."

"I should have known they would come after me," Jesse said. "They always do."

"Big brother's looking for you, Jesse," one of the men called. "Now shoot that fool and dump him in the drink and get your ass back here before it's all our asses."

"Big brother?" Charlie said.

"Well, yeah, Kane, sort of is my brother," Jesse said. "He gives me jobs, but he scares me sometimes."

Charlie shook his head. "That explains a lot."

"Jeeessseeee," they taunted. "Come on, Jesse."

Their boat was getting closer.

"Okay, Jesse, listen," Charlie said. "I either got to bail, or you have to give me that gun of yours, so I have a fighting chance."

"Oh, I don't know," Jesse said. "I don't want to see you have to float home. You could drown. But my gun. Kane said never give up my gun."

"Aren't you running from Kane?" Charlie said.

"I was just helping," Jesse said. "I like to help people."

Just then one of the men from the boat fifty yards behind them fired off a rifle. The bullets thwapped the water all around the boat. Charlie threw his body down into the belly of the rowboat.

"Jesus," Charlie said.

"Don't make us fill that boat with holes," one of the men said. "Kane will take it out on all of us, Jesse. You know how he is. Turn your ass around, or you'll be sorry."

"Okay, new plan," Charlie said. "We're going to capsize this thing."

"You mean turn it over?" Jesse said.

"Exactly," Charlie said. "But we have to do it now before they get too close. After it's flipped, we can get those air pockets underneath."

"Why would we flip the boat?" Jesse said.

"Just trust me," Charlie said. "They're going to catch us one way or the other, Jesse. I'd rather be disappeared when they catch us than sitting out in the open."

"You want to play hide-and-seek with them?" Jesse said.

"Yes," Charlie said. "That's exactly right. But I need that gun of yours."

Charlie didn't wait for permission. While Jesse continued to row, Charlie snatched the gun from his holster and put it in his own waistband.

"Whoa," Jesse said. "You're quick. I never said you could take it, though."

"Jesse," Charlie said, looking Jesse square in the eyes. "You wanted to help, so help."

Jesse dropped the oars. Charlie ignored his pained ribcage and grabbed the edge of the boat on the right side. He had Jesse do the same.

"Okay," Charlie said, wrenching in agony. "We pull back at the same time. It may take a few tries, but eventually, we'll get it. We can overturn it as soon as we get the water to start spilling in."

In synchrony, the two men pulled on the side of the boat while shifting their weight backward. More bullets slapped at the surface of the water.

"What are you guys doing?" one of the voices called.

"Again," Charlie said.

The two pulled back.

"Again," Charlie said.

They pulled back again. The more times they rocked the boat, the easier it tipped up until water started coming in from the left side. Charlie was anguished but continued to heave. Once the boat started to sink, the last pull was all it took, and it flipped over on their heads. Both Charlie and Jesse quickly came up from under the water and caught the air pockets while treading and holding onto the metal seats above them.

"This is kind of cool," Jesse said. "But it's hard to see. They're still coming, you know."

Charlie felt for the gun in his waistband and readied it. "I know."

They waited a few minutes in quiet underneath the boat while the chatter of the other men grew closer.

"What did you do, Jesse?" one of the men called. "It was a stupid thing, you know. Kane won't be pleased with this. You're wasting our time and protecting a man that your brother wants six feet under."

"We know you guys are there," another voice said. "Where are you going?"

"Let's just shoot through the boat and let their lifeless corpses float to the bottom," one of them said. "We'll tell Kane they tipped the boat and they both drowned."

"I'm not going back and telling Kane that his brother is dead," another voice said. "He'll kill us all. The only way this ends is by dragging that fool out by his ears and bringing him back."

"Well, I'm not going under there to get that dumbass."

As the trio bickered, Charlie offered Jesse the universal shush sign and then dipped below the surface. He came out on the side of the boat facing away from them and carefully made his way to the bow. The boatmen didn't notice him as they debated what to do, and that's when Charlie made his move. He carefully raised his gun out of the water, took aim, and with the men only a few feet away, he fired off every shot he had in the gun. Each one hit a mark, and the men crumpled on the boat. Two were unmoving, but he heard the third moaning and shuffling around, but couldn't see him.

"What happened?" Jesse called from under the boat.

Charlie ignored him and swam carefully over to the assailants' boat. He placed both hands on the sides and pulled down and like a jack in the box, the wounded man popped up with his semi-automatic in hand prepared to fire. Charlie quickly let go of the boat and it sprang up quickly, which caused the gunman to lose his balance. He fell backward into the river. Charlie swam under the boat in his direction and collided with his thrashing body under the water.

Charlie hoped the man was at least injured, because he wasn't in any shape to take on a fully equipped equal.

The man struggled to break free from Charlie. Charlie couldn't feel any weapon, so he figured the guy fell off the boat without his gun.

Now what?

He held onto the man's waist and heard him screaming from above the surface of the water. He was panicked. Charlie threw a couple of punches into the man's stomach, but he could tell the guy had a grip on the edge of the boat. Running out of breath, Charlie swam back to the opposite side of the boat and came up for air. He grabbed onto the opposite edge from where his attacker was clinging.

"You shot me, you son of a bitch. You shot me," the man said. "Jesse! You hear me? This is a point of no return for you."

"For you, too," Charlie said. He pulled himself up high enough to see inside the boat. There was a gun within his reach if he could stretch far enough.

He ignored the pain. He tried thrusting his body forward to grab it. The boat had little give because of the man holding onto it from the other side. Charlie tried pulling himself up and over with the help of the other guy's weight keeping it balanced on the water. The man didn't know it, but his clinging to the boat was helping Charlie.

Because of the pain he was in, Charlie couldn't pull himself completely up, but he was able to get up high enough to grab one of the loose guns inside the boat. Once he had it, he fell back into the water and aimed it toward the guy.

"What are you doing over there?" the man yelled. "Jesse?"

Charlie held the gun under the water and fired it. A bunch of muffled shots cut through the water to the other side of the boat and the man screamed. Charlie heard his cries muffled as he sank into the water. The boat suddenly became free. Charlie tossed the gun back up onto the boat and grabbed onto the edge.

"Jesse?" Charlie called.

"Is it over?" Jesse called.

"For them, yes," Charlie said.

"Now what?" Jesse asked.

"We have to get both these boats to shore," Charlie said. "So we can get back on them and continue down the river."

"Are they dead?" Jesse asked from underneath his boat.

"Yes," Charlie said. "They're dead."

"Oh," Jesse said. "Kane won't be happy."

"Who gives a fuck about Kane's happiness, Jesse?" Charlie said. "I'm getting to my friends, and after I do, we're going back and we're going kill that son of a bitch, once and for all. Now come out from under there and let's get these boats back to shore."

Jesse popped out a few seconds later, and each of them towed their respective boats back to the shoreline. They untipped Jesse's boat once it was on land and then unloaded the two bodies from the second boat. Jesse jumped back into his boat and Charlie commandeered the assailants' boat, which had three automatic weapons in it. Together, they headed south toward the green bridge.

Though Charlie was in pain, he had renewed energy—a second wind, adrenaline that only fury could release.

Eleven

THE BOYS, WITH WYATT'S assistance, managed to fill fourteen gallon-sized jugs of water and bring them back to the house. As they finished their task, King alerted them of company coming up the hill and around from the back.

"We got about a dozen armed men coming from all sides," King said, panicked.

"What?" Wyatt said.

"Just what I said," King replied. "Jesus. Get the cocktails ready, and we need to spread out across the floors. Baby and Teddy, bring extra weapons up, quick, and close the shutters. Baby and Wyatt, stay on the first floor at each door. Send Yamil and Miracle up to floor two with cocktails. Teddy, you take floor three, front. Fuck! We're spread too thin. I knew this shit was gonna happen."

"Don't panic," Wyatt said. "We're fortified even with only a few of us."

King grabbed the long-range walkie as the men got closer. "I think we're gonna need help," he called in. "This is messed up. There are just the six of us. Heights? You hear me?"

"King?" Frankie crackled. "We're under attack over here. Our men are mustering. I don't know what I can do."

"Shit!" King tried. "Try to get some of them out and down here. We got a slew of armed men approaching."

"I'll do what I can," Frankie yelled. "Two miles on foot...it's a lot of ground to cover. Thirty minutes?"

"It could be too late," King yelled.

"Charlie?" Frankie called. "You hear me, Charlie? Malayah?"

"Leo, you out there?" King said. "Leo?"

King lowered the device, realizing that there was more going on here. He was concerned about those who were not answering. He picked up the local device.

"Keep low," King said. "Are we in position?"

"We brought up a lot of guns for both floors," Baby said. "The boys are ready with the explosives, but they don't have much of any practice with a real situation. I have them at the front windows on floor two. They have guns too."

"I'm ready on floor three," Teddy said. "I got clear shots and I'll blow these suckers to hell."

King dropped to his stomach and put his eye to the scope. He wasn't the best long-range shooter, but he never dreamed he would have to put himself to the test.

Damn. One more day. All I had was one more day up here. Who are these fucks, anyway? They're attacking the heights, too? Coordinated attacks.

He lined up his sights with a random soldier in the front of the pack and fired off a shot. The soldier fell, and the others sprinted forward. He could only deal with one side of the building. He fired off two more shots. One hit the mark and the other missed. Then the counterattack ensued.

The soldiers opened fire with automatic weapons. Bullets whizzed up in his direction, at the door, windows, and brick. King continued to line men up with his sights and pop off random shots as they returned fire. He heard explosions, which meant Yamil and Miracle were successfully tossing out the Molotov cocktails. He saw two of them impact the street near the men, causing them to disperse. He heard Teddy's shots ring out from the third floor.

King felt that was a good time to get from the topmost roof to the lower to see what was happening out back. As he slid down the small roof to the lower roof, there were men in the back taking shots. He saw several men firing at the backside of the building. Is this what he missed in the battle with Zagan? Shark had died on the roof. Would he as well?

"Are the doors secure?" King asked, taking a moment on the radio.

"They're taking gunfire, but so far, so good," Wyatt said.

"They're in the yard, but not on the side," Baby said. "Kitchen door is secure."

"Baby, take a minute to check on Yamil and Miracle," King said. "Have them switch to guns."

Baby ran up the back steps to the second floor. The boys were there ready to throw another cocktail out the window.

"I'm scared," Miracle said. He had his ears plugged and was on the ground, his back to the wall.

Yamil was doing all the work throwing out the cocktails.

"Yamil," Baby said. "Switch to guns, and be careful not to make yourself a target."

Baby ran back downstairs as Yamil picked up a gun that was half his size. He stood up and aimed it out the window. He had only used small arms up to that point, so he didn't know what to expect. When he pulled the trigger, the kickback sent him flying backward onto his butt.

"Oh, man," he said.

He got back up, held the gun more tightly, and fired again out the window at the bad guys down below.

"I'm scared," Miracle repeated.

"Just stay there," Yamil said. "I got this."

By the time Baby reached the back door, she heard gunfire slapping the reinforced oak on the other side.

"King," Baby cried. "I don't know about this. The weapons these guys have are more intense than what Zagan's people had. These doors won't hold if this keeps up."

As she said that, the gunfire stopped. There was silence.

"They stopped firing," King said.

"Should I open a shutter?" Wyatt asked.

"I don't know," King said. "Wait."

"I can still see some of them," Teddy said. "I can kill 'em."

Baby ran back up the second set of stairs and slid a walkie talkie across the floor to Yamil where he was standing. "Use this, Yamil. And wait."

"They're standing in back, just sitting there," King said. "I don't want to fire. Maybe all they want to do is talk."

"They came to talk with a full-on assault?" Wyatt said.

"I opened fire first," King said. "Maybe they wouldn't have."

"I guess the only thing that makes sense with the pause is to see what the hell they want," Wyatt said. "We may not be able to hold them off forever."

"Stay behind the door for coverage," King said. "And hold down your talk button so we can hear what's going on."

Wyatt crept to the door. He put his hand around the knob, whispered a short prayer, then pulled it open halfway. He pressed down the walkie's talk button, and from behind the door he yelled, "What do you want?"

"We came to announce that this territory is under new order," Wasp said. "We didn't come to hurt you. We came because your home has been identified as potentially housing a cache of weapons, and under the new order, firearms outside the military campus of the island or in the hands of trained soldiers have been deemed illegal. We need to check your residence and confiscate said contraband. In the days ahead, you will receive more information on the new territorial governorship that has been established.

Now, lay down your weapons and allow us to enter, and nobody will get hurt."

Wyatt thought his statement ironic, since the only people that had been hurt thus far had were *Kane's* men.

"What kind of governorship establishes itself with an assault on civilian dwellings?" Wyatt asked.

"The governorship has not deemed your home to *be* a civilian home, but a future resistance outpost," the man called back. "Civilian homes don't typically rain down heavy assault on a policing network just coming to talk."

"Policing network? How can we be a resistance to a governorship we didn't even know existed?" Wyatt said. "Plus, we know damn well you're hitting one of our other locations. You aren't making any sense, son. And if you think we can't keep up with our defenses until the last of you are dead, you'd be wrong. We have higher ground and a fortified installation here. So, for now, you best move along, and if the head of this new...*governorship* wants to enforce territorial laws, he needs to start by involving representatives of other communities to establish those laws. We don't recognize the authority of some wannabe outfit that tries to steal our stuff. That's what pirates do, not governments."

There was a silence. While Wyatt debated with the men out front, Baby commanded Yamil and Miracle to the first floor.

"They want our weapons," she said to them. "You guys need to be fast. We'll hold them off, but you need to smuggle as much as you can from our supply closet through the tunnel to the woods in case they get in. Be fast and make as many trips as you can while we stall them."

Yamil nodded. Miracle was trembling, but he nodded too, in tears.

"Be strong, Miracle," Baby said. "It's fine. You'll be fine."

The boys ran down the basement steps, and Baby ran to the front of the house to where Wyatt was still standing behind the door.

"Buy us time," Baby said. "The little ones are getting our weapons out through the tunnel. We need fifteen minutes. I'll go down and help. That way, if they somehow breach, our weapons will be secure. Well, as secure as they can be."

Wyatt nodded.

"Let me try to be clear with you," the man said from out front. "We're only trying to be proactive with what were deemed to be potential problematic areas, prior to asserting full authority over the territory. Our military is well equipped to keep you safe without the need for warehousing weapons. This is the beginning of a new era. You just need to let us do our jobs, and the life you have been searching for over the last four years will finally be at hand. You won't need to hide anymore. You'll be free to walk the streets safely as we continue to rebuild infrastructure and get back the world we once had."

"First of all," Wyatt said. "You aren't gonna find a group with half a shred of smarts that don't have a cache of weapons on hand in these times. Second, how can we trust you? We could let you in, and you could turn around and kill us without regard. We didn't survive all these years just to go out by letting you walk into our home and shoot us. If we're going to die, we'd much rather die fighting than throwing up our arms."

As Wyatt talked, Baby, Yamil, and Miracle were hard at work running guns, grenades, ammunition, and other important supplies down the tunnel, out the hole, and into the woods. The boys scrambled, carrying as much as they could back and forth as Baby unloaded the supply closet. She left a few random items in the closet and locked it back up as plausible decoy, for if the men got access to the house, they surely would discover the tunnel as quickly as the arsenal closet.

"Nobody has to die," the man said. "Except the men you already killed, unprovoked."

"It sounds like our training is much like yours," Wyatt said. "To be proactive in removing potential threats."

"Touché," the man said. "But I think it's only fair to warn *you*: we can do this the easy way, or a much harder way. You see, at this moment, we have only a fraction of the soldiers with us that compose our military. You know I'm not lying when I say we blew up two bridges, with C-4 explosive. That means we have the resources we need to storm this building by force. Now, wouldn't it be much easier just to let us in, check for contraband, seize it if applicable, and leave without further harm to anyone?"

"Outside of me, we are children here," Wyatt said.

"You have my promise," the man said. "None of the children will be harmed."

Wyatt raised the walkie to his mouth. "Where are things at with the weapons run?"

Baby responded. "We got most of it out. If you are going to let this happen, the timing is right. I sent the boys out into the woods in case things go south."

"King?" Wyatt asked.

"We're not letting these assholes in," King said. "If they get in, that's one thing, but I'll be damned if they think they're just going to show up on our door and march into our home. We were ready to die when Zagan tried that shit, and we should be ready now for the same."

"For Sim," Baby added.

"Yeah, screw 'em!" Teddy echoed.

"Yeah," Wyatt said.

"What's it going to be, mister?" the man called from outside.

Wyatt opened the door fully and opened fire with a spray of ammunition that took at least two men down. The others scrambled. King got up on a knee and fired a series of shots at the men in the yard while Baby ran to the second floor and rained fire down on anyone she could get an eye on.

Teddy did the same from the third floor.

Come and get it, you bunch of assholes. Haha. This isn't our first rodeo!

Wyatt slammed the door shut and flung open the shutters. He didn't see anyone.

The men in the back scrambled to the right and left as King fired off random shots. As he did so, he saw Yamil appear from behind the developing wall. He unloaded a hail of gunfire at men who were running away from King's sniper fire.

Oh, shit. Yamil is no joke. We got another Big Will.

Several men fell to gunfire, and the few left seemed to scatter.

"You see any of them?" King asked from the roof.

"All quiet down here," Wyatt said. "How many were there in all?"

"A dozen or so," King said. "We nailed most of them, though. Baby?"

"I got nothing," she answered.

"We got the guns," a little voice called. "It was Miracle."

"Good boy," King said.

"Those cowards went running!" Teddy said.

They all waited ten minutes or so before letting down their guard. Even then, they didn't move.

"We stay put and on alert until I say otherwise," King said.

Around the corner, the remaining men met up after having fled from the area around the fortress.

"Kane said it wasn't going to be easy," Wasp said. "But I didn't think we would run into that! I told Kane we should bring heavier stuff."

"These damn people have been dug in for four years," another soldier said. "We shouldn't have come here with anything less than our grenade launchers and dynamite. We need to get our asses back to get what we need to take these sons of bitches out."

"I hear you," Wasp said. "We lost a lot of soldiers. There's no doubt about this place, though. It's more than some home with kids in it."

"I counted eight down," one of the other men said.

"Let's get back to the island," Wasp said. "We'll come back with what we need to get in there and clear it. Hopefully the others are having more luck."

With that, the men headed out.

Twelve

KANE'S CREW HIT THE heights first. They approached the compound without warning, fifteen soldiers in all, rushing through with guerilla style blaze and shooting randomly in every direction.

Frankie sounded the muster alarm and radioed her defense team.

"Shoot to kill," she said. "Shoot to kill."

The residents took to their apartment windows and rained fire down. The men took cover behind old cars, trees, and against the building.

Frankie stayed at the entrance of building seven, a central location to all the mayhem. She listened to the exchanging gunfire and decided to leave the safety of cover. She ran through the parking lot of the apartment building, shooting as many attackers as she could.

She took cover behind a vehicle as her people, doing as trained, answered the attack with gunfire from their various apartment windows and at the main doors of each building.

What the fuck is this? She thought of Malayah. These had to be Kane's people. If they were attacking, what did that mean for her and Charlie?

Her thoughts on the matter were interrupted via the long-range walkie.

"I think we're gonna need help," It was King's voice. "This is messed up. There are just the six of us. Heights? You hear me?"

"King?" Frankie answered back. "We're under attack over here. Our people are mustering. I don't know what I can do."

"Shit!" King tried. "Try to get some of them out and down here. We got a slew of armed men approaching."

"I'll do what I can," Frankie yelled. "Two miles on foot...it's a lot of ground to cover. Thirty minutes?"

"It could be too late," King yelled.

"Charlie?" Frankie called. "You hear me, Charlie? Malayah?"

"Leo, you out there?" King said. "Leo?"

Nobody answered back. She thought the worst. She walked into a trap. *Who are these people? What do they want?*

She popped up from behind a car and fired sporadically at every target she saw moving, figuring that none of her people would be out and about after the muster alarm. She ran out from the car and engaged the men as they fired at all the buildings and the people inside. When she ran out of ammunition, she tossed her weapon aside and attacked one of the soldiers, who never saw it coming. He was a young man, and his eyes lit up with surprise when he saw Frankie rushing him.

She drove her body into his and they fell to the ground in a heap. She whipped out a knife from her leg sheath and plunged it into his side. He screamed.

"What the fuck is going on here?" she asked as she jammed the knife into him again. He yelped in pain.

"Stop!" he screamed. "Stop! Please."

"Fuck you, *stop*," Frankie cried. "What do you want?"

"Your weapons," he cried. "Your weapons."

The man sounded like a ferret, crying out like a small child in agony.

"Our weapons?" Frankie asked.

"It's a new order," he said, his voice fading. "A new order."

She grabbed him by the collar. "What the fuck shit are you talking? Whose orders?"

She pulled him up so his face was two inches from her. "Order this, motherfucker." She plunged the knife into him one more time and left him for dead.

Another one of her security men, Merrick, arrived at her side.

"Who are these guys?" Merrick asked.

"Later," she said. "Shoot them all. Watch yourself."

She sprang into action after grabbing the fallen man's gun. As she reached another tree, the gunfire slowed down.

A man came out into the open flailing his arms in the courtyard started yelling. "Cease fire!"

She turned in his direction.

"Cease fire!" he called.

Though outraged, Frankie was curious. She radioed to her commanders and building leaders. "Cease fire. Let's hear what this idiot in the courtyard has to say. Wait for my word."

"Cease fire," he said. "Cease fire."

"We heard you," Frankie screamed. Gun in hand, she made her way to the flailing man. "What the hell do you want?"

The man held firm, not relinquishing his gun, but directing his attention to Frankie, who was coming at him like a ferocious lion with her gun aimed.

"Wait," he said. "It's not necessary."

"Not necessary?" Frankie said. "I'll decide on that. What the fuck did you come here for?"

"Lower your weapon, and I'll explain," he said.

"Screw you," Frankie said. "Your men are at our disposal. Hiding their asses behind trees and shit. I don't have to do nothing. We know you're attacking another outpost of ours too. That's a declaration of war, and we are ready to fuck shit up."

"There doesn't have to be war," the man said. "We'll take submission as the other option. You can shoot me dead now, but soon after, you'll face double an outfit carrying weapons you will have no defense against. You can live today to die tomorrow. Or you can listen to what I have to say, now that we have your attention, and you can have a future."

"If all you wanted to do was talk, then maybe you shouldn't have come here with your guns blazing."

"We *did* come to talk," the man said. "Yesterday. But Charlie ignored our proposal to be part of a new territorial government."

"New government?" Frankie said. "What in the hell kind of shit are you talking about?"

"This territory is being claimed by a government under Ulysses Kane," the man said. "Our first order of business is to warn, engage, and disarm settlements that have resistance potential."

"Kane?" she said. "That heifer with the tattooed neck? That thug ass didn't look like he could govern his way out of a paper bag. If he thinks he's going to walk into town and make this community, or any other community in this area bow to *him*, he has another thing coming."

"Clearly, this didn't go the way we had intended," the man said. "But this won't be the end. Others will be back for your weapons, and they will kill you, as well as anyone else who resists the new government. So, think about your next move for the sake of all your residents hiding in their apartments right now wondering how safe they truly are. Because whether they know it yet or not, they are not safe."

Frankie pinched her chin with her eyes raised for two seconds, pretending to ponder.

"I thought it over," she said.

With that, she fired multiple shots into the man's face and chest, and he fell to the ground. She retrieved her radio.

"Resume fire on anyone who doesn't belong," she said. "Exterior forces, swarm the area and kill whatever you see. We have them outnumbered. They'll either leave or be killed. I will advise when the threat has been eliminated. Be careful."

The defense team did as instructed, and before long, the compound was cleared. There were thirteen dead soldiers on the heights campus, and a couple of others fled. There were no casualties at the heights, and though Frankie wanted to celebrate their victory against the attack, she could only worry about the fates of Malayah and Charlie. As she was about to dispatch backup to the fortress, she heard from King.

"King," she said. "What's your status? We can have people there shortly."

"We have things neutralized over here," he answered. "What about you?"

"No casualties on our side," Frankie answered. "Got a lot them bastards, though. A couple of them fled. They came here like a bunch of drunken cowboys talking shit about Kane and his new government. They want our weapons and basically to kill us all."

"That's the same message we got," King said. "It seems like they thought we would just roll over. Suckers. But they'll regroup and be back with bigger weapons," King said.

"According to them," Frankie said. "We'll just have to figure it out. Do you think Malayah is okay? She hasn't answered."

King didn't answer, but only called, "Anyone else listening out there? Leo? Charlie? Sky?"

The radio crackled with no response.

Thirteen

As THE CREW WALKED the road to the preserve, Timothy, Ember's military host, fell back beside her.

"We're being tracked," he said.

"What?" Ember said. "What do you mean?"

Leo, on the other side of Ember, tuned in.

"Casper and Dietrich signaled from the rear," he said. "We have tails."

"Who?" Ember asked.

"I don't know," he said. "But they've seen a few of them. It's a group."

"Okay," Ember said, staring straight ahead. "What do we do?"

"People are following us?" Leo asked.

Harlow, who was next to him, then joined the discussion. "What? We're being followed?"

"Shhh," Timothy said.

Gigi became interested in the quiet conversation and looked up to everyone as she walked, curious. Parker patted her as she strolled along. "It's okay, girl."

"No, wait," Harlow said. "If we're in danger, I'm scrambling to the drains. If we go too much farther, the network to the Hudson ends. It'll be too late."

"What network?" Timothy asked.

"The storm drainage system that leads to the Hudson," Leo said. "Harlow, where is the nearest gate?"

"We can go back a half mile or up a quarter mile," she said. "After that...forget it."

"We can't go back," Timothy said. "And we certainly aren't leading our pursuers to the preserve. So, we dive in a quarter mile."

"We're going...underground?" Ember asked.

"We have no choice," Timothy said.

"What's the problem with going under?" Harlow asked. "It's not *that* bad."

"Excuse me," Ember said. "I've just never been in a situation like this. I rarely go out on missions, and now I know why. But it also gives me insight into why we have to make Pangea work. Who can live like this?"

"Don't worry," Harlow said. "Me, Parker, and Messiah know the tunnels down below better than anyone. If they try to follow, they'll regret it."

"I'm happy to hear that," Ember said. "Maybe we can even go back a half mile underneath them and come up behind them."

"Wow," Timothy said. "A general in the making."

Ember smiled and fluffed her hair. "Well, I don't want to brag, but I have been known for being quite the strategist."

"In what situations?" Timothy asked.

"Mostly board games," Ember said.

Timothy rolled his eyes.

"Should I radio the others?" Leo asked, holding the long range in his hand.

"Wait on that," Timothy advised. "We don't want to alert the other party with a bunch of radio communications or worry your friends."

A few minutes later, Harlow alerted them of the gate coming up on their right. As they approached it, Harlow signaled Messiah over while Timothy and his men made a shield in front of the gate. Messiah lifted the iron

grate and slid it aside. Parker went in first, followed by Leo. Harlow passed
Gigi down to Leo, then Avi and Ember came down. Messiah, Deitrich, and
Casper followed, and the last one to pass through was Timothy, who slid
the cover back over them.

Once they were all down, they turned on their flashlights. Parker led
them back the way they had come. The next gate they encountered would
take them up so that they were behind the group trailing them.

The soldiers following the preserve group watched from afar as they halted
for what they assumed was a break. As they waited under the cover of trees,
cars, and houses, they noticed the group disappeared. From a distance, it
was hard to tell where they had suddenly vanished to, so the lieutenant, JJ,
stepped out and headed up the road to see if he could put eyes on them.
He stopped in the center of the street, just short of where the outlet to the
storm drain they had entered was, and looked both ways.

"You see anything, boss?" a voice said through the radio.

"Bring the men up," JJ said.

About a dozen soldiers gathered in the middle of the street.

"Where the hell did they go?" one of the men asked.

"Maybe the place they're headed is around here somewhere," JJ said,
confused. "They were all here in this area one minute, and the next...but
there doesn't seem to be anything around here."

"Boss," a man called who was hunched over the storm drain cover. JJ
turned, and the men walked over to it. "Maybe we got gophers."

"Could there be a community in the sewers?" another man asked.

"What kind of community would they have in the ground?" JJ said.
"Anyway, that's not a sewage system. That's a water drain, you idiot. Plus,

we passed twenty of these drains since we left. Why the heck would they dive now?"

"Maybe they're using the system to get wherever they are going more covertly," one of the men said.

"Lift it," JJ said.

One of the men lifted the cover and threw is aside. JJ shined a flashlight down the hole. "A million to one that's where they went. It's the only thing that makes sense. We gonna follow them down there?"

"It's not my first instinct," JJ said. "But if we go back and tell Kane we lost them, he'll be pissed. Why don't I send a couple of you down there to check it out, and the rest of us, we'll hang tight. Ortiz and Dodson."

"I don't want to go down there," Dodson said. "They could be sitting there waiting for us."

"Shh," JJ said. He laid down on the hot pavement and put his ear to the hole. "I don't hear a thing. If they went down there, they aren't just sitting."

"Why don't we just go ahead and find the next outlet," Ortiz suggested. "If they went down, at some point they have to come up."

"These drains are all over the city," JJ said. "How would we know which one they plan to come out of? Now, I'm commanding you two to get your asses down there to observe and report."

"Damn," Dodson said.

Dodson and Ortiz made their way down the ladder. As soon as they were both in the tunnel, Dodson shined the light back up. "It only goes one way."

"Which way?" JJ asked.

"Back the way we came," Dodson said.

As he said this, an outpouring of gunfire erupted on the streets. JJ and the other soldiers screamed as they were all cut down by a hail of bullets fired off by Timothy, Dietrich, and the others who were rushing them from behind. The soldiers, who were all clustered around the drain entrance, never saw it coming.

"What's going on up there?" Dodson yelled.

"Shut up," Ortiz said. "There's someone down here."

"Well, fire!" Dodson said.

Ortiz raised his gun to fire down the length of the tunnel, but before he could react, gunfire echoed, and blasts of orange and yellow light lit up the dark passageway. Ortiz fell dead and Dodson scurried up the ladder. As soon as he popped his head out, there were a multitude of guns pointing in his face. His eyes widened.

"Wait!" he cried. "Don't shoot me."

"Get out," Timothy said.

Dodson climbed out of the hole and observed the carnage around him. All his men lay dead, heaped in a circle around the drain.

"What the fuck?" Dodson said.

Casper emerged from the hole behind him. "Good work, Harlow."

"Hey," Parker said. "I led the way. I think I even shot one of them. I never killed anyone before."

"What the hell is this?" Timothy asked. "Who are you people?"

"You didn't have to do this," Dodson said. "We were only here on Kane's orders to observe and report."

"Report on what?" Avi asked, stepping forward.

Dodson tensed up but held firm. "Communities that could be a danger to Kane's new government. They are to be disarmed or...destroyed."

"You want to take the guns and lives of those who will fight, and then subjugate anyone who is left?" Ember said. "Is that the big governing plan?"

Dodson's bottom lip trembled. "We have established authority in many communities on our journey up the Hudson River from Brooklyn. This was our next stop."

"And it actually worked in these other places?" Ember said. "We must be way ahead of the curve, because the way I see it, we just killed an entire armed unit in less than a minute, and you didn't even know we were there. So, maybe you'll finally discover the first place where you're going to get a little more bang for your buck."

"Say what you want," Dodson said. "We have over one thousand soldiers from here to Brooklyn and more than three thousand residents operating under our protocol. You can kill who you like. It won't change the outcome. They'll just keep coming at you with more people and bigger weapons."

"Maybe we have plans of our own," Timothy said. "You are now our hostage, and will remain so if you continue to be useful. You'll walk with us, but if you make one false move, we'll kill you. Messiah!"

"Yeah," Messiah said.

"Keep an eye on this man," Timothy said. "If he tries anything funny, break his neck."

"Okay," Messiah said, clasping his hands together in front of Dodson's face.

"Radio back and warn the others," Timothy said.

"I tried," Leo said. "These things weren't working in the tunnel."

"We're not in the tunnels anymore," Parker pointed out.

"I noticed," Leo said.

"Anyone hear me out there?" Leo said.

A handful of seconds later, there was a response.

"Leo!" King said. "Thank God. We were worried because we didn't hear from you. We were attacked. We're all right, but some crazy stuff is going down."

"We were followed," Leo said. "But we were able to get around it and take them out. It's that guy, Kane."

"We know," King said.

"We're all good up here," Frankie said. "Those *putas* are just trying to get rid of everyone in the area so they can control everything. We haven't heard from Charlie and Malayah."

"Sky and Misty, either," King said.

"Should we come back?" Leo asked.

"Keep on," King said. "Let's do what we set off to do this morning so we can all come together with a plan to kill this guy. Get there and get back. We have to arrange scouts to the island. Frankie, can you organize that with your people?"

"I'll get on it," Frankie said. "Over and out."

"I'm worried about Sky and Misty," Leo said.

"They seem tough to me," Harlow said, placing a hand on Leo's shoulder.

"They are," Leo said.

"Then let's keep this journey going," Timothy said. "At a faster clip, perhaps. It's probably best that we shave as much time as possible off this round trip."

"I agree," Ember said.

The group continued with Dodson in tow. Before they got too far, Harlow pulled Leo aside.

"What is it?" Leo asked.

"Now that I know what's actually at stake here," she said. "I feel I need to go back to the tunnels and get my people more invested," Harlow said. "Messiah and Parker can continue with you, but I have to let my people know the dangerous position they're in, or we'll be living in the ground forever."

Leo smiled. "Do that. Meet us at the fortress. The more communities and people we meet and have on our side, the stronger we will be to beat this guy. It's the last step in becoming what we need to become."

Harlow nodded. "Take care."

"We got this," Parker said, raising his weapon and regarding it as a valuable jewel.

"Don't let having a weapon go to your head," Leo advised. "More important than a weapon is the person using it."

"Goodbye for now, then," Harlow said.

Harlow ran back in the opposite direction. Leo kept eyes on her until she disappeared through the same gate where the fight had taken place.

Fourteen

CHARLIE AND JESSE ROWED down river until they got to the green bridge. Charlie pulled the boat up to shore, and Jesse positioned his alongside Charlie's.

"Where are we going?" Jesse asked.

"Up the bank, not too far from here," Charlie said. "We have an outpost."

Charlie led the scrawny brother of Kane up the bank and to the entrance of the bridge out of Troy. They proceeded slowly to the intersection and up the hill leading to the fortress. Charlie clutched his side the entire time. King saw him coming up the hill and yelled.

"Charlie!" he yelled.

Charlie wasn't sure what he would be walking into, so he was relieved to find that things seemed relatively normal. He hunched over and clutched his knees. "Thank God."

"Who's that?" Jesse asked.

Charlie ignored him and moved forward to the beacon of hope that was the fortress. The light. It was the first time since the ordeal on the river that he allowed himself to dwell on what had happened. When the doors to the fortress opened and Baby was standing there, Charlie broke down.

Baby came to his side; Yamil and Miracle, as well. They all hugged him as Jesse stood waiting in uncomfortable silence. The children could see his brokenness and helped him into the fortress. Wyatt ran to him from the kitchen.

"Charlie," Wyatt said. "What happened out there? Where is Malayah?"

Charlie just shook his head as he cried. Jesse bowed his head as he realized Malayah's fate.

"We knew it couldn't be good, Charlie," Wyatt said. "They attacked all of us at the same time."

"They told me they were going to, right before he dumped us in the river," Charlie said.

King ran down from the roof. "Charlie!"

"King," Charlie said. "Hold off on telling the others. Malayah didn't make it. I need to tell Frankie in person."

"We got to fix you up, Charlie," Wyatt said.

"Who the hell is this?" Teddy asked.

"Meet Jesse," Charlie said. "Kane's brother."

King pointed a gun at him. "Kane's *who*?"

"Brother," Charlie said. "He helped me escape. He could prove to be useful."

"Like Ms. Betty," Baby said, warily.

"I just like to help people," Jesse said, raising his hands.

"Well, I'm going to help you out the door," King said.

"King, wait," Charlie said. "It's fine. He's harmless, but Kane might come looking for him."

"His men will be back, regardless," King said. "They blew those bridges with C-4. They can probably take the entire fortress out with that stuff. We may have to string him up on the front wall in order to keep this place safe."

"You should send people from the heights down to the river," Charlie said. "We can take them out as they cross. Or destroy their boats. Once we know they're all there, they can't get off the island unless we *let* them out, right?"

"I'm way ahead of you," King said. "Let's box this bastard in. I contacted Frankie and told her to do just that. Are their boats on the Troy side?"

"They were on the Troy side when we arrived," Charlie said. He turned to Jesse. "Is that where they generally keep the boats?"

"They keep them on that side when they're waiting for the soldiers to get back from a mission," Jesse said. "When the soldiers are on the island, the boats are on the island."

"I should have figured," Charlie said. "I guess all the boats being on the Troy side when we arrived should have been a red flag. I walked us right into a situation and got Malayah killed."

"You couldn't have known," King said. "She was a good woman."

King got back on the long range. "Frankie, you copy?"

"What is it?" Frankie replied.

"Did you get a group together to surveil the island?" he asked.

"They're leaving pronto," she said.

"Tell them to hole up and stay concealed until we can be sure that every soldier that left the island today has returned so we know they're all in one place," he said. "Send some of the men to the Green Island side, as well, to keep the perimeter. And if they try to cross on either side, we can take them out."

"You got it," Frankie said. "I have Merrick and Watson leading two teams. Each has a long-range com. I told them to keep them on low, but we can get hold of them if we need to."

"Nice," King said. "It's time to turn these tables."

"I'm worried about Malayah, though. They haven't answered."

King paused and looked at Charlie, who closed his eyes.

"Look, Frankie," King said. "When they entered the island, I'm quite sure that Kane would have confiscated their weapons and walkies. It's the same protocol *we* follow. Just keep the faith, but I understand your concern. Just know, no matter what happens to either of them, you have our support. They risked their lives going there, and we're all hoping for the best."

There was a brief delay.

"I know how the rest of that mantra goes," she answered.

"Good luck, everyone," Leo said. "We're rocking forward. We have a hostage!"

"I got to get back," Charlie whispered. "I have to tell Frankie."

"What about your long-range?" King said. "The one you brought to the island? I hope to hell Kane hasn't been listening—"

"It's okay," Charlie reassured. "We stowed them in a garbage can before we ferried across in case things went bad. And they sure as hell went bad."

"Thank God for small miracles," King said. "Now, what do we do with *this* guy?" King turned to Jesse.

"I don't know," Charlie said. "Sequester him for now until we can meet with the committee."

Baby walked in with a bunch of medical supplies. "Did they break ribs?"

"I think so," Charlie said. "I'll live."

"I don't know if there's much we can do about that anyway, but if you have any open wounds, we can cover those and put ointment on them."

Baby went about mending Charlie, and after she did so, he headed off for the heights. King went back to the roof.

"What about Misty and Sky?" Teddy asked via local walkie. "We haven't heard from them."

Fifteen minutes later, Misty chimed in. "Guys, you read me? Misty here."

The gunfire stopped as Mike and his men were scurrying to the back door of the ranch house. Misty and Sky dusted themselves off and rose to a crouch.

"What the hell?" Misty said. "This has to be the same group that's attacking the others. I'm guessing Kane's people?"

"Well, yeah," Sky said.

"Sky!" Mike called. "Keep low. Get out here. We're leaving."

"I doubt that," Sky said.

Just then, Cypress called from the kitchen door out back. "They got men in the back, too."

"Told you," Sky said.

"Hell if they think they're just gonna walk up to this property and shoot their way in," Hawk said.

"You, in there," a man called from out front. "We only want to talk. Come to the door."

Sky jumped to her feet and ran to the window beside the door. She peered out, and a row of men were standing beyond the fence, guns lowered. Misty came up from behind and peered over her shoulder.

"Should we go out?" Misty asked.

"Hell no," Mike said, running to the door. "If anyone is going out there it's going to be me."

"It's not like I haven't done this before," Sky said to him.

Mike looked her in the eyes. "It's *my* turn."

"How many we got?" Cypress asked.

"Five back here," Fisher answered.

Click, click, click. "Eight out front, by my count," Zippo said as he looked out the window on the other side of the living room.

Mike took a deep breath. He felt the beads of sweat roll down the side of his face. He was angry that these men would put his niece in this compromising position. He thought of all the times Sky must have been in similar situations in the past that he hadn't been there for. The reality stung.

Thirteen. We have enough ammunition to fend them off. Let's see what they want and go from there. I won't let them hurt you, Sky. I'm here now.

He opened the door and stood at the threshold. "I'm listening. What do you want?"

A young man stepped forward in front of the others.

"We are representatives of Ulysses Kane," the man said. "We are securing the area and initiating a new territorial government. We need to confiscate your guns and check for other munitions storage and seize them if they exist. After that, we'll go. If you resist, whether today or tomorrow, you'll regret that you did."

"Well, unless you consider a barn full of horses munitions, you'll be out of luck here, my friend," Mike said. "As for guns, the only guns I see are the ones that you guys have used to tear apart my house. And I really love my house."

Sky's heart raced. She worried about her uncle being exposed to a bunch of delusional, gun-toting followers of this new menace, Kane.

"Based on what we've observed, you have more than a half-dozen armed people in that house with you right now," the man said. "Have them toss out their weapons and let us search the rest of the property. If there is nothing more to find, we'll leave peacefully."

"As you came, huh?" Mike said. "We've been defending this area for four years, and you're darn right we're armed. If you think we're going to toss our weapons out to some snot-nosed punk who's following the orders of the latest psychopath in town, you have another thing coming. I'm quite sure we have more than enough...*munitions*...to hold you off for about a week. We'll probably kill most of you by then, though."

"Kane is not a psychopath," the man said. He sounded as if he believed it himself. "He is a leader and offers protection and security to those who comply with directives."

Sky stepped up behind her uncle and pushed by him with her M-16 assault rifle. "Direct this."

She fired her rifle as Mike ducked back into the house. The men scrambled for cover. There was nowhere for the soldiers to hide. She thought she got a few of them before retreating into the house.

"Yahoo!" Cypress yelled as he jumped out the front door alongside her and fired off his gun. "Kick ass, girl."

Misty broke the front window and fired her weapon, and a cacophony of bullet spray ignited the open sky.

Mike ran to the rear of the house while mayhem ensued. Eddie, Fisher, and Hawk sprung open the back door and leapt to either side while firing at the men covering the rear perimeter.

Mike threaded the needle between the four men and bolted from the house to the barn. Once there, he unhitched his horse and quickly mounted it. "Go!" he yelled.

His horse kicked forward. Mike drew his pistol and fired off a series of shots as his horse excited the barn. Gunfire continued from all points as he rode his horse in circles around the house, chasing down men and shooting them dead.

As enemy fire dissipated, Cypress and the others also mounted their horses and chased fleeing members of the assaulting party away from the property. They tried to escape, but the land was open and there was nowhere to hide.

The men on horseback returned to the house and secured the perimeter. Sky, Misty, and Zippo exited the home when they realized their opposition had been squashed.

"How dare them sons of bitches interrupt a good breakfast like that," Cypress said.

"What the hell were they thinking?" Mike said.

Sky walked to the horse Mike was straddling. "We know about this man...Kane."

"What's to know?" Mike asked.

"He's an old acquaintance of Charlie, the leader of the heights," Sky said. "He only recently made himself known, but he secured an island in Troy for his army of men. We just didn't know what he was up to...until now."

"He thinks he's going to organize a government for *this* area?" Mike said. "Isn't that what we're proposing to do?"

"It's either us or him," Misty said.

"Man, they messed up your house good," Fisher noted.

"At least you aren't blind," Mike said.

"We need to get back," Sky said. She turned to Misty. "Radio the others and tell them we're on the way. I thought I heard them reaching out while we were fighting."

Misty picked up her walkie. "Guys, you read me? Misty here."

After a few seconds of silence, the radio crackled. "Thank God. We were waiting to hear from you."

"What's going on over there, King?" Misty asked. "We got attacked. We're fine, though."

"Seems to be the theme," King said. "They attacked us all. We fended them off, but they swore to come back with heavier stuff. Frankie sent a team from the heights to monitor the areas around the island. If we keep them from leaving the island, there isn't much they can do."

"We're coming back," Misty said.

"Leo is fine too," King said. "Our only casualty is Malayah."

"What happened?" Misty asked.

"Kane killed her when they visited the island," he said sullenly. "Charlie managed to escape."

Just then Frankie crackled in. "What did you just say?"

There was a long silence. It was clear to Misty that King screwed up in sharing that information over the long range.

"Oh, Frankie," King said. "So sorry. I forgot these were long range. Charlie was on his way to tell you. I can't believe I said that. Frankie..."

There was no response.

"Frankie," King said. "Forgive me."

Misty lowered her walkie and addressed the others. "Damn. King messed up. This is all messed up!"

"Let's get out of here for now and back to the fortress," Sky said. "Uncle Mike, your arsenal is secure at Misty's?"

Mike looked around. "I don't see anyone here that's going to try to look for it." He held out his hand. "Come on up."

"You can hitch with me, Misty," Cypress said, extending his arm to her. "We'll be back to your place in no time at all."

Sky climbed aboard the nag. "Sorry about your house," she said.

Mike looked back at the ranch, riddled with holes. "We'll fix it."

Together, they set off on horseback headed to the fortress.

Charlie arrived at the heights nearly an hour later. He saw Frankie in the courtyard pacing with large strides. He froze immediately, sensing that something was wrong. Frankie froze as well when she saw Charlie standing there. They stared at each other for ten long seconds and Frankie dropped to her knees.

"No!" she cried. "No, Charlie. No."

Charlie made his way to her as quickly as possible and knelt in front of her. The two embraced.

"I was hoping what King said wasn't true," she said. "I turned the radio off. I couldn't hear anymore."

She continued to wail. She had never dreamed that sending Malayah off to the island would be the last time she ever saw her.

Charlie wondered how Malayah's death had gotten communicated to Frankie so carelessly, but it mattered little. He would have had to have told her anyway. It wouldn't have made it any easier.

Charlie nurtured her as best he could until her cries became whimpers. Some of the residents came over to see what was going on, but Charlie shook his head as if to indicate that they shouldn't interfere. The one exception—Mrs. Chandler. Though heavy-set, she got right on her knees and took over for Charlie.

"Okay, now," she said softly and empathetically. "It's so hard. We know how hard it is, dear. You're with friends. We're going to get you through this."

Charlie pushed away and sat back on his bottom. He was exhausted. His clothing was damp, his body bruised and cracked, and his mind weary. He gazed into the blue sky and closed his eyes. He tried not to picture Malayah's last moments, but he couldn't help but see them in his mind.

He watched Mrs. Chandler go to work. She was a jack of all trades. Ever since intervening to save the community from the coup, she had become an entirely different person. She was a true leader. Though she may have assumed, she didn't even know what the situation was with Frankie, but it didn't matter. She saw her pain and answered it, no questions asked.

Frankie settled down enough to have her wits about her, and when the shock of the news of Malayah's death passed, she separated from Mrs. Chandler, and they sat on the lawn wondering who would speak first. It was Frankie.

"What happened?" she asked.

Charlie shook his head. "It went well enough when we first arrived. Then, just before we were set to go back across...Kane ambushed us with a couple of soldiers. They laid into me good and he just...shot her. Cold."

Frankie closed her eyes and clenched her teeth. "And they left *you* alive?"

"I can't figure that one out," Charlie said. "They laid a beating on me, then dumped us both in the river. I think he believed I would probably drown, but his...one of their own came to my rescue by boat."

There was no way Charlie was going to detail Malayah's exact manner of death, as it was too gruesome a fate to reveal to Frankie. He also did not think it smart to tell her that Kane's brother was at the fortress.

"So, that's where she is, then?" Frankie said, becoming teary-eyed again. "Floating alone down the dirty river."

"I'm so sorry, Frankie," Charlie said. "I never dreamed in a million years that this could have happened, or I would never have taken us there. We arrived just after his men left the island to attack our settlements. He's trying to take this area by force. According to him, he's been occupying territories all along the Hudson as far south as Brooklyn. He has some sort of Napoleon complex."

Frankie stood up and wiped her tears. "I'm leaving to join the others on the Hudson."

Charlie and Mrs. Chandler stood as well.

"Frankie," Charlie said. "It might be better if—"

"No, Charlie!" Frankie said. "I'm not sitting on my ass while that son of a bitch who killed Malayah is alive. I will cut the fucking head off that snake and do us all a huge favor."

"Frankie," Mrs. Chandler said. "Are you confident that Dylan can secure the heights while you're away with the stronger defense leaders?"

"He can do it," Frankie said. "Because there won't be anyone attacking us. We have them right where we want them. Those idiots fortified themselves on an island from which there is no escape with us surrounding them. And this guy thinks he's Napoleon?"

"I said he had a complex," Charlie reiterated. "At least hold off on the major fireworks until our people get back from the preserve and Misty and Sky return from Pinewood with the group from there."

"They can hold off," Frankie said. "But I plan on swimming over there, finding that *puta*, and slitting his throat."

Frankie marched off to the armory. She loaded up guns, grenades, and ammunition and headed off toward the island.

Fifteen

"YOU'RE STAYING HERE," KING said as he sat Jesse down at the table in the library room on the second floor.

"I can leave," Jesse said. "I just wanted to help people. That's all."

"We can't let you go either," King said. "I know you helped to save Charlie, but if you leave this room, I'll kill you."

King closed the door tightly behind him. It didn't lock from the outside, so he was taking his chances. Wyatt met him as he was coming out.

"You're just gonna leave that guy in there?" Wyatt asked.

"What else are we going to do with him?" King asked. "He's Kane's brother. There's no way we're giving him the key to the house."

"We at least have to feed him," Wyatt said.

"We'll feed him," King said. "Sky is on her way back, and we can all discuss together what we should do. I think supporting the heights people at the river is a good idea for all of us. We're going to have to bring some serious weaponry over there in order to keep them from getting off. If we had some more heavy artillery, we could inflict a lot of damage to the island from our positions."

"We don't know what kind of weapons Sky's uncle has, or the preserve, for that matter," Wyatt said. "Maybe they have some of what you're looking for."

"Scud missiles?" King laughed.

"I wouldn't count on it," Wyatt said. "Back in the day, they'd just fly a military drone over there and wipe them all out with a few quick flicks of a joystick."

"Yeah." King recalled fondly his days playing *Call of Duty* on his Xbox. "It's damn well caveman days up in here."

"We'll figure it out," Wyatt said. "At least we know they won't be showing up on our doorstep again guns blazing as long as we have them all trapped on that island."

"Can you take the roof for a while?" King asked. "I need a break."

Wyatt shrugged. "I can do that."

Wyatt left for the roof and King touched base with the others. Teddy was walking the first floor like a tin soldier, rifle slung behind his back. Yamil and Miracle were in the kitchen washing vegetables for dinner, and Baby was on the deck beating an area rug.

"You better be washing a lot of veggies, boys," King said. "Misty and Sky are on their way back with a bunch of people."

"Baby gave us this," Miracle said. "This is all we have."

"We have reserves in the basement," King said.

When he ran into Teddy, he gave him a wink. "What are you practicing for, *The Nutcracker*?"

Teddy laughed. "You said *nuts*."

"No," King said. "I actually said 'Nutcracker,' and you don't need to be marching around in circles. You're making me dizzy. I see you're still wearing your knight necklace."

Teddy put his chin to his chest as he looked down. "Yup. This was way cooler than dollar bills. So, what's up with that guy in the library? He's creepy."

"We're just keeping an eye on his ass until Sky and the others get back here," King said.

By the time he got back out to the kitchen, Baby was lugging the carpet inside.

"You were really beating the hell out of that thing," King said. "Were you thinking of anyone special while you hammered away at it?"

"Yeah, you," she smiled.

While everyone was in the kitchen, Teddy sneaked up to the second-floor library to get another look at the visitor. He pushed open the door with the barrel of his rifle. The door creaked on its hinges, and upon first glance, Teddy didn't see anyone. He took a step back and steadied his rifle.

"Hello?" he called from the hallway.

He angled his head to see behind the walls that joined to the door.

Is he hiding, or did he leave the room?

"Uh, guys," Teddy called. "We have a problem."

King yelled up from the kitchen. "What?"

"This guy doesn't look to be in the library anymore," Teddy said.

Seconds later, King flew up the stairs. Baby was behind him. King was less shy than Teddy about going into the library and led the way. Baby and Teddy followed behind. Jesse was gone.

King radioed up to Wyatt. "Wyatt, check the perimeter and see if you see Jesse anywhere. He's not in the library anymore."

He lowered the walkie. "Go back downstairs, Baby."

Baby turned around and came face to face with Jesse, who entered the library from the hallway. Baby backstepped and they all froze as Jesse stood there with a grenade in his limp hand. He had the lever pushed down and the pin removed.

King, Baby, and Teddy stepped back as far as they could until their backs were against the rear bookcase.

"What are you doing, Jesse?" King asked, keeping his eyes on the grenade.

Wyatt then crackled in. "I don't see anything up here, over."

KINGDOM   161

King didn't make any sudden moves. He wondered how many times something like this had to happen before they learned their lesson about letting unknowns into the goddamn house.

"Low-hanging fruit," Jesse said. "Low-hanging fruit. That's all Charlie was. This...this is bigger. This...Kane will finally be proud of me. I can go home and tell him, and he'll let me do things now."

"No, Jesse," King said. "This isn't the way to earn respect. You'll get yourself killed, and us along with you. Now, let me come over to you and take the grenade."

"I can't," he said. "I just can't. This is the perfect plan. He'll be proud."

"I thought you only wanted to help people," King said. "How is this helping?"

"I'm helping my brother," Jesse said. "He's helped me a lot. He's always helped me."

"Jesse, don't do this," King said.

"King," Baby fretted.

A gun fired off from the hallway. The bullet entered Jesse's back and he fell to his knees. The grenade dropped from his hand and the lever popped off.

Miracle, standing beside Yamil, had shot Jesse as they stood in the doorway.

"Get down!" King yelled as he tipped over the library table.

In a second's time, Baby and Teddy dove behind the table and King hurdled it to get to the boys where they remained standing at the doorway. The grenade went off as he got to the threshold of the door. He had pushed the boys to the hallway floor but caught part of the grenade explosion. It sent him hurling over the second-floor railing. His body landed on the middle of the staircase and rolled down the rest of the way until he hit the foyer floor at the main entrance.

Wyatt, having heard the explosion, arrived from the rooftop to observe the mayhem. Smoke was billowing from the library and the wall to the right of the library had a large hole in it. The little ones were getting to their feet in the hallway, and he heard coughing from inside the room.

"King!" he yelled.

As he entered the library Baby and Teddy were waving smoke from their faces. Pieces of Jesse's body were everywhere.

"Where's King?" Wyatt asked.

"King!" Baby yelled.

Wyatt ran from the library and looked around. When he peered over the railing from the second floor, he saw King lying motionless on the foyer floor.

"King!" he yelled.

He rushed down the steps and knelt beside him. "King, King, are you okay?"

Shit.

Wyatt checked for breathing and a pulse, and he was relieved that he found both.

There was blood oozing from his body. Wyatt turned him over as Baby and Teddy and the little ones arrived from the second floor.

"Oh, no," Teddy said. "King."

Teddy ran to his room on the third floor and closed the door. He paced his bedroom floor in a fright.

Once King had been turned over on his stomach, Wyatt saw that his shirt was shredded and he had sustained numerous injuries to his body.

"Baby, go get the first aid, and a long-range radio," Wyatt said. "Yamil and Miracle, go get a towel."

Baby returned seconds later with first aid supplies and the radio. Wyatt cut away King's shirt. There were several lacerations and small puncture wounds that were all seeping blood.

"Goddammit," Wyatt said. "I don't know what I'm doing. Baby, call to the heights. Tell them we need Doctor Bennett down here fast."

"Stop the bleeding!" Baby said just before radioing the heights.

Yamil and Miracle returned with the towel, and Wyatt dabbed and wiped the wounds. "Fuck, we need the suturing kit."

"Is he breathing?"

"He's breathing, yes," Wyatt said.

"What happened?" Sky said frantically over the radio after hearing Baby's plea for the doctor. "We're minutes out."

"Just get here and we'll explain," Baby said. "There's no time to get into it, but King is in serious trouble."

"Oh, no," Leo chimed in. "We're almost to the preserve. Stay in touch."

Wyatt used the towel and continued to put pressure on King's wounds. He checked his head and ears to see if there were any cuts or welts that could indicate head injury.

"If he's breathing, why isn't he waking up?" Baby said.

"We just have to wait," Wyatt said. "Get this bleeding stopped and get him stitched up and hope for the best. I don't see any head injury, and his pulse is strong, but who knows. He could have internal damage or some sort of head trauma."

"Where did Teddy go?" Baby asked.

"He went upstairs," Yamil said.

"Go see that he's okay," Baby said.

The littles ones ran upstairs as Sky appeared through the door with Misty, her uncle, and a gaggle of men. They were all stupefied with the sight of smoke in the house and King lying face down in a puddle of his own blood.

Sky immediately had flashbacks of when Flip died in the same place, lying across Sim's legs. "Oh, my God."

The men poured in. Mike took charge.

"Hawk, tend to him."

Hawk was a former EMT.

"Okay, tell us what happened," Mike said, pulling Baby aside while Sky took a knee near King.

"Where did these wounds come from?" Hawk yelled out.

"A grenade," Wyatt answered.

Sky's eyes widened. Misty ran to the second floor to assess the damage. She ran back down a minute later.

"It's bad up there," Misty said.

"Charlie brought Kane's brother back to the fortress," Baby said. "The guy helped Charlie escape after he was attacked and thrown into the river, so I guess he trusted him. But we made sure to sequester him to the library. We were just waiting for you guys, but then he got a grenade...or had a grenade...I don't know. King saved us all, and Miracle shot the guy, but the grenade went off."

"Where's Teddy and the boys?" Sky asked.

"Upstairs," Baby said. "Teddy ran off."

"Okay, his pulse and breathing are steady," Hawk said. "A lot of the wounds are superficial, but there are a few deep ones. We have to remove the shrapnel, clean it up, and get these wounds closed. How did he get down here if the explosion happened somewhere else?"

"I didn't see, but the explosion must have blown him over the railing and down the stairs."

"So, he took a fall," Hawk said. "He could have a head injury. We're going to address the wounds we see and move him to a bed."

Sky stood up and went to Baby. "How could Charlie have left Kane's brother in our care? I thought since the Ms. Betty days, we were done with taking chances like this."

"I don't know," Baby cried. "The guy saved Charlie's life, and then turned around and did this."

"We need someone on the roof," Wyatt said.

"Fisher," Mike said. "The rest of you do a perimeter check and stay outside."

"I'll show you," Misty said as she led Fisher away.

Cypress, Eddie, and Zippo left out the front door while Hawk and Wyatt tended to King.

"Mike," Hawk said. "We need a board so we can mobilize him when we're done here. A plank or something so we can move him. Tear up a sheet or something into strips so we can use them as ties. Misty, we need more water and another towel."

Misty set off to get more water and a towel while Sky and Mike left to get the other things that were needed.

An hour later, they had King's back freed of shrapnel, cleaned, and sutured. They turned him over and laid him on the plywood plank. They tied down his head, chest, and legs. Cypress and Zippo came back in to help move him to Sky's room on the first floor. They untied him once they got there and slid him off the plank onto the bed. He still had not woken up.

"What's the latest?" Leo asked.

"King's been caught in an explosion," Misty said. "Kane's brother was here at the fortress and set off a grenade in the library."

"What was Kane's brother doing in the fortress?" Leo yelled.

"It's a long story," Misty said, frustrated. "Too much to say now. King has been stabilized but he hasn't woken up yet. He's in a coma or something. I don't know."

"Oh, shit," Leo said.

"Kane's brother set off a grenade?" Charlie chimed in. "The man who saved me from drowning and brought me back to the fortress? Christ, King? Dammit, I've screwed up all over today."

"Don't blame yourself, Charlie," Misty said. "This has been one heck of a day for everyone. How's Frankie?"

"Distraught. Outraged. She left to join the group at the Hudson," Charlie said.

"We'll keep you posted on things," Misty said.

Once King was in bed, Sky went to the third floor to check on Teddy.

Misty made time to talk with Mike and Hawk. "Is it bad?"

"If he has brain swelling, it could go down," Hawk said. "Without any medical equipment, it's hard to say what's going on inside his body. We also have no way to provide IV fluids, so he'll only be able to endure a short-term period of unconsciousness, or he'll dehydrate and starve. We'll have no way to sustain him long term if he doesn't wake up."

Misty looked to the floor.

"I'm sorry, Misty," Mike said, placing a hand on her shoulder. "We'll let him rest and hope for the best."

"We've been hearing that phrase a lot today," Misty said.

"We'll help you get cleaned up around here and then figure out a plan for resolving this issue at the island."

Sixteen

"I'm hungry," Leo said as they got deeper into their journey. It was late afternoon, and the residential areas they had passed through gave way to woods and isolation.

"We're almost there," Ember said. "We'll make sure you get fed. Your dog looks thirsty too."

"Her name is Gigi," Leo said as he patted her. Gigi was panting hard.

"How could I have forgotten?" Ember said.

Soon after, she led them through a wall of trees where they met with a path that led deeper into the forest.

"Stick strictly behind me," Ember warned. "Our perimeter is set with covered pits and other traps."

As they proceeded down the path, they saw people everywhere walking with guns, and others cutting down trees. They saw a man with a pad and paper taking notes, and as the trail hit a curve, they saw a body of water through the trees. The sun's rays were fading, but still cast a sparkling light upon the water. Leo smiled and felt at peace.

As they walked toward the edge of the pond, they saw a series of blue panels pointed toward the sky. The sun was reflecting off them, and Leo wondered what they were. He also saw a couple of rowboats out on the pond with people in them, and he started to feel more comforted by the environment. Nobody seemed to notice or care as they passed through the forest except for the couple of people on the path who gave them a double take.

Ember stopped one such person and introduced her. She was a tall but slight woman with gray and white hair that ran down past her shoulders. She had wrinkles on her face, and she bore a friendly smile.

"Grace, I want you to meet my new friends, Parker, Messiah, Leo, and their dog, Gigi."

Grace froze on the path and her blue eyes widened. She had a pack on her back and a walking stick in hand. She didn't speak, but she put her hand over her chest and looked at them as if they were aliens from another planet.

"They are from the fortress," Ember said. "They've come to see our compound and we hope a partnership is imminent."

A tear from her eye followed the path of one of her wrinkles. It trickled slowly and dripped off her chin. "You look just like my Ricky."

She was eyeing Parker. Grace dropped her walking stick to her side and held out her arms. "Can I hug you?"

Parker shrugged, "I guess. Nobody's hugged me in years."

Grace approached him and put her arms around Parker and sobbed. Though Parker didn't return the hug, it didn't seem to matter to Grace. Gigi went up to her and sniffed her and licked her cheek during the embrace.

She let go of him and wiped the tears from her face. "What you must think of me," she said.

"It's okay, Grace," Ember said. "It's a special day. Different than any other we've seen since we've all been together. I would imagine many in our community who had children before the fall will feel emotionally overwhelmed at seeing our visitors."

Graced sniffled and stood after grabbing her stick. She kept her gaze upon Parker as she addressed Ember with an update. "The panels are servicing seven huts, as of today."

"That's two more than last week," Ember said. "Progress."

"Where are you going with them?" Grace asked.

"I was just planning to give them a quick tour," Ember said. "We haven't much time. Perhaps just enough to visit a cottage and the visitors' center. I'm trying to make them feel welcome and at home, but time is of the essence."

"Can I come along with you?" Grace asked.

Ember smiled. "Of course. Be advised, though, we have a prisoner. We were attacked on the road."

Grace regarded Dodson, who was under the careful eye of Messiah. "Understood. I guess we all knew there would be inherent risks of venturing out. We weren't wrong, then."

"It'll prove all for the better that we followed Mike's advice," Ember said as she walked them down the path. To her visitors she said, "The world in this place hasn't changed all that much from what it was, except for what we added to it so people could live here. Back then, they could only visit. I worked here for many years, and so it was quite natural for me to make this my home in the end times. The problem with people back in those days was that they never listened. They never observed. There is so much to be missed when one is distracted. As we walk along, I encourage you to listen and watch. The world that will open to you is one that you've never known before."

Ember continued to lead them through a forested maze, and Leo continued to observe, which was the purpose of his mission. Observe and report. To assure trust. The trees swayed and birds flew from one to the other, chirping their songs. Men and women abided in the trees, each with his or her own agenda. Work? Leisure? It was hard to tell, but everyone seemed at peace.

Leo observed what he believed to be the cottages that Ember had mentioned. They were small rectangular dwellings in the forest every hundred feet or so. Each looked built the same way. They were made of wood and looked more like double-sized sheds one would find behind someone's home to store lawnmowers or other equipment, except these homes had small chimneys on the top. He observed someone exiting one of the dwellings to shake dirt from a small carpet.

"We have one hundred and six cottages in the preserve," Ember said, as if reading Leo's mind. "Each has a fireplace, a loft that sleeps two, a bathroom, a mini kitchen, and even a living room, if you can believe it. All that in one small space. Mr. Sheridan, our resident architect, formulated the design, and our construction people made it reality. It was to our benefit that he designed and even helped build tiny homes before the fall. Do you know what a tiny home is?"

Parker and Leo shook their heads in unison.

"Whoa," Parker said. "They look much nicer than the sewer."

"*Now* you're calling it a sewer?" Leo said. "I thought it was a storm drain."

"Well, now that I see *this* place, it's definitely a sewer," Parker said, standing in awe.

"And you didn't think as much when you saw the fortress?" Leo asked.

"You never invited me in!" he yelled. "It looked just like a regular house to me."

Ember laughed. "These are just regular homes too. Only...tiny." She laughed. "Some of us live in the old visitors' center, but that's just until we can get more of these houses created. We felt if the Native Americans and pioneers could thrive in small dwellings, so could we. It made no sense, living in a larger and more dangerous new world at the time. Now that we've made progress...it's starting to make more sense. Still, here we have everything we need. Food, water, and natural resources to survive. Our efforts are still to conserve and preserve, above and beyond what we use to meet our survival needs. So, we retain the best of both worlds here. We're in the process of expanding our solar energy project, which will ultimately bring light electricity to every home in the preserve. Only about one hundred more homes to go."

Leo thought of the fortress, and though seeing the preserve gave him a glimpse of a community startlingly more sophisticated, he still missed his own cozy home, because his home was more than the structure of the fortress. Yet, part of him couldn't wait to tell the others about the preserve.

As Ember led them down the earthen path, Parker left the trail. He pushed through some trees, making his way to the edge of the pond. Grace, Ember, Leo, and Gigi followed him as he stepped over fallen branches and hopped over large stones to reach the water. The soldiers, along with Messiah and Dodson, remained on the path.

At the edge of the pond, Parker stood in awe of a rainbow that cast an array of colors over the pond. Gigi lapped up some of the pond water as Grace put a hand on Parker's shoulder.

"Isn't it beautiful?" Grace stated. "If only every moment of our lives could be as serene."

For several more seconds of silence, they stared at the rainbow before it began to fade. Parker then turned around and led them back to the path where the others were waiting.

"Why don't you guys take Dodson and Messiah to the observatory?" Ember suggested. "You can hold Dodson in one of the smaller conference rooms for now. Organize the group, and we'll be there in an hour. We'll have a quick meeting and then head back out after sundown."

"Got it," Timothy acknowledged.

"Messiah stays with me," Parker insisted.

Ember nodded. "I understand."

Timothy and his team led Dodson away while Ember and Grace led Parker, Leo, Gigi, and Messiah to one of the little homes that was nestled in the trees and stopped short of the door, which had a small window on either side of it.

The house was unpainted pine with a gabled roof covered with aluminum. A small chimney protruded from the top. Leo saw an upper and lower window on the right side of the home as well.

"Wow, that's little," Leo said. "Cool, though."

Ember and Grace exchanged looks. Then Ember went and knocked on the door. An older man with a balding head, wearing a sweater and jeans, answered.

"Ember!" he smiled. His eyes panned left, and his smile quickly faded as his face slightly contorted to a look of surprise and wonderment. "Do my eyes deceive me?" He smiled.

"I thought you would appreciate meeting some of our new friends," Ember said. "They're from the fortress. The place Mike told us about. It's true."

Grace and Ember laughed as the man stepped from his doorway and onto the ground. He looked at them the way they had all looked at the rainbow moments earlier.

"We're just kids," Parker shrugged. "But, if you want a hug, too, bring it in."

Parker held out his arms and everyone laughed. Mr. Dumas gave Parker a quick hug as he too laughed.

Mr. Dumas released Parker and smiled at him. "I searched all over after the fall to find children. I found only one." Mr. Dumas sighed. "The boy, Avi, whom I believe you met. He was fifteen at the time. We have seven other children between the ages of one and three, but the people in the preserve have not seen children *your* age in many years. There are lot of people here that had children your age who didn't make it. So you'll get a lot of attention today, I'm sure." His eyes skirted from one visitor to the next as he considered another thought. "You would only have been six or seven back then. How on earth did you even survive?"

"We actually were hoping to come in, Pierre," Ember said. "So I could show them a cottage and give them something to eat. I know your fish soup is the talk of the preserve. We could talk more while they eat."

"Absolutely," Mr. Dumas said. "I can serve you up my finest recipe. The secret is in the spices, boys. Did Ember tell you about the spice gardens?"

"No," Leo said.

"Oh, my goodness," Mr. Dumas said. "You know what, young fella, I think we're going to get along fantastically. And do you know why?"

Leo shook his head.

"Because we're unique, in this world," he said. "Two tween children and a French man. I am almost as rare as a young child. We are gems."

"What about Messiah?" Parker asked.

"And Gigi," Leo said.

"Oh, my goodness," he said, looking up and down at Messiah as he patted Gigi on the head. "I think Messiah is going to educate us all here at the preserve, about how we're constructing these tiny homes. He is already teaching us that we must not make one-size-fits-all homes. Every day is a new learning experience. And as for Gigi, she is quite the beautiful dog."

Parker and Leo smiled.

"I hope we can all fit in for soup," Grace said. "I wish to join you, though my work is not done."

"Who could think about work when we have children, a warrior, and a dog standing on our doorstep?" Mr. Dumas said. "We have stories to share, and we should have a community to ignite! We've waited for this moment for four years."

"We don't have much time," Ember said. "We were attacked on the road, and the other communities were as well, simultaneously. People have died and were injured. We must leave for the fortress this evening."

"Very well, then," Mr. Dumas said, kicking open his pine door and welcoming them into his house.

In the center of the room was his square dining table. It sat four, but he had two lounge chairs, one in each corner of the room, enough room for six to sit comfortably. He popped on some battery-operated lights, only softly complaining that his house was not one of the first to be powered with solar electricity. He set the table with four bowls and placed two more on the end table that was between the two corner chairs. Gigi laid beside the table and Mr. Dumas brought her a bowl of water.

In the corner on the left side was a wood burning stove, which kept the 320 square feet of space warm and cozy during winters, but on this day remained unused.

Mr. Dumas lived alone, which would not last forever. While there was a waitlist for housing, every cottage was required to be filled to maximum capacity. Yet, they did not randomly assign people to homes. They assessed compatibility of roommates with an intensive survey. None of the current waitlisted were deemed compatible with Mr. Dumas, as Mr. Dumas wanted to share his space with someone his approximate age, and most of the current waitlisted were much younger. He often noted his hope to Ember that the production of cottages would soon outpace the need, so he wouldn't have to share.

I lived my life privately and alone before, and I hope to retain this status at the preserve.

Ember took seats at the table while Grace and Messiah sat in the corner chairs. Grace cried silently watching Parker's toothless smile shine while he held onto his spoon in eager anticipation of a meal.

She saw her son, Ricky, in her mind. He was nine when he died, and had the same freckle-loaded face with sandy hair, and even some of the same expressions. She had thought Ricky was going to make it. Several weeks into the plague, he was still alive and healthy. She thought it was God's plan that they both survive when most families were being torn apart by death. But it was not to be. When she heard him cough for the first time, she broke down and begged the universe for a reprieve. She thought of ending her own life, but always believed in purpose. She believed that life was a gift granted by the stars; that taking part in this world required understanding that the happenstance of human creation meant only fools would have an expectation of how life would play out.

Still, it was hard. The miracle of life. The human predicament, as some called it, of being alive but having to figure out how best to live.

Mr. Dumas anxiously served them his soup and sat down at the table so he could chat. Ember was more inclined to give them time, but Mr. Dumas had no plan to wait. Perhaps that is why Ember brought them to him, and not because he made the best soup at the preserve. He had a way about him. People immediately trusted him and felt comfortable with him.

When he discovered Avi, he took personal care of him during a time when there were no little houses. Avi, even though he was an older child, relied on Pierre for everything. He was his teacher, friend, and father, and the two were inseparable. Pierre wanted Avi to join him in his new home when his turn came around, but Avi, then eighteen, decided he wanted more independence. Pierre respected this decision, and when he left the visitors' center, they embraced, and then Pierre said, "See you at dinner!"

Avi laughed, and the two remained close.

"Now, boys," Mr. Dumas said. "Tell us about this fortress and your survival there. We've heard stories."

Parker swallowed a spoonful of soup.

Leo looked at him to answer.

"It's where we live," Leo said. "Sim found us all, but he died in a battle we had with a lunatic."

Ember put down her spoon as Grace leaned forward in her chair.

"Who was this man?" Ember asked.

"His name was Zagan," Leo said.

"That's *his* story," Parker said. "The two of us just kind of met recently. Me and Messiah have always lived underground in the storm drains. Not as exciting, but I did get my teeth knocked out by one of the tunnel rats not too long ago. It hurt like hell, but, hey, I'm still here."

"Resilient," Mr. Dumas said.

"Tell us more about Sim," Ember said.

"He was our dad," Leo said. "Not our real dad. He just...found us. I was at my house playing with Legos. My parents were dead. They killed my dog, too. My mom tried to kill me also. But, she didn't mean it. She just loved me too much."

Grace gasped.

"That must have been hard," Mr. Dumas said.

Nobody was eating their soup. Grace put her bowl on the end table and Mr. Dumas pushed his bowl to the side while Ember remained frozen with her spoon halfway from her bowl to her mouth.

"Yeah, but it ended up okay," Leo said proudly, continuing to eat his soup.

"Well, I'm sure glad we found you," Mr. Dumas asked.

"Yeah," Leo said. "So are the others. We're ready to make shit happen."

Gigi raised her head from the floor as if noticing Leo curse.

Everyone laughed.

Ember placed a hand on his arm. "So are we, and I think with the ingenuity of all of us, we can do just that."

Mr. Dumas raised a glass. "*Faire de la merde*—to making shit happen."

Everyone toasted.

The evening gathering was an informal assemblance of the residents to introduce the visitors and discuss the merger of the communities.

It was a rushed affair. No sooner had they finished their soup than they cleaned up and headed to the observatory. Ember had left in advance to prepare for the event.

Mr. Dumas and Grace walked them from the tiny home and through the forest via a windy path that led to a central area, where there stood a large building made of wood with more of those blue panels affixed to the top of the roof, which were encircled by a vegetative green roof. Surrounding it were driveways, parking areas, sections of grass that were neatly manicured, and a small pond, at the edge of which were informational stands.

The building had many large windows, as wide as they were tall, and when the boys and Gigi entered through a set of glass doors, they didn't know which direction to look. The ceilings were high with embedded skylights like the one they had at the fortress in the attic, and the inside was awash in brilliant fading sunlight. There were tanks displaying all sorts of small animals, including fish, frogs, and salamanders, as well as an assortment of taxidermized animals like owls, hawks, and beavers. There were even real trees inside.

Parker and Leo were mesmerized as they were led through to a large room where Ember was setting up chairs. Messiah, too, gawked, but remained his quiet self, and Gigi followed their every move.

When Ember saw them, she smiled wide, her red cheeks puffing out in welcoming glory.

"Boys!" she said. "We're just getting ready."

She walked over and stood before them.

"Thank you, Mr. Dumas, for escorting them," Ember said.

"It was my pleasure," Mr. Dumas said as he bowed to the boys. "It's been an honor meeting all of you. For now, if you'll excuse me, I must take a seat."

"How do you like this place?" Ember said, holding out her arms. "Isn't it amazing?"

"I love it," Parker said. "Harlow would love it too."

"It's great," Leo said. "It's interesting. The displays."

"You like it, big guy?" Parker said to Messiah.

"There's a lot of things to see," Messiah beamed.

"There is indeed a lot to see here," Ember said. "Thankfully, this place hasn't changed too much since the bad times hit because we were dealing with nature at the preserve all along, and nothing about nature has changed. The many people who live here helped to maintain it so we could see it thrive."

"We have gardens and trees too," Leo said. "And a well. In our basement."

Parker looked at Leo. "You have a well in your basement?"

"I didn't say we had a well in the basement," Leo said. "Just that we have a well."

"Ahh," Ember said. "We didn't get to see your basement, but Sky explained."

"This place is better," Leo said matter-of-factly. "But I still like the fortress better."

"I know what you mean," Ember said with a laugh. "No matter where you roam, there is no place like home."

"This is big," Parker said looking around the room.

"Yes, they used this room as an assembly area before the world changed, so it's the perfect place for meeting." She then turned caring eyes upon them. "You'll meet lots of people, so I hope that is okay."

"It's fine," Leo said. "That's the point. It's why they sent me. You know, they call me the mayor of the fortress."

"Interesting," Ember said.

"Where is that prisoner guy?" Parker asked.

"He's being held and guarded in another room until we can figure out what to do with him," Ember said.

Over the next thirty minutes, Leo, Parker, and Messiah visited the many exhibits in the visitors' center. They explored freely. As people entered for the gathering, many of them pointed and gawked at the little boys and the tall stranger. Leo noticed but was distracted by the interesting things to see and do in the center. It wasn't like any place they had ever been.

Some of the windows overlooked the forest and there were mounted telescopes they could use to spot the wildlife. They saw birds and deer up close. As they gazed upon the trees, bedazzled, Leo turned to his new friend.

"So, what do you think?" he asked.

"Why do people keep asking me that? I love it here," Parker said. "Who wouldn't?" Parker said. Then he went back to his telescope.

He had only a few seconds more to gander, as Avi called for them from across the room. "Let's go, guys!" he said.

They proceeded to the room, which had since filled. Avi was standing at the open door to the assembly area, smiling.

"Are you ready?" he asked.

"Yeah," Leo said. "Let's do this."

"Do what?" Parker asked.

Leo grabbed him by the arm. "Never mind. Just don't go pulling your gun out during the meeting."

"What meeting?" Parker asked. "Messiah is shy, you know." He turned to Messiah. "Are you going to be okay?"

"Yeah, I'm okay," Messiah said.

There were sixty-eight guests in the conference hall, and all were anxious to get a formal introduction to the boys who had come on a journey from the fortress. Some had seen them in passing, and others not at all.

When they walked into the hall, it was as if time had stopped, and the rest of the humans had vanished from the world. The people sitting in their chairs looked like statues made of stone with frozen faces and unmoving limbs.

Leo raised his eyebrows as he proceeded across the front of the room toward Ember, who was standing in the front of them all. As the boys closed the gap, they turned to face the unflinching crowd. There were old people, young people, men, women, and two people holding babies.

Finally, Leo shrugged his shoulders. "Why is it so quiet?"

The tension broke and everyone burst into laughter. Leo regarded this as strange, as he didn't quite understand that they were the center of attention. Parker seemed to relish it and took bows. Leo hit him on the side of the arm. Messiah stood ignorant of the attention, and many eyes had shifted when they saw him for his size alone.

Out of the blue, a man with gray hair stood and began to clap his hands. One after the other, everyone else stood and the hall erupted in thunderous applause. Gigi, not understanding the noise, began to bark and turn her head back and forth.

When the clapping subsided, everyone sat down, and the trio remained with Ember, wondering what the attendees would do next. Parker spotted Grace, Avi, and Mr. Dumas seated together at one of the tables and waved excitedly, which evoked more laughter.

"Thank you all for coming," Ember said. "Earlier today, the universe delivered to us the most precious fruits of the fallen age. Children who fought for survival in a place known as the fortress, which was led by a man who passed away but left behind a family entrenched in love and loyalty."

"Me and Messiah, here, actually spent those years in a sewer system," Parker said.

There were some more giggles and gasps.

Ember began to pace, and Leo thought of Sim. Sim loved to pace while he talked. It helped him think.

"We have led them here from the fortress to see what we have grown, in hopes we can finally forge a partnership with several other local allies and secure the area with new governorship. So we can start over again. Pangea." The word drifted over the crowd like a magician's spell. "We'll have a security force, a school, a centralized arsenal, and as we continue to rebuild, a new way of life that will take us beyond the confines of the preserve."

"Can we trust them?" a woman asked in the crowd.

"We've done so well over the years," another voice said. "We don't wish to jeopardize what we have built by sacrificing our autonomy and risking our lives to a bunch of strangers. Pangea is an initiative, if you remember, that was not fully endorsed by the whole community. There is still a lot of reservation about the timing being right for this."

"I am aware of this," Ember said. "But our timing should align with the opportunity that presents itself, even if it means we must take a risk and step out of our comfort zones. My instinct about the fortress, and their allies, is strong. As far as jeopardizing what we have built...If we don't share our work and take some chances, we could be hiding in the forest forever. And a great many people, like these children, will miss out on what we have to share."

Leo stepped forward confidently. "You talk about risk. Our father, Sim, took many orphans in, and we lived together as a family for years. Over this past year, while you were fishing in the pond and building little houses, many of us died defending our home. Flip was a good friend and barely ten years old. Ace was seventeen. Shark, fifteen. JZ, fifteen. And Big Will, our dog Gigi's caretaker, only eight." Gigi whined at hearing Big Will's name. "They all died by gunfire, except JZ. She was stabbed and crucified. I wasn't supposed to know that, but I found out." He then put his hand on Parker's shoulder. "My friend Parker had his teeth knocked out by a man while living in the storm drains for the past three years, and only lived because Messiah, here, came to his rescue."

There was not a sound as the crowd stood witness to Leo's traumatic past.

Leo continued. "One of our other brothers, though, King, reminded us a few months ago to never let our trauma control us. He said to let it give us power so that it didn't become our Achilles' heel...our weakness. And Sim told the first orphan he found that she should prepare her heart as a fortress, for there is no other! Elizabeth died before he found the rest of us, but her legacy lives on in our hearts, because *she* showed Sim the way from despair to hope. Without her, there was no Sim. Without Sim, there was no us. She wondered, 'why a fortress, and not a kingdom?' And do you want to know what he said to her?"

There was silence. The group was captivated by Leo, resolute in his stance.

"What?" Mr. Dumas finally asked, for all of them.

"He said that *we* are a fortress," Leo said. "And that from *us*, a kingdom can rise. He didn't say a kingdom *will* rise. He said a kingdom *can* rise. So, I say, let *all* of us prepare our hearts as a kingdom, for there is no other. The fortress...is not a kingdom. But the fortress, along with the preserve, the underground, the heights, the group led by Mike, and all the other communities that are out there, not yet found...*is* a kingdom. And we can all...make it rise. Or we do nothing and become slaves to someone else's vision. Like that of this man hunting us. Kane. He can't win. *We* must win."

Mr. Dumas stood immediately and started clapping. Soon after, everyone in the room stood in ovation. Ember smiled, and Leo remained, not feeling celebrated, but understood.

"Then we must leave now," Ember said. "For there is an enemy we must vanquish...together. An enemy that has attacked us all, as well as the fabric of future democracy. On the road, and at our homes. We must send him a message that this territory is *ours*. And the dawn of a new day...Pangea...the kingdom...shall rise."

Leo put his arm around Parker. Messiah, though perhaps not fully understanding the significance of the moment, smiled.

They were invited to view the preserves arsenal. They were captivated by the cache of high-tech and long-range weapons, courtesy of Timothy and his marine buddies who knew right where to go to obtain them.

They set off on the road at sundown on foot, toting a wagonload of firepower and two dozen volunteers from the preserve.

It was time to kill Kane.

Seventeen

Wasp arrived back at the island soon after his team's unsuccessful attempt to secure munitions at the fortress. He and his remaining soldiers crossed the river with a few of the boats that lay in wait under the Green Island bridge.

Kane saw them coming from his balcony and went down to the parking lot to greet them. He only counted nine men, and realized that a handful of others charged with the mission were not among them.

Wasp approached him, a look of unease on his face. He knew going back to Kane with word of defeat would not be well embraced.

Kane threw out his hands. "I see you are missing a few men. Hopefully casualties not lost in vain."

"I wish I had better news," Wasp said. "They weren't the submissive types. What can I say? There was no way a dozen men with a modified arsenal were going to breach that place, and they sure as hell weren't going to drop their guns and let us in. With all due respect, Kane, the people we seem to be fighting in this area are far more equipped than in any other area we have seized to this point."

Kane rubbed his chin as he turned away from Wasp. "Interesting. The men who escaped from the heights seem to have said the same thing. Sven was killed there, and his team nearly wiped out. I haven't heard anything from the teams that were following the two groups on the road either."

"That means, potentially, we've lost nearly fifty soldiers," Wasp said.

Kane appeared bewildered. "How could that be? Is it so much different here than in all those other places? We've never seen such resistance. And even my own brother has gone AWOL."

"These communities in the area seem more connected than in any other place we've been. It's going to be harder to nail them down. In the other places, they had less time to get their shit together and organize. Here, it may just be too late."

"It's never too late," Kane protested. "We lost some battles, Wasp, but not the war. We need control of this area before we head farther north."

"Then what's our next move?" Wasp asked. "If the other teams aren't coming back, we'll need to engage more of our soldiers to go back at them with heavier artillery. In the case of these communities, requesting they lay down arms is not going to work. We need to eradicate them with force."

"That's exactly what we're going to do," Kane said. "We have plenty more soldiers at our Hudson territory who we can bring up, but we need to plan a secondary assault immediately. Let's start by sending another team to the fortress with our heavier stuff, and we can simply blow it to hell. Then, we'll go to the heights and do the same. You can lead another team to the east bank where I've seen some of them trying to covertly assemble." Kane clenched a fist. "I'm done with this shit. Turf wars. I'll show them all who's turf this is!"

"What about your brother?" Wasp asked.

Kane reflected momentarily. "I can't imagine where he could be. I sent some soldiers after him when he fled south in a boat, and they never returned. I think he helped Charlie escape down the river. If you can get him back to me safely, then do so. But he's not a priority. Not anymore."

Wasp nodded and set off to assemble the teams.

While Wasp was preparing for his next mission, fifty security officers and civilians armed with numerous guns and grenades from the heights' arsenal arrived at the eastern and western sides of the Hudson, creating a gauntlet with the island in between. From both shores, the island was but a football field length's swim.

"Our teams are in place down here," Watson said. "We have both sides covered. We have boats on Troy side and there are a couple of boats on the island side. It's hard to tell if everyone who went out has come back."

"Likely so," Charlie said. "Two of the groups were fully disposed of, so I'm guessing by now, those soldiers that fled the heights and the fortress area have returned. Though we shouldn't make assumptions, it's a good bet all his people are now on the island."

"What do you want us to do?" Watson asked.

"Frankie is on her way," Charlie said. "Just stay put and lie low until she gets there."

"We're on our way back from the preserve," Leo said. "We'll travel fast and be back in three to four hours. How's King?"

"The same," Misty said.

They kept the chatter on the long range to a minimum until they noticed two boats setting off from the island. Watson turned on his night vision binoculars and saw people boarding two of the boats.

"Uh, this is Watson. Charlie, you read me?"

"I hear you," Charlie said.

"We have some people boarding two boats," Watson said. "It's hard to see how many, but it looks like they are going to cross over to Troy. How should we proceed?"

Just then, Frankie sneaked up behind him. "We should proceed by smoking them motherfuckers that killed Malayah. And after that, I'll swim across and finish this. I'm gonna send Kane's head across the river like a fucking coconut."

"Though it's inconvenient having to show our cards early, we can't let them escape," Charlie's voice came over the walkie talkie. "They may be planning another assault on us. Can you wait until they hit land and take them out quietly?"

"Yeah, we can do that," Watson responded. "By the way, Frankie is here. She is planning to swim across and...make a floating coconut out of Kane's head."

"Frankie," Charlie said. "Try to avoid letting your emotions dictate your actions. Play it safe."

"This is the fortress, here," Mike said over his walkie. "Me and my men are headed to the river with some weapons. Things are secure here, so it makes more sense that we join the team at the river. We can all help put an end to this."

"Should we join you there?" Leo asked. "We have two dozen people and a lot of weapons from the preserve. Together we can *all* end this."

"Leo," Sky said through comms. "Play it by ear. If you all make good progress on foot then, yes, it may be helpful to have more numbers there. It's just hard to tell if and when this conflict is going to ignite."

"I want to be there with you all," Charlie said. "My body is broken, though. I wish I had more to offer at the moment, but I won't be able to make it back on foot. For what it's worth, I'm sorry to everyone. About Malayah. About King. About Kane. I feel like everything bad that has come of this situation is *my* fault. And here I sit, immobilized."

"We're going to take care of this," Sky said. "*All* of us. If King was conscious, he would be the first one there, like you. This is what community is all about, Charlie. It's about all of us. Not one of us."

"We'll keep this attack quiet, but it's possible Kane could have night vision too and is monitoring things from the island. So, maybe we should take them out in the city after they've docked and set off."

"No, no," Charlie said. "What difference does it make if he sees or not? He's a rat in a box. He just doesn't know it. Don't give these soldiers an opportunity to break free."

Frankie snatched the radio from Watson. "Don't worry, we're going to sink these motherfucking *putas*. They ain't going nowhere."

Watson said to Frankie, "If they're loading weapons in the boats, though, we could seize them instead of watching them sink to the bottom of the river. I think we should take them as soon as they hit shore on this side."

Frankie shoved the radio back at Watson. "Fine, Watson. We just better not miss any of them."

Watson radioed to everyone else. "Okay, we're going to radio silence."

After the two boats set off from the island, Watson, along with Frankie and half of dozen other men, crept over to the docking point beneath the remnants of the bridge. They stayed concealed under the darkness of the overpass.

As the rowers took their boats across, Frankie clenched her teeth. Her rage nearly bubbled over. She had to fight the urge to jump out and cut them all down in the middle of the river so they would drown.

"Just hold tight, Frankie," Watson said. "We got this."

In the middle of the river the boats slowed down.

"What is taking these bastards so long?" Frankie muttered.

For the second half of the voyage, the boats slowed to a snail's pace. Abruptly, they started to turn back around.

"What the hell are they doing?" Watson asked.

Gunfire then erupted from the west side of the river. Watson turned the radio back on.

"We got eyes on another boat traveling north, almost at the northwestern shore," Merrick radioed from the other side. "They were too far across for us to target."

"These boats are nothing but decoys," Frankie said. "They know we have eyes on them. Go up-river and try to intercept them and warn the fortress."

Frankie slid down the embankment leading from the underpass. "Wait for my signal flare then light that island up with everything we got!"

With that, she dove headfirst into the river.

"Frankie!" Watson yelled as she swam off.

Watson watched distractedly as she swam her way toward the island and then finally broke with his men. They sprinted up River Street trying to spy through the buildings and restaurants where the boats were docking. Eventually, they made their way to a dock behind a large parking lot.

They ran through the urban lot to the river's edge and saw two rowboats docked, but nobody was in them.

"Shit," Watson said.

He grabbed the long-range. "Be advised we have soldiers who made it across, probably with heavy guns. Fortress should be on red alert. If you have enough people, I suggest trying to cut them off."

"Let's sink these boats," one of the men said.

Watson and the men expensed short rounds to fill the boats with holes. Though they were tied to the dock, they filled with water and sank halfway.

Back at the island, Kane laughed as he watched the men on the western shore scrambling after realizing the two boats that they had eyes on were decoys. Wasp and his team set off north from the island and landed at a dock a mile up and split before Watson arrived.

"Sir," one of Kane's guards said. "It may be too early to celebrate. They have this island surrounded. We're otherwise trapped here."

Kane stepped in from his balcony and fired a shot between the man's eyes.

To the other guard in the room, he said, "You are paid to protect me, not advise me. Take this heap of shit and toss him into the river."

The other guard nodded and dragged the dead man out by his feet.

"Trapped?" Kane said to himself. "It's all in the eye of the beholder, my friends."

He stepped back out onto the deck and peered out over the dark river. He smiled fiendishly.

Eighteen

BEFORE WORD OF ANOTHER potential attack sounded, and after King was settled in bed, Sky took a moment to visit Teddy in his room.

Yamil and Miracle were with him, sitting side-by-side on Leo's bed. Teddy was on his own bed, ears plugged.

"Teddy," Sky said. "Teddy, listen."

Teddy rocked on his bed with his ears plugged.

"Teddy, stop it!" Sky said. "How much have you been through? To be sitting on the bed behaving like this is not what King would want from you."

Teddy lowered his hands from his ears.

"Boys," Sky said. "Go downstairs and see what you can do to help."

Yamil and Miracle left, and Sky turned her attention back to Teddy.

"Is he dead?" Teddy asked.

"No," Sky answered. "He is in bed, and the wounds on the outside fixed, but we don't know what's to become of him. He needs your prayers and attention. We all hope he'll get through, but we don't know what's wrong with him inside."

"He saved everyone," Teddy said. "That's twice, for me."

"That's what he does, Teddy," Sky said. "It's what we all do if we need to. It's what we will *always* do, and you would have done no different, had you thought faster. But King is older, and therefore is more prepared to think quickly in these kinds of circumstances. It's his job to protect you! Now, we need to be strong, like always."

"Where is he?" Teddy asked, sliding his body to the edge of his bed.

"He's downstairs, in my room, resting peacefully," Sky said. "And let me make one thing clear: If he doesn't make it through, you know as well as I, he wouldn't have changed a thing about how he responded to the situation."

"I know," Teddy said. "It just sucks."

"A lot of things suck, Teddy," Sky reminded. "All the time. But a lot of things are good, too. Kellogg's coin reminds me of this whenever I need it."

Sky reached into her pocket and drew out Kellogg's coin. She held it up and smiled.

"He gave me this for luck," she said. "At first, I thought it was a curse, but then I learned why he carried it."

"Why?" Teddy said.

"Because he was still alive, and being alive is a thing to behold in any time," Sky said.

"But he died," Teddy said.

"Not before he could pass on the coin to me," Sky said. "I've been alive ever since."

"Maybe King needs the coin," Teddy said.

"Maybe," Sky said, "he needs something else."

Sky gazed downward to the necklace around Teddy's neck. Teddy took her cue and took the knight on a necklace and held it in his hand. He smiled and jumped off the bed.

"I'll be in charge of watching him," Teddy said.

"Yes, Teddy," Sky said. "That'll be good."

Before Teddy went to King's room, he grabbed the wooden king's piece from the chess game and ran into the basement. There he stayed as he carefully used a boring tool to create a hole through it. He found another shoelace and ran it through the hole before inspecting his work. He beamed with pride.

He raced back upstairs and grabbed one of the chess games that had all the pieces. The wooden chess set was down two pieces, but the plastic set was fully intact. He went back to the first floor and stopped short of Sky's bedroom door. His heart skipped a beat. He closed his eyes and took a deep breath before entering.

He saw King lying in bed, covered up with a blanket up to his chest. His eyes were closed, and he was unmoving.

Of course he isn't moving. He's not awake. He's sleeping. Just sleeping. He'll wake up soon.

Teddy had the chess set tucked under his arm and two necklaces strung around his neck. It was quiet. Too quiet. He didn't like it.

He walked to King's bedside and put his fingers under his nose. He felt King's warm breath of air on his fingers.

Good. He's still breathing.

Teddy walked around to the other side of the bed and put the chess game on top of it. He licked his lips as he wondered what to say. He took the necklace he had just made from around his neck and slipped it over King's neck.

"Hi," Teddy whispered. "King. I just put a necklace on you. I know it is kind of copycatting, but it is a little different. It has the king's piece on it. I also brought the chess game down. Sky says I can watch you. Like you watched me when I almost died. I guess you did what you had to do. Sky said it's what *I* would have done too; you just did it quicker. I want you to know I'm wearing my knight necklace. It reminds me about what a knight is. A knight is a protector. He wears his armor and goes to battle." Teddy felt tears welling in his eyes. "King. I'm fighting for *you* now. I hope you can hear me, at least, so you know...I will never stop fighting. Because you never did. Wyatt says alone we break, but together we can *never* be broken. We all love you. When you're better, me and you are gonna go home together. Just like we talked about. To say goodbye one last time." Teddy wiped away his tears. "Don't leave me."

Sky listened at the doorway and put her head against the wall. She wept quietly and then stepped in with a chair.

"I thought this would come in handy," she said, as if she hadn't been listening.

"Yeah," Teddy said, trying to make it seem as if he wasn't crying.

He took the chair from Sky and brought it back around to where the chess set was.

He set it up with all the pieces.

"Here's what I'm going to do," Teddy said as he watched King sleep. "I'm going to play the board. I'll play my pieces, and then I'll play *your* pieces. Just as you would. No cheating, I promise. We'll see who wins."

Teddy made his first move and then studied the board to see what King would do.

He then made King's move.

After Mike and his men had departed from the fortress to give aid to the group at the riverfront, the call came in from Watson about how Kane's men had tricked them and made it to the eastern shore, possibly headed toward the fortress with bigger guns.

They held up their horses a mile into their journey to the riverfront.

"Whoa," Mike called. When he stopped, the others behind him did as well.

Their horses met in a cluster on Fourth Street.

"Looks like we're holding up," Mike said. "They could be heading straight for us."

"What if they come from over the bridge?" Cypress asked.

"I doubt it, if they crossed on the eastern bank," Mike said. "Hawk, ride ahead and keep an eye on the bridge. The rest of us will hitch our horses behind the gas station at the intersection and set up on either side. If they intend to get to the fortress, they'll have to go through a gauntlet of gunfire first."

"Go," Hawk said. His horse sprinted off back toward the bridge.

"Let's head back. We'll set three of us behind the stone wall on the road leading to the bridge, and two of us on Morrison Hill a little further up. We have to make sure they don't make it beyond that."

Mike radioed. "Sky, we're coming back your way. We'll try to make sure nobody gets by, but Wyatt, keep your eyes peeled. I'll keep you posted, but be prepared to move to the basement if need be. I don't know what kind of weapons they're bringing back with them for round two."

"What about King?" Misty chimed in. "We can't move him."

Mike paused. "Let's hope you don't have to."

"Doctor Bennett and a few other backups from the heights should be there any time," Charlie radioed.

"We'll keep an eye out," Mike said before raising his voice and calling to his men. "Let's go!"

They raced back to the intersection to take up positions after hitching their horses behind the gas station.

Mike, Cypress, and Zippo spread out along the road under the cover of a low-rising asphalt wall that ran the length of the road to the bridge.

Fisher and Eddie took up a position across the way on a hill that was adjacent to the fortress hill. If anyone came from Fourth Street, they wouldn't be able to pass without going through them.

Hawk had the bridge covered.

"Wyatt," Mike said. "We're down here. Keep a good look out. If you see anything, give us a heads up."

"No problem," Wyatt said. "Got the ol' night vision scope going as we speak, but so far, I ain't seen anything suspicious."

Another thirty minutes passed in silence. Sky, Misty, Baby, Yamil, and Miracle moved the weapons from the woods, where they had earlier been taken, back to the fortress. They stockpiled everything in the kitchen in case they needed to use them.

"I'm scared," Miracle said.

"Stop being scared all the time," Yamil scolded. "You shot that one guy."

"He was going to hurt us," Miracle said.

"That's why," Yamil said. "You have to kill the bad guys. Whenever we use guns, it's so nobody hurts us. So be brave."

"Okay, okay," Miracle said.

The seconds passed slowly as Mike and his men waited, and Wyatt kept eyes on Fourth Street from the roof. Ten minutes felt like ten hours, but then they came. Wyatt spotted them on Fourth Street. They were weaving between cars and keeping away from the middle of the road. He tried to see what weapons they were toting, but he couldn't tell.

"We have bogies coming from Fourth," Wyatt said. "Can't see what weapons they have, or determine how many, but they are approaching fast."

"Hawk," Mike said. "You can come back this way. Quietly. Get ready, everyone."

Minutes later, seven men emerged from the shadows of Fourth Street. Mike observed that they had semi-automatic rifles, as well as large-scale weapons including what looked to be grenade launchers being carried by two men. Those were double-handled, with enormous cylinders.

Holy shit, Mike thought.

"Wait," Mike said, as the men moved further along. "Wait."

"It looks like seven," Wyatt said.

"Wait," Mike said.

"They got some big-ass guns," Wyatt said.

As they approached Morrison Hill, Mike yelled. "Now!"

Mike and his men stepped out into the open and lit the area up with gunfire. The soldiers approaching were not surprised, acting almost as if they were anticipating it. A few of them stopped to return fire in the direction where shots were coming from, while the two soldiers with grenade launchers pressed forward as if football players heading for the endzone.

"Cut them down!" Mike said.

Although multiple rounds of ammunition echoed in the streets from both sides, they only managed to hit one of Kane's soldiers, who fell to the ground but continued to provide cover fire for his counterparts from his wounded position on the street.

From the fortress rooftop, Wyatt fired off rounds with the rifle, but hitting the moving targets proved difficult, and he was not the best long-range shooter.

Six of the men, including the men with the grenade launchers, made it past Mike and the others stationed behind the roadside barrier. Mike continued to fire at them from behind. Fisher and Eddie were ready at Morrison Hill for the second wave of attacks on the advancing soldiers.

The men, not expecting a second assault, were taken off guard when Eddie and Fisher stepped out from each side of Morrison Hill and sprayed them with bullets. Two more of the soldiers fell, including one of the men with a grenade launcher. Two others stopped at the intersection and fired up hill. Bullets struck Eddie in the leg and side, and he fell.

Fisher continued to lay down fire, and with Wyatt shooting from the roof and Mike, Zippo, Hawk, and Cypress firing from behind, there were bullets whizzing from every direction. The muzzle flare from the exchanges lit up the night.

Another of the soldiers collapsed at the intersection, taken out from the hill. Cypress had jumped the barrier and took out the injured soldier who was in the middle of the road providing cover fire.

"We got two more!" Mike said. "It's a warzone down here! We can't let the guy with the launcher get any closer to the fortress."

The soldier with the grenade launcher made it to the foot of the hill leading to the fortress while the two remaining soldiers continued to lay down cover fire. One of them fired at the roof, causing Wyatt to take cover. The bullets slapped at the shingles, which sent pieces flying everywhere.

The night was ablaze with gunfire. On the east side of the fortress, Sky opened the shutters to the fortress on the first floor and fired at the men from her window. Above her, Misty and Baby were shooting from second-floor windows. Yamil was firing from the third-floor window. Though, when he turned to see where Miracle was, he noticed his best friend and brother wasn't there.

Mike and the others continued to pursue the men to the hill in a relentless attempt to kill the remaining men. Of the three left, one of the men was hit. He fell to his knees and kept firing. A bullet grazed Mike's leg, but with his adrenaline pumping, he barely noticed.

The last soldier with the grenade launcher made it part way up the hill just as Miracle sprung from the front of the fortress firing a pistol. Miracle ran down the length of the hill firing repeatedly.

From the side window, Sky saw him approaching the men down below. "No!" she screamed.

Her heart raced and she bolted for the front door in hot pursuit.

When she made it to the street, she screamed his name in agony. "Miracle!"

"Get him!" Misty cried from her window.

Miracle didn't respond. He just kept going as fast as his little legs could take him. Sky couldn't even fire for fear of hitting him, but the timid boy kept running with his gun blazing wildly. Instantly she recalled when he and Yamil had found their way home from Valley Hall, and how profoundly relieved and amazed she had been. She remembered running down the hill in much the same way she was presently, only feeling elation and joy at that time.

In this instance, her muscles were tense, and she felt unbelievable pain and loss, for in her mind, she saw Miracle running to his death—a death from which she might never be able to recover.

Miracle ran with purpose, trying to aim his gun at the soldier with the big weapon. One of his bullets struck the man that was beside the soldier with the grenade launcher, as that bad man was already wounded and distracted by Mike and the others, who were in hot pursuit at the intersection. The soldier fell to the ground, and Miracle continued to close the gap between himself and Kane's last man, who was preparing to shoot a grenade at the fortress.

Miracle made it within a couple of feet of the final man and took aim. "And now you. You're bad."

He got to within steps of the soldier with the grenade launcher. He heard Sky crying behind him, and Wyatt from the roof. He raised his gun at the man, who lowered the launcher with a surprised look on his face.

Then Miracle fired.

Click.

Miracle's revolver was out of bullets. The small boy lowered his gun and put on his growly face. The man smiled and then kicked Miracle in the chest, sending him to the ground. Then, the soldier pointed the grenade launcher at the fortress and aimed true. Before he pulled the trigger, though, he heard a mysterious voice beneath his feet. He looked downward.

"Boo," Harlow called from the street vent.

The barrel of a gun was pointing out of the storm drain. Gunfire rattled from beneath his feet and struck him in the chest and head, but as his body convulsed, he squeezed the trigger on the launcher, hurling a misguided grenade at the fortress.

"Look out!" Sky cried from the middle of the road.

Her stomach dropped knowing that Baby, Misty, and Wyatt were all on the east side of the building, vulnerable.

The errant grenade, veering from its original course, hit the roof and chimney. A massive explosion lit up the sky from the fortress crest.

"Wyatt!" Sky yelled as Mike and his men ran up the hill.

Mike scooped Miracle into his arms as he hobbled toward the fortress, following Sky's lead.

With all of Kane's soldiers finally dispatched, everyone but Fisher who was helping Eddie with his injuries on Morrison hill, proceeded to the fortress.

They burst through the doors. Baby and Misty were on the second-floor landing.

Sky cried. "Where's Yamil?"

"He's fine," Misty said. "He's on the third-floor landing."

Teddy emerged from the first-floor bedroom. "What was that explosion?"

"The roof," Sky said.

Everyone ran up the stairs. Yamil was running down the third floor set of steps, coughing. "It's smoky. The roof has a hole."

Sky was thankful that Yamil was fine, but was overcome with fear about Wyatt's well-being. She ran to the third floor with the others behind her. She sprang open the door to the attic and dashed up the steps.

Through the smoke she saw Wyatt coming through the skylight. When he was all the way in, he was waving smoke away. "Gosh dang, that was some scary shit. Good thing I know how to jump."

Sky ran to him and hugged him tightly, and he returned the embrace as the others behind Sky broke into laughter.

"The roof is messed up, though," Wyatt said.

Sky pulled away from him. "*This* fortress we can fix," she said. "But the human fortress...if something happens, we can never fully fix it."

The two hugged again.

"There is for sure only one of me. How is everyone else? Did we get those sons of bitches?"

"I was grazed," Mike said. "I think Eddie was hit too."

Sky, Wyatt, and the others ran back downstairs and out the door as Fisher was coming up the hill, helping along a limping Eddie. He had been hit, but there seemed to be no mortal wounds.

Behind him were two dozen people who had emerged from the storm drain behind Harlow. They were all standing in a large cluster on the hill.

Sky smiled at Harlow. "Thank you."

"It was nothing," Harlow said. "The timing was perfect, though, I have to admit. And I hardly ever carry a gun, but after a couple of days with you guys...I felt it was probably a good idea."

Sky laughed. "Yes, a gun usually helps around here."

"Speaking of which," Harlow said, "I left Leo and the others to convince my fellow tunnel rats that a life in the sun may be worth taking a chance on. Most of them agreed."

Sky looked beyond Harlow to the men, women, and children that stood before her in the street.

"You're right," Sky said. "It is. And together, we'll make sure that the sun will shine. Now, let's invite them all into the fortress to talk."

Harlow nodded and tended to her people.

Sky then made her way to Miracle.

"What were you thinking?" she yelled as she took a knee in front of him. She then wrapped her arms around him. "You know I could never stand to lose you. You're a crazy little boy."

"He was a bad guy," Miracle said. "I didn't want him to hurt us."

She held him on both sides and looked into his eyes. "You have the most amazing heart, but you scared the heck out of me!"

Yamil then came up to him. He slapped Miracle on the head. "How could you do that to me? Don't you ever scare me like that again! *I'm* not even that crazy!"

Sky smiled.

Miracle shrugged. "I didn't want them to hurt you," he said to Yamil. "I didn't care if the bad men hurt *me*, as long as they didn't hurt *you*."

Yamil smiled and hugged Miracle tight.

In that moment, the fortress shined.

Mike limped over to Sky. "We're going to head back out to the river. Carryout our original plan."

"I'm going too," Misty said. "I'll take Eddie's horse and he can stay here. I know how to ride."

"Let Baby patch up your leg before," Sky said.

Baby dashed off to fetch the first aid supplies.

Sky turned to Wyatt. "Can you hold things down here?"

He looked around at all their visitors who had crowded the house.

"Sure, why not," Wyatt said. "Though I thought we weren't entertaining guests anymore. Is this safe? We don't even know any of these people."

"I'll keep them in line," Harlow said. "I know them all. They're good people."

"Keep them on the first floor under guard, but feed them," Sky said. "Don't let them roam, and frisk each one for weapons. Let them know we'll need to hold any of their weapons for now."

Baby came back with the first aid. She tended to Mike's wound, which was more significant than a graze. The bullet had passed through the meat of his thigh. Baby sterilized it and tied a bandage around it.

"You'll need stiches when things settle," Baby said. "But that will do for now."

"Then let's ride," Cypress said as he headed to the door. "There's more work to be done."

As they opened the door, they came face to face with a balding, spectacled man holding a black bag, and three armed men. Cypress took a step back and raised his weapon.

The spectacled man held up his hands and three armed men quickly raised their weapons.

"Wait!" Wyatt yelled. "They're from the heights!"

"The doctor," Sky said with an air of relief. "Baby, show him where King is. The rest of you come in. There are a lot of visitors. Wyatt can fill you in."

"Come on in, boys," Wyatt said. "You just missed a crazy-ass battle."

"We heard an explosion," Doctor Bennett said.

"It was right here," Wyatt said. "We're going to keep you busy tonight, doc."

After welcoming the men from the heights, Mike's team, along with Sky and Misty, hightailed it to the gas station down the hill where the horses were hitched. Misty hopped on top of Eddie's horse while Mike helped Sky onto his.

"Misty and Hawk, we'll split at the Congress Street Bridge," Mike said. "You two will keep straight to the west edge, and the rest of us will cross the bridge to the east edge where more of the action seems to be taking place."

"Sounds like a plan," Hawk said.

"Go!" Mike said and the horses sprinted off over the green bridge and to the highway.

Nineteen

AFTER FRANKIE JUMPED INTO the Hudson River, she made her way across to the island. She didn't care if the enemy saw her. She was not going to die in the river. She was going to make it across, find Kane, and kill him.

The boats that had turned around reached shore before her, and whoever was manning them retreated to the island. When she came to shore, the boats were empty and the island seemed quiet. She had a .57 Magnum, a Remington 750 rifle, and a long knife tucked neatly into a belt sheath.

She crept up the very rocky shore that Malayah had been carried down before being thrown into the river by Kane's soldiers. She made it to the paved parking area in front of a strip mall plaza and proceeded to the endcap. She peered around it and saw two guards at a booth at the apartment complex perimeter.

She checked her rifle and said a quick prayer.

Dear Lord. Let me kill everyone. Amen.

She then rounded the corner with her rifle poised to shoot.

The two guards saw her approaching and immediately left the booth, a bit confused.

"Hey," the bubblegum popping man who earlier had frisked Malayah said. "Where are you coming from?"

"Your momma's house," Frankie said as she fired multiple shots. Each one ripped through the man's body. He fell instantly. The other guard tried to flee, but Frankie cut him down with multiple bullets to his back.

She made her way into the booth and confiscated their weapons. She slung a few rifles around her back and tucked another pistol into her waistband. She continued, looking to find someone who could tell her where Kane was. Though she had just fired off her gun, her intrusion had not garnered a response.

She ran under the cover of night to one of the apartment buildings, which were much nicer than the apartments at the heights.

Bougie motherfuckers.

She entered the complex and proceeded down the first-floor corridor, randomly checking apartments for residents. The first three apartments were empty, but when she burst into the fourth apartment, there was a scared group of women and children filling the space wall to wall.

What the fuck?

The women tucked their children into their bosoms and let out audible cries as Frankie entered, guns drawn, and scanned the area with a readied weapon. When she realized there was no threat, she lowered her weapon. The room was lit with several candles and battery-powered lights, but it was a gloomy scene.

"Where's Kane?" Frankie cried.

None of the women spoke at first. Multiple children were buried in their arms. Frankie empathized, but still yelled, "Where is he!"

One of the women stepped forward. "Building C. Apartment 11."

Frankie scanned the area. "What are you doing here?"

The woman said, "Kane made the women and children report to a few of the apartments on a code red. We don't know what's going on. But we heard the gunfire."

Frankie nodded. "Let me tell you what's going on. Kane has attacked our communities, and I'm here to track him and down, and kill his murdering ass."

Frankie turned to leave then the women uttered, "Will we be free?"

"I promise you," Frankie said. "You'll be free. Because this bullshit ends here."

The woman smiled, and Frankie returned the sentiment, though she wasn't much in the mood for glee.

"Just stay here until it's done," Frankie said. "I'll be back."

Frankie left. She was on a quest to find building C.

She stayed in the shadows of the complex building as she made her way across the island.

A.

B.

C.

She clenched her teeth and entered the glass doorway to building C on her way to apartment 11.

Across the river, Watson returned to the rest of his men from upriver.

"We disabled the boats that got them across," Watson said. "It's up to all of you, now. Frankie jumped into the river headed toward the island. I couldn't stop her. Nobody could. She's on a damn mission. She was talking about sending us a signal flare before we launch any kind of assault."

"If she succeeds," Charlie said from the heights. "It can only help us. If she doesn't..."

"You want us to just hang tight?" Watson said. "They obviously know we're here."

"Yes," Charlie said. "We need to keep our presence strong on both sides of the river to make sure nobody else gets off."

"Roger that," Watson said.

Little did Watson know, Kane's teams, who landed at the east side dock, split into two groups. Half the group went to the fortress to destroy it, while Wasp took another group of six men to designated areas along the Hudson near where the resistance took up position.

Wasp's men spread out along the river's edge where the detonators, attached to long wires leading to bundles of dynamite, lay obscured. Kane not only wanted to protect himself and his people through isolation on the island, but he also had the wherewithal to booby trap the land around him.

As Wasp and his men coordinated, each of his six men found a distinct detonator and stationed themselves there. While Watson and more than twenty other men from the heights waited and observed, Wasp radioed his men.

"Is everyone in position?" Wasp asked.

Each of the men acknowledged his position, and Wasp smiled. Kane was right. They would wipe them out on the east bank, and in the chaos bring the rest of their soldiers across from the island to finish off the heights. Then they would bring more soldiers up from Hudson and subdue the entire area. True, this area had been harder than all the rest to get under control, but they would do it, notwithstanding casualties, and then move farther north to continue their conquest.

"Okay," Wasp said. "Once my charge goes off, they'll panic. Wait until they scramble. Hit your detonators when the potential for more casualties is likely. Use your small arms and knives to take out anyone who we miss with the blasts. They won't see you coming."

Wasp then smiled as he saw a pocket of heights people close to the dynamite connected to his detonator. He pushed down on the detonator handle and a massive explosion ignited the area. Men flew screaming in every direction. Wasp then pulled out his pistol and charged.

Watson, nearby where the first explosion hit, shouted. "Where did that explosion come from? Take cover!"

The heights people started to scramble just as a second explosion ignited. More men cried out. Watson jumped on his radio.

"Be advised, we're under attack. Western team, watch yourself. The land perimeter is wired. It's a trap—"

Just then, a third explosion went off and Watson found himself hurling through the air, down an embankment, and into the river.

On the east bank, explosions continued to rock the area one after the other. When the series of detonations ended, Wasp and his men attacked with small arms sending the heights people fleeing in random directions.

The two dozen men guarding the western side of the Hudson could only watch, as there was no easy way to get there in time to help. Kane had detonated the bridge that cut through the island, so the only way to cross was to swim or go all the way around by way of the Congress Street bridge, which was a distance away.

"This is Merrick," came the call as he watched the explosions from across the river. "There's nothing we can do. We're trapped over here. By the time we get across, whatever is done will be done."

"I hear you," Watson cried, making his way up the bank. "Wish us luck. It's a shit show over here."

"Yeah," Merrick said. "I can see that. Godspeed."

Twenty

ON THE ROAD BACK to the fortress from the preserve, Leo, though exhausted, kept his group moving at a jog.

Messiah and Avi chugged along pulling the weapons cart on wheels while the others tried to keep pace.

"Come on," Leo said. "There's no time to waste."

"My legs are killing me," Parker said. "We didn't even sleep. I'm tired."

"We're all tired, Parker," Leo said. "But it's life or death. Harlow could be in trouble too. Sleep later."

Leo kept the lead alongside Timothy and Gigi while Casper and Dietrich pressed from the other side.

Along with Avi and the soldiers, Mr. Dumas, Grace, Ember, and nearly two dozen others joined the return journey.

"Are we ready to get these guys, or what?" Leo screamed, his attempt at a pre-battle pep rally.

"We're ready, Leo," Avi said. "If we live through this, what do you say you introduce me to Sky, more formally?"

"Stay focused," Leo said. "We're not going back to the fortress."

"Where are we headed?" Ember said.

"To the riverfront," Leo said. "These weapons will reach the island. We're going to light them up! Just like the Fourth of July."

"Hoorah," Casper said from the back.

Gigi barked.

Though they all had been in constant motion since early morning, they pressed forward, mentally preparing for confrontation.

"Let's hope we get your endorsement of our community after all this, Leo," Ember smiled.

"Don't worry," Leo said. "You had me at solar electricity."

They kept a steady pace, and as they got closer to the city, they could hear explosions at the riverfront, and it motivated them to push themselves through the final leg.

"Faster!" Leo said as he heard the drama over the long range. "We have to get there!"

Everyone was chugging along, and though exhausted, they kept pace. Once they heard the explosions they ran even faster.

"We have a problem," Timothy said. "Even when we get there...we won't know who's who if they're tangled up. It's hard to even see out here."

"We can just get there and see," Leo said. "I guess if anyone comes after us, we'll know then. The people from the heights may just have to fight their one-to-one battles."

"I don't hear anymore explosions," Avi said.

The group finally arrived at the city center, and behind some buildings and a former restaurant laid the edge of the river. They heard screaming and yelling. Gigi started barking.

"Calm down, girl," Leo said.

"Unload the cart," Timothy yelled. "Arm yourselves! We're headed down that bank. Wait for my call."

Everyone scrambled to take up arms just as Mike and his horsemen arrived, racing down First Street.

"Mike!" Ember cried.

"Sky!" Leo cried. She smiled with relief.

All the horseman stopped on the roadway. They hitched their horses to the cart and jumped off. Gigi ran up to Sky and hugged her.

"Perfect timing," Mike said. "Now let's get down there."

Parker went to Messiah. "You stay here and guard the rest of the weapons. Shoot anyone that looks like they want to hurt you. You're better off than I am. I have to go down that hill. What the hell did we get ourselves into, big guy?"

"I don't know," Messiah said, his deep voice resonating calm. "But I like meeting people."

Parker smiled and shook his head.

Timothy, Dietrich, and Casper led the way with night vision goggles past the restaurant and down the bank. The rest of them, including Leo, Sky, Gigi, the preserve reserves, and Mike's team all fanned out as they proceeded down the hill into the unknown.

They saw some men exchanging gunfire, others fighting hand to hand, and witnessed the carnage of the sneak attack, several bodies lying on the ground. The smell of smoke filled the air.

Despite several losses on the heights team, they had managed to kill four of the seven men who initiated the explosions.

"Watson," Sky said into the radio. "We have about thirty of us coming down the bank. We don't know who's who, though. Your people won't either. You copy?"

There was no response as everyone halted in the trees ahead of the remaining skirmish until there was nothing more but silence.

"Watson, do you copy?"

"Watson is dead," another voice came through. "We got them all but one, though. He fled up the bank."

"There are about thirty of us here," Sky said. "We're coming down, so hold your fire."

"It's clear," Timothy said.

Everyone rose from crouches and came down the embankment, where they all gathered with about six of the remaining heights reserves. They approached one guy who was disheveled and covered with black soot.

"I guess we came too late," Mike said. "Sorry, but they ambushed us at the fortress."

"They ambushed us here, too," the man said. "They had explosive devices all over."

"Let's not sulk," Casper said. "We were coming here before we even knew about the booby traps. We have high-powered weapons that can reach the island. We can attack them from here. They may have had some tricks up their sleeves, but they're still trapped on that island."

Dietrich and Casper stepped forward with rocket launchers. Avi was holding a grenade launcher, as were Cypress and Fisher.

"We'll pummel these assholes," Cypress said, eyeing his weapon up and down with glee.

"Yeah," Fisher said. "And I thought *we* had some cool shit, but nothing we got comes close to matching this firepower."

"There's plenty of ammo for these things and more rockets in the cart," Timothy said.

"We have one of our own on the island though," the man said. "Frankie swam out there and told us to wait for her signal flare before we did anything."

"Shit, she could be dead already," another one of the heights people said.

Just then, Merrick jumped on the comm as the sound of gunfire echoed across the river. "We're under attack over here. About twenty-five men just came straight out of the river. They're forcing us north. They could have this side rigged with explosives too."

Everyone gathered at the edge of the river, mouths agape, listening to the gunfire and seeing the muzzle flare from dozens of guns volleying bullets across the way.

"Misty and Hawk are headed there, if they aren't there already," Sky noted, panic in her voice.

Leo offered her a look of shock before turning his attention back to the sight of the firefight.

"We're gonna send you rocket support," the heights man holding the radio said. "We got eyes on the more southern group of shooters. You say that's Kane's soldiers?"

"Yes, they're closing in, though," Merrick said. "We have about fifty yards between us. Make sure you put those rockets in the right place."

"Dietrich!" Timothy said. "He's got this."

Dietrich stepped ahead and put the rocket launcher on his shoulder. He lined his sights up with the area where he observed the muzzle flare amongst the southernmost group.

Three, two, one.

He pressed the trigger, and with a hiss, the rocket sprang from the tube and soared across the river, leaving a trail of firelight behind it. The entire group watched as the rocket flew across the water and hit the west bank. The explosion rocked the land.

"Wow," Parker said.

Gigi kicked into an incessant bark as she watched the lighted spectacle.

"Give me another one," Dietrich said.

Casper handed him another rocket, and in a repeat of the first round, he sent off another rocket. It, too, exploded where the pocket of Kane's men was attacking. Soon, the group could only see the muzzle flare from the north end group—the heights reserves.

"Now, go get the rest," the man told Merrick.

While all of the others watched the ongoing volley of gunfire across the river, Messiah stood guard at the cart. He was stargazing when a person he did not recognize crept up the bank and rounded the corner of the riverside restaurant.

Messiah crouched down behind the cart as best he could and watched as the man approached. He heard the man's footsteps and his heavy breathing as he got closer.

"What the hell is this?" the man said to himself as he saw the horses and cart.

Messiah realized he had left his gun leaning against the cart, so he did his best to remain concealed.

The man, the lone soldier who fled from Kane's unit, approached the cart of weapons and stared at them as if seeing a pot of gold. He then turned his gaze to the horses, salivating. He would take their weapons and ride off on one of their horses.

Many of the weapons had been deployed by the reserves who were now at the banks, but there were still several more along with extra bullets, rockets, and grenades.

The soldier leaned over and started loading himself up with weaponry when Messiah slowly rose from the front end of the cart. The man froze in place as Messiah hovered over him.

"Holy shit," The man said gazing upward at the mammoth boy.

He tried to grab for one of the weapons, but Messiah advanced upon him quickly and hammered him in the face with a solid fist. The soldier crumpled to the ground like a paper doll and moaned as he spit out teeth. Messiah then grabbed him with both hands by his clothing and bench pressed him over his head. The man screamed as Messiah threw him the distance of ten feet and as he crashed landed on the concrete.

Messiah went to the cart and grabbed a grenade. He walked back over to the maimed man, released the pin on the grenade and stuffed it into one of the man's pockets. He quickly picked up the soldier, spun him around and flung him. The man, screaming, was in midair when the explosion went off, blowing his body to bits.

Messiah wiped his hands together, then went back to the cart as if nothing happened and continued watching the stars.

Twenty-One

SHORTLY AFTER HIS PERIMETER explosions rocked the east side of the river, but before Leo and the others arrived to lend their support, Kane watched the lighted mayhem from his balcony with much satisfaction.

"Whose turf is it now?" he mumbled.

He then turned to his lone soldier standing guard. "Go alert the third unit that they need to get in the water, covertly, to the western bank while that group is distracted by the explosions. We'll sneak attack them. Once we crush these cockroaches, we'll pay a visit to each of their communities and finish them all to claim our victory."

The soldier nodded and left to alert the third unit. Then, Kane, still celebrating on the balcony, broke into a song and dance to a familiar tune.

This land is my land
This land is my land
From Green Island
To New York City
From Poughkeepsie
To Saugerties and Kingston
This land was made for me and me

His celebratory dance ended abruptly when the preserve group arrived with the rocket launcher and lit up the west bank. During this turn of events, and as his men were being obliterated by rocket explosions and gunfire, Frankie made her way to his building. She stayed in the shadows alongside Building C as she saw random soldiers patrolling. She didn't want to give her position away, so she resisted the urge to step out and kill them.

She found an entry point to the building and made her way inside. The hallway was quiet as she cleared floor one, looking for that magic number eleven. She moved up a stairwell to floor two, and as she was on the stairs, a soldier came through the doorway from the second floor. He made it halfway down the steps before he realized she was there, pointing a gun at him. He froze, but when he realized Frankie was not one of their own, he drew his weapon.

Frankie lunged and snatched the soldier's leg out from underneath him before he could react, and he lost his balance and fell on the stairs. Frankie jumped on his back as she pulled a knife from its sheath. The soldier clawed at the steps as he clamored to get out from under her, but she wrapped a hand around his forehead and pulled his head back. She leaned forward and whispered into his ear.

"This is what I'm gonna do to Kane," she said.

She slid the knife in a swift motion across his neck and opened an inch-wide gash from ear to ear. The soldier spit and sputtered as she continued to keep backward pressure on his head with her hand until the bloodletting was through and his writhing body came to rest.

When she got to her feet, the stairs were dripping with blood. She stepped over his corpse and made her way to the second floor.

She burst through the second-floor door. The corridor was clear. She proceeded to her left and realized the numbers were going down from nine, so she reversed her direction, and two doors down from the stairwell, she found it.

Eleven.

Fury surged within her as she stared at the number, thinking how beyond it lay the man who took Malayah from her. She tried the doorknob to see if the apartment was unlocked, but the knob didn't turn. So, she stepped back, raised her foot, and with blunt force, she thrust her foot into the door. It sprang open on the first try and she went in, gun drawn.

At first glance, she didn't see anyone. Then, Kane quietly stepped from the balcony into the apartment, staring at Frankie with a piercing gaze.

"Ahh," he said. "I remember you. The heights."

Frankie stared at him, seething inside. She kept the gun trained on him as she took in the sight of this grotesque man who had stolen half her life away.

"How was your swim?" Kane asked.

"Swimming is much better than floating, which is what you'll be doing in that river as soon as I kill your ass. Maybe you'll meet up with Malayah down river and she'll smile seeing you, knowing what I did to avenge her."

Kane smiled. "Oh, the girlfriend. Now it makes sense. It was nothing personal, you know. I was just sending a message. This area will belong to my people. If not today, then tomorrow. Or next month. It's...inevitable. My associates don't give up so easily. I am merely one piece of this puzzle."

Frankie clenched her teeth. "This isn't about tomorrow. It's about yesterday."

"Then shoot me," Kane said. "My men are fucking everything up anyway. To the victor go the spoils."

"The thing is," Frankie said as she unbound herself from her numerous weapons. "I told everyone I was going to slit your throat. So, shooting you is just not going to do it. But just know, once you're dead, I'm gonna cut off your fat head and throw it into the river. That's *your* fate."

"My fate...will always be mine...regardless," Kane said. "It's the one thing you can never take from me."

"Who would want to," Frankie said as she tossed her gun aside, whipped out her knife, and charged at Kane.

He grabbed her knife wielding hand, but the force of her body sent them both out the balcony door, where they slammed against the railing. She struggled to get her hand free, but he held it firm. He held her other hand also, and the two were stuck.

"Want to dance?" Kane asked with a laugh.

Frankie drove her knee into his groin, and though he still held firm to the wrist of her hand wielding the knife, he released her other hand. With it, she punched him in the jaw. He recoiled but quickly returned a cuff of his own that sent her reeling backward and away.

Frankie rubbed her mouth and wiped away the blood, and quickly lunged at him again. Kane moved out of the way, and Frankie hit the railing, face-forward. From her right side, Kane struck her in the back, then delivered another sock to her jaw. Frankie didn't allow herself to be subdued. She quickly drew further away from him and held out her knife. He stood only a few feet away, sneering.

"Really?" he said. "This is a bit disappointing. Had I given Malayah a chance to fight, she probably could have done better. But she didn't see it coming. I shot her in the stomach before she even had a clue. But that wasn't even the best part. The best part was when I dropped a boulder on her head. It's got to be a tough way to go, having your skull crushed."

Frankie screamed and rushed Kane again. She hit him with so much force that both toppled over the balcony railing and fell ten feet to the ground below. Frankie used Kane's body as a cushion, but when they hit, she flew off him in another direction. On impact, she released her knife, and it rocketed from her hand.

Kane lay on the ground coughing and laughing. "This land is my land. This land is my land..."

As he sang his tune, Frankie recovered on all fours. She turned to him as he lay there staring at the sky.

"From Green Island, to New York City...," he continued to sing, cough up blood, and laugh. "This land...is made for me and...me."

Frankie got to her feet and recovered her knife. She stood over Kane.

"You don't want to do this," Kane said. "Women...and children. If you kill me. They'll all die. They are housed in an apartment complex rigged with C-4. The rest of it that we had. If I don't contact my guy with the code word every thirty minutes, he'll blow them all to hell."

Frankie would doubt him if she had not seen the terrified women and children herself. She grabbed Kane by his collar. "If you want to live, you better tell me that code, or I swear to God—"

Kane laughed. "The only way they live is if I live. Now get the fuck out of here, and maybe some other day we'll finish this."

Frankie released his collar. She had no idea when the last time was that Kane and his contact had communicated. She could have twenty-five minutes, or two minutes. It was unknown. Then she saw a watch on Kane's wrist. She grabbed his limp arm and pulled it up to her. It read 2:15 a.m.

Fifteen minutes? She wondered. But she knew she was going to take a chance. Kane was likely in no position to get back into his apartment and radio the code anyway.

Leaning over him, Frankie said, "They may live, or they may die, but it isn't going to save *you*."

She spit in his face and then slashed Kane's throat. She watched for thirty seconds as he choked on his own blood. Then she sprinted off to the apartment building where the women and children were holed up.

As she ran, she heard a series of explosions on the west bank, along with gunfire. She wondered what her people were dealing with, but knew she had to get to the women and children before the apartment blew up.

She entered the building and burst through the doors of the apartment she had seen them in earlier. They were all still there cowering.

"We have to get the others and get out of here!" she yelled. "This building is rigged to blow. Move it!"

Everyone fled for the doors and filled the apartment hallway. Some of the women knocked on the other apartment doors to alert the other groups. Within minutes, the building was flooded with people fleeing.

Frankie waited outside the building and directed them to the norther side of the island. "Get to the other side!"

As the women and children ran north on the island a few perimeter soldiers started firing. Frankie returned fire as the others ran for cover.

"Move it!" she screamed.

She faced off with several soldiers who were closing in on her. Once the building was clear, she pulled a flare from her pocket and sent it up. A bright red light lit up the sky as Frankie stole off into the night. She followed the mass of women and children as they fled across the land isthmus to the northern end of the island and stopped in a fielded area.

Seconds later, the apartment building they were in exploded with an unprecedented thunder and flame that shook the island to its core. Soon after, rockets and grenades soared from the east side coast and immersed the southern end of the island in a barrage of intermittent explosions.

From the field, Frankie watched in glory as the rest of the island was annihilated.

A short time later, as the fires simmered and the threat abated, Frankie turned to the crowd of onlookers whom she had saved from a fiery death.

"Kane is dead!" she yelled to them all. "But *your* life is just beginning. We will rebuild here, and you will have a new chance, along with many others in this area."

They all looked at her frightened, but not oppositional. Frankie had no idea what life had been like for them on the island under Kane's rule, but she was excited to paint a picture of a new future for them.

"For now," Frankie said. "It looks like there are plenty of apartments on the northern end of this island for you to relocate yourselves. Me and my people will clean up here while you tend to your children, and we will see you tomorrow."

As the crowd dispersed, Frankie returned to the south side of the island where Kane still lay amongst the rubble and destruction. She stood over his lifeless body thinking about what he had done to Malayah. His death did not repair the sting of her murder, and she knew that come morning, the painful feeling of intense loss would still remain.

But it was a start.

She spat on his lifeless corpse before dragging it down the embankment and rolling it into the river. She watched as he floated away.

"This is our island now," she said.

Merrick radioed the east side a short time after they sent the rockets over to assist.

"Five casualties," Merrick said. "We got most of them bastards. A few of them ran off, but we're secure over here. What the hell was that explosion on the island?"

"We don't know," came the message. "But we saw the flare Frankie sent up and lit the south side of the island up. Hopefully that'll take care of that."

Sky grabbed the radio from the heights' crew member.

"Did you see two people on horseback?" Sky asked. "Are they okay?"

There was a short silence.

"They got here just after the attack," the man said. "We're sad to report one of them was struck and killed in the gunfight."

Mike put his arm around Sky. Leo grabbed Sky's hand.

"Was it a girl or a man?" Sky asked.

Just then static came across the line.

"Hello?" Sky said. "Do you copy?"

After another brief thirty-seconds of silence, Merrick came back. "The deceased horse rider was a male. The other is here and wants to speak with you."

Leo and Sky breathed a sigh of relief while Mike turned to his men, who had to contend with Hawk's death.

"Sky?" Misty came through on the other end. "I'm here. Tell your uncle I'm sorry about Hawk."

Sky closed her eyes. "He's listening."

"I think it's over," Misty said.

"Is it ever?" Sky asked.

Sky hated the thought of one of Mike's longstanding family members being killed, but she was relieved that it wasn't Misty who fell. She had lost enough of the people she was close to. Which brought her to another thought: could she ever care about the survival of everyone else as much as she did about the people she personally held dearly?

The answer was no. Even in a larger colony, the fortress would always be the fortress, as much as it was the kingdom. It would remain itself as it became part of everything.

Sim's house, bringing the light to those who were lost.

Frankie left Kane's women and children behind as she rowed across the water to the east side where she was met by hordes of people, many of whom hadn't been there when she left.

They were happy to see her, and she told them about her mission and its results.

"We need some people to join me over there for the night," Frankie said. "There are a lot of innocent women and children in limbo. We want them to feel safe and to make sure the island is clear."

Several people from the preserve and the heights volunteered to go back with Frankie to watch over the island while the rest of them returned to the fortress and the heights for some well-needed rest, after which a new era would be born.

Twenty-Two

BACK AT THE FORTRESS, everyone celebrated the news of Kane's defeat and the destruction of the island. The underground network led by Harlow seemed supportive and amenable to change, and as they dined, they stressed their appreciation of the warm welcome.

When Sky and the others returned, the walls inside the fortress were packed from end to end, but it was a great crowd. There was talk and laughter, as well as victory cheers despite the loss. The place was full of life, hope, and promise.

For the orphans and Wyatt, the moment was a bit sullied by King's condition and unknown future, and it was Sky's first order of business when she got back to touch base with Doctor Bennett.

"I'm afraid I can't tell you much more than what you might have already assumed," he said. "I checked his heart and it seemed strong. His lungs are clear of fluid, and I examined the cuts on his back. Though some of them are deep, none of them would prove fatal, and they do not seem to be fostering any kind of infection. His comatose state could be temporary or long-term, but we do not have the ability to keep him alive long-term. We do have other tools at the heights that will allow us to run an IV to keep him hydrated, at least, but I'm not sure to what end. You may have to consider that he may not make it."

Teddy, from King's bedside, heard this, and though he wanted to cry, he held strong for King.

"Don't listen to anyone, King," Teddy said. "You're a fighter. If you were meant to die, you would be dead. You will wake up. I know it."

Mike caught Sky on the second floor as she surveyed the damage to the fortress.

"Hey, girl," Mike said.

"How's your leg?" she asked.

"Many others have suffered a lot worse than this," Mike said. "Including Hawk. He was a good man. At least Eddie will make it."

"I'm sorry," Sky said. "But now you know what it's been like for us all this time. It hasn't been easy."

"Look, I know I still have a lot to prove, and I can never truly make up for the years lost. I'm just thankful you survived, and we could...be together again. I'm here now. That's not going to change. Unless...you're not comfortable with that."

"I came looking for you, didn't I?" Sky said. "Truth is...I've always been looking for you. Since that day. Part of me always new you weren't dead."

"Your mother and father would be eternally proud of you, Alyssa...Sky," he said. "I'm proud of you too. You're an inspiration, truth be told."

"And you're...an asshole," she laughed. Uncle Mike joined her and the two hugged.

It was a hug she remembered, but one she had not had in four years.

Dear Journal,

There are twenty-five entries to write about what has happened in these last few days. My uncle has returned. It was me who was planning to set off on a journey to find him, and he was there the whole time. It would be easy not to forgive, but nothing has been easy about these past years, so why should I try to make it easy? I remember that expression I read about how if you love something you set it free. And if it comes back to you, it is yours, and if not, it never was. Let's not look at the past and be crippled by it, but look forward to the future.

I saw how my orphans have shined since Sim's death. From King and all the others lying their lives down so their loved ones could live, to Miracle, still a little boy, running down the street ready to die to save his family.

Something miraculous has happened since the fall of man. It has given rise to something else. Something special. At least in this place. To think, from a few flowers, a garden will still blossom means that the nature of life is still something to behold.

Sim, look at the garden that has grown from the seeds you have planted. This kingdom, at heart, will always be your garden. A garden of life. A garden of love. A garden of hope. And you and our fallen, the sunlight, forever shining upon us helping us grow. I will always love you.

When Sky was done with her journal entry, she went downstairs to check on everyone else when Harlow called.

"You're just in time," Harlow said. "Parker was about to sing a song."

"Sing a song?" she said.

"I was a chorus boy before," Parker said. "The best soprano in the choir."

"You never told us this." Sky said.

Parker raised his shoulders. "I've only known you ten minutes," he said. Everyone laughed.

"Let's hear it, then," Leo said.

Everyone gathered in the living room, and it was a full house. Sky stood in the foyer, and Yamil and Miracle joined her at either side. Teddy was the only one not in the room, as he was keeping vigil by King's side. Yet, he kept the door open wide so he could hear.

Parker stood in front of the fireplace. The handprint banner was pinned to the wall above him. He placed his hands in front of him and started ever so softly, the *Ave Maria*. The group was transfixed as Parker's soprano voice filled the room and beyond. His song choice served the moment as a temporary escape as well as a tribute. Everyone listened to Parker intently as they hugged their loved ones, sat pensively alone, or simply enjoyed the peace of a song they hadn't heard or maybe even thought of for years.

Teddy sat back in his chair and listened to the adoration of Mary while Parker sang, and when it was over, he sighed. He looked at King through candlelight and shook his head in despair. He wanted to sleep but couldn't.

On a whim, he moved one of the chess pieces to make *his* move, then sat back again in his chair.

"It's your move, King," he said. "You know, we never played enough. Big Will was your sparring partner in chess. I was never really good, so I was afraid to play. But then, I realized after you were lying here that you never get to play anymore. I'm gonna stop being afraid so we can play. If you wake up, I'll play every day with you. You can teach me more. We'll go find a good set. Not wood or plastic. Crystal. What do you say?"

King didn't respond. Teddy sighed again as Sky entered the room.

"Why don't you go to bed, Teddy," Sky said. "Things have settled down for the moment. King isn't going anywhere."

"I will," he said. "King just has to make his move first."

Sky nodded sympathetically. "Don't stay up too much longer, Teddy. It's not healthy."

After Sky left, Teddy surveyed the board to prepare for King's best move. He glossed over the board for a few minutes and then sat upright. "What the hell? Are you serious?"

Teddy realized that after making King's move, his fate would be sealed. But he couldn't deny him this, so he moved King's pawn into place.

Then something marvelous happened.

"Checkmate," King said from his bed.

Teddy looked up and King was staring at the board with a smile.

Teddy jumped into the air and his knees knocked the chess board over and the pieces flew everywhere.

"King!"

Teddy threw his arms around King as he lay there and bawled. Sky came running back in after hearing Teddy scream and saw that King was awake. She called to the others. Misty, Leo, Yamil, Miracle, and Baby came running in, and they all celebrated around his bed.

The doctor came in and gave him a check-up after the others dispersed. Before Teddy left for the night, King asked him to stay behind. Teddy took up his usual seat.

"I knew you would make it," Teddy said. "I *knew* it."

"You can't beat me in chess even when I'm in a coma," King said. He reached up and took hold of his necklace. "I love this, though."

"It was all I could think of to do," Teddy said.

"It was enough," King said. "You know...I heard you."

"You heard me?"

"Yes, everything you said," King said. "Maybe if I hadn't, I wouldn't have been able to come back."

"It's what I did while the others were fighting," Teddy said. "We won, though. Again."

"So, I hear," King said. "But remember what we learned...No matter what happens...ever...we won a long time ago."

"Yeah," Teddy said. "We still have a trip to take, you know."

Teddy held out his hand and King grabbed it. "I'm looking forward to it."

"Me, too," Teddy said.

Twenty-Three

AFTER A FEW WEEKS of mending, King was ready to leave with Teddy on the road trip. The boys saddled up for their journey as everyone else organized their plans for the first territorial summit to take place at the preserve.

As Teddy and King prepared to leave, Holly, Rodger, Jack, and his contractor crew from the heights were just arriving to fix the damage to the library and roof. They were planning to go to Mike's house after they were done at the fortress, though Mike was looking at places to relocate closer to Sky. Sky insisted he and his men stay where they were, so as a whole, the kingdom could cover more ground.

It's only two miles. I'll be fine. Ember and I have talked. We're looking to create a circular perimeter. Ten-mile diameter. We'll discuss it further at the upcoming summit.

"Are you sure you guys are good doing this on your own?" Sky asked.

Each had a pack full of the essentials and was carrying a gun.

"We can handle ourselves," King said. "Right, Teddy?"

"We'll be fine," Teddy said. "Stop being such a worry wart. That's what my mother used to tell me."

"Someone has to worry around here," Sky said. "Did you pack your energy bars and flashlight?"

"Yes, Mom," King said. "We have everything. Including the map Charlie gave us to find Teddy's old apartment."

"And you remembered where *your* house was?"

"I used to think I didn't remember," King said. "But I was only making excuses not to go back. I'm ready, though."

"Good luck," Sky said. "And don't forget to keep your eyes out for things we could use."

"We got you," King said.

The boys set off down the hill after bidding farewell to the others. They decided they would go to Teddy's old apartment first. Blue Creek Apartment Complex. Charlie gave them directions. Teddy had a vivid recollection of his apartment, but not so much of the surrounding area.

They went over the green bridge and took the highway south before crossing over to the west. They passed a former military arsenal that they had explored in the earlier days in search of weapons. They kept south before veering into a residential area. They passed a former Dollar Store, fast food restaurants, parks, markets, a church, and homes. The two enjoyed quiet conversation but stayed alert to their surroundings. They crossed paths with a middle-aged woman at one point who was coming out of a convenience store. All parties froze, and had their weapons raised.

"It's all good," King said. "We're only passing through, but we are part of a much larger group. We're trying to organize this area. You interested in hearing more?"

The woman didn't answer. Her eyes were wild. She backed further away from them, continuing with her guns raised. Then at one point she swung around and dashed off.

"We'll have to figure out a way to reach all these people in a way that they'll listen to if we're going to get them to follow us."

"It's something that'll come up at the summit, I'm sure," King said. "Building trust with the people that are still out there is going to take a special set of skills."

The two looked at each other and at the same time said, "Mrs. Chandler."

"Ember seems like she could be good at that too," Teddy said.

"Yeah, that job has to be ladies," King said. "Nobody is going to listen to a couple of dirty, punk-ass kids like us."

"I'm not dirty!" Teddy exclaimed.

King shrugged. "I am."

If anyone could lead a mission to unite a territory of apocalyptic nomads, it would be Mrs. Chandler and Ember.

The two continued on, up a hill and around the corner, until they saw the complex.

"That's it!" Teddy said as if finding the end of a rainbow. "I remember it now. There's the playground where Mom used to bring me. Once, she pushed me on the swing so hard that I fell off backward. I used to play with my neighbor, Dexter. He would tease me, but he was the only other kid my age in the whole place. There's a pool on the other side. I learned to swim there."

"Do you remember where your apartment is?" King asked.

"It's 11-8," Teddy said. "I remember the numbers. It's the one right next to the storage units. I remember that, too. It's the only apartment on a hill, too. I used to ride my sled on it every winter."

The two walked closer, and Teddy could hardly contain his excitement. Peripherally, King could see him smiling and he could hear his breathing getting heavier.

"You know what I think about?" King said. "This place, for instance, and Sim finding you here. It had to be like finding a needle in a haystack.

There are a ton of houses and complexes around here, and you know Sim couldn't have checked them all."

"I got lucky," Teddy said.

"Exactly," King said. "But it makes me wonder about how many other kids weren't so lucky. There were just too many places to look. There were probably lots of kids our ages out there at the time who were never found and just died...scared and lonely."

"That's grim," Teddy said.

"I'm just trying to fathom how lucky we were," King said.

"Or maybe it was fate," Teddy said.

King laughed. "What do you know about fate?"

"I know that if we're standing here, then we were meant to be standing here, right?"

"I guess you believe in either luck or fate," King said. "A minute ago, you said you got lucky."

"Okay, then," Teddy said. "Maybe I wasn't lucky. Maybe the universe planned it so that Sim, out of all the places in this huge area, checked my apartment complex. My building. My apartment. Or maybe he was led by some higher power. Whatever the case, I was meant to live. I was meant to be here. Or...I wouldn't be."

"You're making my mind hurt," King said as they got to building eleven.

The two opened the door and stood at the landing. There was a set of stairs that went down and a set of stairs that went up. Teddy led King up the steps and stood in front of his apartment. He hesitated.

"Oh, my God," he said. "This is it."

"Whenever you're ready," King said, thinking about what his own journey back home would be like.

Teddy opened the door and stepped over the threshold into the apartment. He took a few more steps in so King could come in behind him. The boys stood in the middle of the open room. The living room was on the right and the dining room table to their left with the kitchen beyond it.

The empty food cans and bottles of water were still where he remembered from when he was little. He walked over and sat at the dining room table. His plate was still in the same place as it had been years ago when Sim found him. His mind was awash with memories of his mother.

"Will you say the Our Father with me?" he asked King.

"What's that?" King asked.

"Sim knew it," Teddy smiled. "You can listen."

"Sure," King said.

He walked over and sat down at the dining room table. Teddy bowed his head and King took his cue.

"Our Father, who art in heaven, hallowed be thy name. Thy kingdom come, thy will be done, on earth as it is in heaven. Give us this day, our daily bread, and forgive us our trespasses, as we forgive those who trespass against us, and deliver us not into temptation, but deliver us from evil. Amen."

After the prayer, Teddy got up and walked to the corridor behind the dining and living rooms. It ran in two directions. To the right was his room, and the left, his mother's room. He turned left and made his way to her door. The door she retreated behind after she became sick. The door she locked. The door he had nightmares about not being able to open to find her.

He remembered being much smaller when trying to get in a long time ago.

King turned the corner as Teddy stood before the door reading the message his mother had scrawled across it in black marker. The same message Sim had read to learn his name.

My boy is Teddy. If he is still alive, please take him and protect him. He's hyper, but very loving. I'm scared for him, but I couldn't take him with me. Always remind him how much I love him. His mom.

Teddy started to cry. King came up from behind and put a hand on his shoulder.

"Do you want me to get you in there?" he asked.

Teddy shook his head. "I can't. I won't. All these years I thought I had to. But she didn't want me to see her like that. It's time to let her rest. And for me to just...remember her like she was. But if you could give me a moment."

"Sure," he said.

King turned the corner and went back near the door to wait.

"Mommy," he said. "I can read your message now. I *was* hyper, wasn't I? I still am. You don't have to be scared for me anymore. And by the way, Sim always told me how much you loved me." He passed his hand over the message on the door. "I will *always* love you for protecting me. I still remember your face. I'm sure, behind this door, you're still pretty. I have missed you and always will. I'll see you again. But not like this. Bye, Mommy."

Before he left, Teddy found the same marker his mother had used to write her message on the door. He went back to the door, and beneath her message, he wrote his own message.

Behind this door is the best mom ever. She died four yeers ago saveing me. Keep closed. Rest in Peece. Her loving son Teddy.

When Teddy came back out, King was examining a smart phone. "You okay?"

"I think the nightmares will stop now," Teddy said heading for the door.

"Hey," King said. "This was probably your mother's phone. We'll bring it with us. Once we get electricity back, we can try to charge it and you'll have pictures. I'm sure she took a lot. Moms always did."

"Cool," Teddy said.

King placed the phone in Teddy's backpack, and they headed off. They went back the way they had come, but instead of crossing the green bridge back home, they kept straight on the highway. King led the way past the

Congress Street bridge, the island, where Frankie was spending her time resettling Kane's refugees, and into another part of the city beyond Troy. Ultimately, they ended up in a trailer park behind a school.

"You lived here?" Teddy said.

"It looked a little better before the fall," King said. "But not too much better."

Eventually they made it to a gray trailer home that had black shutters. It was King's time to lament.

"Jesus," he said. "Now I know how you felt back there, Teddy. But I ran away from this place months before the sickness spread. It's so weird."

"It's okay," Teddy said. "Whatever you find in there...it'll probably help with the nightmares."

King turned and looked at him with a raised eyebrow. "I never had any nightmares. Only regrets."

"Same thing," Teddy said.

Was it? King wondered. *Maybe Teddy was right.*

"Okay, let's do this," King said. He opened the door and stepped into the trailer.

They entered the living room, and it looked the same way as King remembered it. The furniture was as he recalled, and there, lying on the couch were the skeletonized remains of a man. King remembered his clothing. It was his abusive stepfather. The one who caused him to run away. King half-expected the man would still be , ready to pummel him when he walked through the door.

Thank God.

"Sorry," Teddy said.

Teddy was not fully aware of King's past.

"He was a dickhead," King said. "At least it's good to know that not every asshole survived the plague."

"Oh," Teddy said.

King pressed forward beyond the living room and turned left into the dining room and kitchen. The dining area led to the master bedroom. Teddy explored the right side of the trailer to allow King space.

When King entered the master bedroom, his heart sank. He wasn't sure if it was relief or sadness that he was feeling. Or maybe he was only feeling a level of closure from finally knowing his mother's fate. Though, he wasn't sure how he would ever feel full closure, given the choice he made to run away.

She was there in her bed, under the covers. Peaceful.

God damn, Mom. I should have come back when this whole plague shit started. I was so stupid. I'm sorry. I know that's not enough. I was just a stupid kid.

He stepped closer and noticed a piece of paper on the nightstand beside her bed. He walked alongside the bed, trying not to see his mother in such a state. As he got closer to the nightstand, he saw that the piece of paper was a note.

He realized after picking it up, that it was for him.

Jimmy,

You may never read this. But I thought I would write it because some people are not dying. I hope you are one of them. As for me, my time has come. I want to tell you how sorry I am about everything. I lost my way when your father died. I know it hurt you too, and I just didn't know how to deal with Randy when he was hurting you. He hurt me too. But I was your mother and I should have figured it out. Instead, I messed this all up, and then there ended up being no time to fix it. But I don't want you to think I didn't miss you when you were gone. I looked every day. I drove around in my car and asked people. Believe it or not, even Randy looked. Probably just so I couldn't have any excuses to leave the house. I was so sad when I couldn't find you, but it's my fault. I understand why you did what you did. I wish it hadn't come to that. I'm so sorry, baby, and I hope if you survived all this death that you someday read this and know I've always loved you, and that I would never blame you for anything. I failed you, but you are my boy forever and always. Remember all those good times when your father was alive. There were so many beautiful years. Those are the years I remember now as I await the end of my life. In every thought, I see you. I love you, Jimmy.

After reading the letter, King fell to his knees and cried, in relief, in sorrow, but more than those, in a feeling of freedom from the mental prison he convinced himself he had been trapped in for all these years.

Teddy heard King sobbing from the kitchen and stopped short of going into the room. He only hoped that whatever pain King was feeling that it would free him, as this is what their daylong journey was for...to close the circle and free their minds.

By the time they returned to the fortress, they both agreed it was one of the most important missions they had gone on since the beginning, and well worth it in the end.

Twenty-Four

THE DAY OF THE summit arrived. It was held in the visitors' center at the preserve. The orphans, along with Charlie, Harlow, Mike, Mrs. Chandler, and Frankie were among those who made the journey.

Mike and his people toted Yamil and Miracle on horseback while the others walked. Among many things, they planned to discuss finding more horses for messengers, policing, general travel, and how to make outreach easier.

In the week since Kane's defeat, so many plans came to mind as the idea of having a unified territory in which they would be safe to travel and rebuild became more likely. The fortress wall, still not completed, would be but a small feat compared to a new perimeter fence they discussed placing around the area at a three-mile radius in all directions.

That's about nine and a half miles of fence, Leo pointed out. *And what about the preserve?*

It's far out. If we made our radius ten miles, we would need sixty-two miles of fence. Anyway, they have been managing just fine and have their own perimeter safeguards.

A central armory for their weaponry was also discussed as part of the plan once their twenty-eight miles of circular territory was secure.

After arriving at the preserve, the visitors spent the day sightseeing, meeting people, having lunch, and discussing their excitement for the future. It was during this time that Sky ran into Avi. She had only seen him in fleeting glances since that first day his group arrived at the doorsteps to the fortress. Letting down her guard for only a second, she offered the boy a smile.

"There it is," Avi said. "The smile I've been waiting to see. I knew you couldn't be that serious all the time. You'd have a stroke by the time you were twenty."

"I think I've already had a few," she said. "Anyway, what is it with boys? All they want to do is play. Perhaps if boys were more serious, it would give *me* some extra time to have fun for a change."

"And if you had that extra time, what would you do?" Avi asked.

Sky pondered. "Come to think of it, I don't know."

"That's sad," Avi said. "Let me show you something."

Avi led her over to the visitors' center viewing windows that peered out over a small pond.

"Go ahead and look through the scope," Avi said, adjusting the end of it upward.

Sky leaned into the telescopic tool and viewed the pond. She spotted a pair of trumpeter swans wading across the surface.

"Are those...swans?" she said, mesmerized.

"They sure are," Avi said. "Not the most common bird to see in New York. Do you want to know what a pair of swans represents?"

Sky pulled herself away from the scope and noted Avi's wide grin, but she shied away from staring too long at him in a desperate attempt to ignore his handsome dark features.

"What does a pair of swans represent?" she asked, awkwardly taking the bait.

"Soulmates for life," he answered with confidence.

Sky giggled. "You made that up."

Avi laughed. "No, it's true. I promise."

Then, Sky looked at him again. This time, for a longer duration. Avi returned the stare, and Sky felt stirrings in the pit of her stomach that she had never felt before in her life.

It was a good feeling. It was a good day. Maybe the best one in years.

In the late summer afternoon, and after the prisoner Dodson was brought to the edge of the preserve and exiled, the summit commenced, and included Sky, King, Misty, Ember, Wyatt, Charlie, Frankie, Ember, Avi, Mr. Dumas, Grace, Mike, Cypress, Harlow, and one of her trusted and more senior members of the mole community who wished to lend a voice to the changes.

Frankie resolved to oversee the redevelopment of the island community as its newfound leader, and make it a special place for the women and children that had been caught in the middle of the siege that resulted from Kane's assault on the city.

There was some concern about Kane's soldiers attacking once again from their southern territories to finish what he started, but with eyes at the gates of the city from the fortress, and on the river by way of the island, they could monitor it closely.

They were told that, considering not having a formalized prison, the prisoner Dodson had been exiled. Timothy had escorted him to the edge of the city and told him that if he was ever seen again within their newly devised perimeter, that he would be killed.

As the meeting began, Ember closed the door to the conference room and welcomed the group.

"It's an amazing privilege to be here today with all of you fine people who share the same progressive vision for a new future. To see this is beyond what I thought we would ever see happen in our lifetimes. We must wonder how many other communities are out there, established within this area, that can aspire to be part of our newly founded kingdom. We have a daunting task ahead of us, ladies and gentlemen, but a thrilling challenge as well as we look to set the stage for future generations."

"Before we start," Sky said. "I would like to acknowledge a short silence for all those who died so that we could be here today."

Everyone bowed their heads and held their own thoughts as the brief time passed. Sky remembered her parents, Sim, Ace, JZ, Shark, Willow, Flip, Big Will, and Malayah. She said a silent prayer in their names.

"Now, let us begin with our pledge," she said.

In one voice, they softly decreed.

We, the leaders of the new world, pledge to: do our best, work together, defend our territory, live and die for one another, love, lead, remember. We are the kingdom, and the kingdom is us.

THE END

About the Author

T.A. Styles earned his B.S. in Elementary Education and Mathematics and his M.S. in Developmental Reading. He taught in elementary and junior high schools for twelve years before launching his own childcare enterprise, TSL Kids Crew, which he has operated since 2009. He has had a passion for writing stories since he was a teenager, as it was a hobby and skill for which he realized at a young age he had a knack for and loved. He has two grown children and has traveled extensively including to Iceland, Australia, Greece, Italy, South America, and many other places nationally and internationally.

Connect with him at www.tastyles.com.